D1532319

THE
HIGHWAYMAN'S
FOOTSTEPS

NICOLA MORGAN

CANDLEWICK PRESS
CAMBRIDGE, MASSACHUSETTS

First U.S. edition 2007

Library of Congress Cataloging-in-Publication Data is available.

Library of Congress Catalog Card Number pending

ISBN 978-0-7636-3472-8

2 4 6 8 10 9 7 5 3 1

Printed in the United States of America

This book was typeset in Cochin.

Candlewick Press
2067 Massachusetts Avenue
Cambridge, Massachusetts

visit us at www.candlewick.com

With thanks to:

Elizabeth Roy, my agent, for her calm wisdom and for always fighting my corner with steely charm.

And Chris Kloet, my editor, for consistently and enthusiastically battering my books into shape, for generously sharing her knowledge, and for being great fun to work with.

Elizabeth and Chris have been with me since my first novel. I owe them huge gratitude. This book is for them, though by now they will have read it more times than they would want.

CHAPTER ONE

I felt cold metal on the side of my skull before I heard the voice. I knew at once what it was. A pistol. Resting on the bone just behind my ear. The favorite place for murderers, robbers, highwaymen — because, by angling the pistol slightly inward, they could be sure to blow a man's brains out before he might have time to scream.

I had been warned of them. Many times. But this evening, my mind had been occupied with other worries. What would my father say if he discovered the trouble I had found myself in earlier that day? His own son, on the run from soldiers?

What would he say if he never saw his son alive again? I had been running away, yes, but this was not how I had planned it to end. Perhaps he would care little. My mouth was dry with fear and I tried to swallow. Above all, I tried not to faint with terror.

Then came the voice. It was an odd voice, uneven and croaky. Muffled, too — I supposed he spoke from behind a mask.

"Drop what you carry. Take four paces forward, slowly. Then lie face down on the ground." When I hesitated, trying to do everything just as I was told, the voice snapped, "Now!" and I could hear the heavy, rasping breath.

Lying on the ground, my face pressed into the earth, I tried to think. I turned my head to one side, the better to breathe. "No!" came the voice, tight as a whip. "Face down!"

The damp soil was in my nostrils, and more than soil, for this had been a dwelling and the ground was steeped in the stinking rot of people's lives. My neck hurt as I twisted it, pushing my nose as far out of the dirt as I dared. Now I could feel the hard, round mouth of the pistol beneath my shoulder blade, on a level with my heart, I guessed. The man's knee was pressed into my back. I could move no part of me.

I tried not to think about what would happen. How could I die like this, unnoticed and unknown? If I could only think hard enough, think deeply enough, perhaps some trace of my thoughts would find a home and someone would know that I had died here. Perhaps I could leave a ghostly breath behind to speak of me to others coming later to this place. These moors were haunted, were they not, riddled with the specters of royalists and Roundheads, dying in agony for their chosen cause? If they could speak from beyond death, then could not I?

And so, squeezing my eyes closed, the better to concentrate, I repeated these words in my head: *I am William de Lacey. I am fourteen years of age. I live — lived — at Hedley Hall, some miles from Hexham, until some days ago, when I ran from my home. I had no choice. I could not stay. My father and my brother had both insulted me. If I had been a true gentleman, and truly honorable, I would have challenged them to a duel for what they said to me, even though they are my father and my brother. But perhaps they were correct: I am not a true gentleman. I am a coward. A gentleman cannot be a coward, can he?*

If my mother and father discovered me dead with a pistol wound to my back, it would be proof of what they already believed: only a coward would be shot in the back. It would be proof that I was bolting like a frightened rabbit, instead of standing and facing danger.

They were right. They had wished me to become an officer. But I knew I would be of no use, whether in the King's army or the militia so beloved of my father: my fear would turn me to stone. If wishing for a better life than fighting is cowardly, then I am indeed a coward. If I want something more than to die on a distant battlefield, shattered by the musket of a man who has never heard my name, then I must be a coward.

I could not say what frightened me the more — the thought of losing my life and the terrible pain as the lead ball entered my body, or how God would judge me when I came to Him. Would I deserve to go to Heaven with the stain of cowardice on my character? Would God judge me as my parents had done? How could He not, when I judged myself in the same way?

The pistol remained pressed into my back as the man's hand expertly searched through my pockets. He found what he was seeking — a purse weighty with guineas. The purse I had stolen that day, because my hunger drove me to it. I wished I had never taken it. Another day of hunger would have been better than this. If I had not stolen it, I would not have hidden from the militia in this ruined hovel, and I would not now be at the mercy of this robber. And, furthermore, if this man did not shoot me dead, the hangman would be pleased to put his rope around my neck.

How had I stooped so low? Why was I, William de Lacey, the second son of a gentleman, High Sheriff of Hexham, colonel in the militia, and Member for Parliament, now choking on dirt in a ruined peasant dwelling instead of sitting at a table weighed down by rich food?

The man's knee was lifted from my back. I could no longer feel the pistol. I heard the soft click of metal on metal. The pistol being cocked, ready to fire. I held my breath, waiting for what was to come. His heavy breathing disturbed me — if he was ill at ease himself, he would perhaps be more inclined to shoot. Should I speak, to plead with him, to reassure him that, if he would let me run away, I would never speak a word of his whereabouts? But my voice was trapped within me, and my mind could not grasp what I should do.

Distant sounds assailed my ears. I could hear the evening curlews on the darkening Yorkshire moors, the soft crunch of wheels and the clattering of a horse passing on the nearby track, the occasional call of sheep settling for the night, the swish of northern wind through the hanging doorway. And still I held my breath, still waiting.

I thought of my home far away: my sisters, my elder brother — the one whom my parents respected and favored. I thought of my mother and her weak and frightened face and how the way she gently stroked my hair meant nothing if she did not stand up to my father's sternness. And I thought of my father, and how little he thought of me. And of my friends at school, especially Harry and Robert, my age and my equals in everything. Would they ever understand why I had run away? I had never told them — or anyone — of my feelings. But when I thought of my horse, Blackfoot, and my new spaniel puppy, that was when I had to struggle hardest against the tears. Who would care for them as I did? People said I had a special skill with animals, though when they said that my father would only turn away with a small sneer.

Now, I feared I should never see them again.

I could no longer feel my hands, my feet, my legs, my arms. A cold numbness was creeping through my body. Perhaps I was dead already? Perhaps the shot had come and I had not heard it? Some say that death is merciful. Perhaps this is its final mercy — that you do not hear it come?

And then the words, as sharp as gunshot. "Stand up!"

What was this? A way to torture me? A way to draw out the moment that must come? I had heard of worse things than death, things that murderers can do first.

I stood up, slowly and with some difficulty. As I did so, I carefully turned toward the man.

"No! Face the door." Something strange hung in his voice, as though he were afraid. But he could not be. Not standing near me with a gun, and me unarmed.

Or perhaps as though he was in pain. His breathing was even harsher now and faster than ever.

Before I turned away, I had caught a glimpse of him. He was smaller than I had imagined, and thinner. Slightly hunched; clothed entirely in dark or black; his face masked from the nose downward, below narrowed eyes.

"What do you want of me?" I asked, trying to make my voice sound strong. "You have my money. I have nothing more."

He did not reply. Only the sound of quick breathing filled the space between us.

Then I heard a soft groan and a sound as though of something falling. I turned to see him crouching, head almost touching the ground. One hand was held to his side, under his jacket, and when he took his fingers away, I saw dark liquid glistening on the black glove. Even in this gloom, I knew it was blood. A quantity of blood. The pistol lay on the ground. I leaped to pick it up. I could not see its pair anywhere.

I could shoot him now or hold him as my prisoner until I might alert passing soldiers. I would earn a large reward for capturing a highwayman or a robber. Then, surely, everyone would know that I was not a coward.

But no! I had stolen a purse full of money. We could hang together, this robber and I. I could turn him in no more than I could go back home. And shooting him would serve no purpose other than perchance to draw the soldiers toward the sound.

No, must I not take the purse back and leave the man to die as he deserved? Who knew how many poor souls he had killed in his life of robbery. His death would be of value to the world. I could not be sure of the nature of his crimes but from his apparel he was a highwayman, in clothes of a certain quality: the coat with large cuffs turned back and sewn with ebony buttons, a black kerchief over his lower face, and a tricorne hat edged in silver.

More than that I could not see, though I did notice his long, thigh-high riding boots without spurs. But there was no horse, nor any sign of one. Perhaps it had been lost in whatever action had caused the man's injury. A highwayman would not easily give up his horse.

With my foot, carefully, I pushed him, trying to see where my purse might be. He moaned, a strange mewing like the sound an injured cat might make. He raised his head and as he did so, his kerchief slipped from his face. He was younger than I'd imagined, much younger. His cheeks were smooth and unshaven. He was no older than I.

Standing there with the pistol in my hand and an injured boy in front of me, I began to feel less fear.

He had sweat on his forehead, from a fever perhaps, and his face was twisted in his effort not to cry out. Groaning again, he began to slip sideways until he lay curled on the hard floor. But it was as his head touched the ground that I had my greatest surprise. His hat was dislodged from his head, revealing black tresses of long, thick hair.

This highwayman was no man, but a girl.

CHAPTER TWO

At first, I made no movement, too shocked to know what to do. She groaned again, twisting slightly and sliding one hand beneath her, to where the wound was.

I moved to the doorway, still holding the pistol in my hand, ready to use at any moment. And I could have used it, accurately, although not willingly — I had been taught to aim and to handle a pistol. Tutored in Latin and Greek at my grammar school, as well as mathematics, poetry, and the like by a tutor at home, and shooting, swordplay, and horsemanship on my father's estate. Though no better than average at my books, I was proficient at such physical pastimes — I could shoot a pigeon with ease and jump the highest hedges without hesitation. But could I ever shoot a girl? Even if she were about to shoot me? I knew I could not. It would not be proper.

I peered through the doorway. No one moved in the darkness. The hovel was some distance from a village — about a mile, according to the milestone that I had passed only shortly before. It was set back forty or fifty paces from the road. I could see the winking firelights of the village down in the valley, and occasionally even hear the floating noises of drinkers in a tavern, when the wind brought the sounds to me. But there was no one nearby who was likely to show an interest in this ruin. I turned back to the room. A nearly full moon on a crisp and cloudless night splashed its beams through the windows, providing a milky light.

The air was cold, but thick walls sheltered us from the worst of the February weather. There was no glass in the windows, but they were small and quite high up, and the roof seemed sound, at least in this part. The door hung on one hinge and moved with an irregular creak. I carefully lifted it and closed it as best I could. Now, we would have warning if someone tried to enter. Even a moment or two could mean the difference between life and death.

On the other side of the room was an open doorway, pitch black, leading into another room, or perhaps a store.

I was safe enough for now. But what about the girl? What should I do? She was no longer a threat to me. Should I leave her? Perhaps to die? But what could I do to help her? I had nothing, no physic. My only knowledge of injuries or fever was in animals.

Besides, she had meant to kill me and had stolen my money. Who knew what evil her life contained? Her face was somewhat dirty, her hair loose and undressed, and her skin was slightly darkened by the weather, though not coarsened as with most countrywomen. She was, I assumed, not highborn, though her voice had hinted at some quality, which I found strange. I had heard tell of gentlemen turning to highway robbery through a desire for adventure or because they had fallen on hard times, but I did not know if these were simply stories. My father had always said that the marks of a lady were her pale skin and gentle, soft disposition, in which case this was no lady.

But then I wager you would say that I was no longer a gentleman. Gentlemen did not steal, did they? I had been well schooled in all the virtues that would ensure my place in Heaven. It seemed to me that I had failed to obey at least two of them: "Thou shalt not steal." "Honor thy father and mother." I folded my hands, as I had been so often taught, in case God watched me then. More than ever now did I need His protection.

I tried to gather my confused thoughts, to decide a sensible plan.

To retrieve my purse — that was my most pressing need. I moved toward her, holding the pistol falteringly in front of me, pointed at the center of her body, not trusting myself to aim at something as small as her head.

I could hear my heart beating hard and fast, feel the blood pounding in my ears. My palm was slippery around the pistol.

Chapter Three

What if she were to move? What if she lunged toward me? I would have to shoot her then, would I not? To save myself. I had never killed anyone before, and I had no wish to do so now. If I had no stomach to kill unknown soldiers from another land, how should I then shoot dead a young girl as she lay bleeding from her injuries? "Thou shalt not kill."

I knew I could not shoot her. I could not live with myself if I did.

With one hand, I wiped the sweat from my brow. I sank to my knees on the earth and placed the pistol on the ground, sliding it away from both of us. She could not reach it now. And I would not pick it up again. Not unless I had a different enemy.

Her eyes were closed, and pink patches glowed on her cheeks, sweat beading across her pale forehead. Her mouth was open in a slight grimace, her teeth clenched as she breathed, fast and shallow, her chest and throat rising rapidly. One arm was on the ground in front of her, fist squeezed oyster-tight, the sinews standing out on the back of her hand.

I looked to the ground beside her. There did not seem to be more blood than before, but I could be certain of little in this gloom.

She had fainted, I felt sure. It was the way of females. How else could I explain her sudden collapse? One moment she had been standing fiercely over me, and the next she was in this helpless state. Now I knew why her breathing had sounded so labored before. She must have used all her remaining strength to fight her pain and to capture me when I had stumbled unwittingly into her refuge. I imagined her fear as I had come through the doorway, her relief to find only a boy.

Slowly and with caution, I leaned forward and touched her cheek. She twitched but did not open her eyes. Her skin felt hot, burning with fever. I had never seen anyone with such a fever, and I did not know what to do. I searched my mind for anything that I might have been told, but found nothing.

What now? My own hunger and faintness were

increasing. And thirst. I had had nothing to drink for some hours now. The thirst was worse than the hunger. My tongue clung to the roof of my mouth, tasting of metal.

I had need of that purse, needed my money. *My* money? Well, even though it was not mine, I needed it now.

My plan before I was held up by this girl had been to go to the village for food and drink, and it was not yet too late. I must retrieve my purse and then go. It did not seem right to touch a young girl's body as she lay helpless, but I had no choice. Quickly, and turning my face away, I slid my hand under her shoulder and around her back, until I found what I was looking for. I pulled the purse out and put it in my pocket. I noticed, as I did this, that there was no other pistol.

Her lips were moving now as she started to mutter, though at first I could not make out the words. I put my head closer to her mouth, pushed the hair away from her face. Still she muttered.

"What is it? What are you saying?" I asked, my voice sounding suddenly loud in the darkness.

She mumbled again, and I realized she was asking for water.

"I have none," I replied. "I have nothing. Try to sleep and I shall find food and water. In the morning light." Would I? Should I not simply disappear and put myself as far as possible from this place? What did I owe her? Did I not have my own troubles? Even if I could help her, which I doubted, why should I? Why risk my own life for a stranger, and a criminal at that?

She was still muttering, trying to move. I put my hand to her shoulder to keep her still. She seemed to be pointing. I looked around the room. She was pointing to the black doorway into the next chamber. At that moment, the moon disappeared behind a cloud and suddenly we were in deeper darkness. Now the only sounds were our breathing, rustlings from the rafters, and the soft whirring of the wind before it rains.

I must wait. Still she mumbled and pointed. "Hush," I said. "Wait a little."

"Water." Her voice sounded slurred, as though her lips or tongue were swollen. "My bag."

As I tried to quiet her, the moon at last returned and I could see the darkened doorway once more. With my heart thumping faster now, I walked toward it. Inside was dark as pitch. I entered, straining my ears in the silence, my arms in front of me, ready for what I might find. My feet stumbled on an object. I crouched down. It was soft — a cloak, and the bag. Beneath them lay something hard — the matching pistol. I picked them all up and went back to the girl.

Inside the bag I found a bottle, corked. I pulled the cork out and sniffed. It had a slightly musty smell of old water, but not excessively old. I was about to put it to my lips, but, despite my terrible thirst, I could not do so. I held it to the girl's mouth and carefully trickled some between her lips. Most of it was wasted as it trickled out again.

"You," she said, licking at her lips. "You drink."

I did as she told me, surprised that she had the grace to think of me. Feeling somewhat guilty, as though I should be helping her and not the other way around, I took only what I needed. I poured some more between her lips.

I knew not the proper way to behave toward her. She was a criminal; she had tried to kill me; she was no lady; yet, despite everything, I had been born a gentleman, and she was weaker than I. But these were strange times, and I must do what needed to be done. Whatever that seemed to be, I must try to do the right thing.

There was bread in her bag, too, a part loaf, dried at the edges but edible. I broke some and offered it to her, but she closed her mouth and shook her head. I tried again but still she would not eat. I knew not if it was right to eat or not to eat with a fever. But I recalled that animals usually knew what was best for them during illness, and I hoped this might be the same for her.

In the moonlight, I looked at the bread. My hunger now was intense and my mouth watered. This was not the time to wait, not the time to remember my manners. I was hungry and she was not. I ate as quickly as I could.

I listened to her strained breathing, watched her closed, flickering eyes with dread. I did not know her but I could not bear the thought of her — anyone — dying here, now, in front of me. And then my being left alone.

I must help her. Whatever the foolishness of it, despite the fact that she had planned to kill me, despite the fact that I was on the run myself and did not want to be held back by an injured girl, despite the fact that she was a criminal, and that I had nothing in common with her, I had to help her. As one person to another, as two people in need, we were linked.

Chapter Four

"How were you hurt?" I wanted her to stay awake, not to drift into a frightening place, frightening for both of us. I thought that if I made her talk, she could not die. It had begun to matter to me that she should not die.

Her voice was little more than a soft moan. Her breathing seemed so faint that at any moment it might float away entirely. "Pistol."

A pistol wound? If so, then what chance did she have to recover? "I need to see. I need to move you a little," I said.

As I carefully turned her onto her back, she made no sound, but I could feel her muscles tighten and her breath freeze as she tried not to cry out. She kept her hand pressed against her side.

"I must move you a little more. Into the moonlight. So that I may see." I crouched behind her and slid both hands under her body, shifting her as gently as possible toward the place where the moonlight pooled on the ground. A whimper escaped from her as I settled her down again. I took her black-gloved hand and eased it away from her side.

I winced for her as I looked at it. A long straight slice through the thin flesh over her ribs. The lead ball must have been a hair's breadth from entering her, ripping the clothes as it passed. It was not a new wound, from the look of it. The edges were an inch apart, raw, and swollen. Blackened, too, from the heat of the bullet's passage. There was now only a slow trickle of blood. She must have sustained the injury some days ago, and it had come apart in the sudden effort of stealing my purse. Although I may not have known how to deal with fever, I had seen wounds before. Would my knowledge of the treatment of animals help me with this girl's injury?

My father had always told me to leave such things to our servants, but I could not agree. It was one of the things he despised about me — my softness in the face of suffering, whether human or animal. If I could not bear the pain of others, how could I face pain myself? He told me that if I could not toughen myself then, by God, he would toughen me himself in his militia. His harsh words, his contempt, did nothing to toughen me, only drove me to anger and hurt.

I had wished to attend boarding school, like my brother, but my father said that I was not clever enough for the Law or the Church, and I would be better having lessons at home like my sisters. But when my tutor died, more than two years past now, I had begged to be allowed to go to the grammar school. My father agreed — he was glad, I supposed, to have me away from the house. The happiest days of my life were spent with Harry and Robert and the other boys, reciting Latin verbs, tables, the dates of the Kings and Queens of England — and trying to trick the masters into amusing diversions. And, as I grew taller, and broader and stronger, I had felt myself to be something of a leader, well liked and respected. There was nothing they could do that I could not. But these feelings disappeared when I returned each evening to my home, where bitterness took over and I felt small and weak.

I put these thoughts away now and tried to decide how to help the girl's injury and fever. I knew that if this was a wounded horse I should need a mixture of certain herbs, pounded and mashed into a poultice to draw out the poison. Surely the same would work for a person? But I did not have the herbs, nor any way to find them. For now, all I could do was to pray that she would survive the night. In the morning, I would go to the nearby village and buy such physic as I could. And I would find us food.

Meanwhile, I made a pad of the only clean shirt I had brought with me and pressed it firmly to her wound, keeping it in place with her own torn shirt and jacket. I shut my ears to the pain she suffered while I did this, but she knew why it had to be so. The wound must be closed as much as possible and protected from the terrible poisons of the night air. I made her the best pillow that I could with her bag, and covered her with her own warm cloak.

I explained what I would do in the morning. I could not tell if she grasped this, as she drifted in and out of wakefulness, sometimes muttering words I could not understand. Sliding down onto the ground, leaning against the wall, I sat close to her and began to wait for the morning to come. Once, after a short while, her hand moved toward mine in her sleep and I clasped it in the darkness, unseen by the world. I do not think she knew what she did, though I blushed in the night for such impropriety and hoped she would not remember in the morning. As I took her hand, our fates were sealed, locked together by chance and the foolish things that humans do to each other.

As the night settled into its heavy silence, my heart slowed and sank, and dark thoughts flooded my mind. What had I done? What would happen now? How long could this girl and I survive? She was a criminal — how could I trust her? Would we be caught and face the hangman's noose or would we manage to escape for a few hours or days or weeks, spending every moment terrified, only to be shot down like dogs in the dirt when the soldiers eventually caught us? What did it feel like to die? And who would ever know or care about us?

I knew only that at this time, there seemed no choice. I did not wish to be alone. You may say I stayed with her because I was too afraid of loneliness. Or you may say I stayed because I could not honorably leave her to die. I do not, in all honesty, know which would be closer to the truth.

CHAPTER FIVE

I slept little and lightly. This was the fourth night since I had left my comfortable bed at home, and a hard, damp floor no longer seemed strange to me. But my head was full of what I must do the next day. Besides, I was afraid to sleep too deeply, in case an intruder came and I did not hear until it was too late.

The winter iciness seeped through my skin, chilling me to my bones. The girl muttered in her fevered sleep, and I fretted for her condition in this hostile cold. I moved my body closer to her, for both our sakes, though not too close. It would not have been proper. And I did not look at her.

I wondered about her, however. How could I not? What sort of villain was she? She appeared to be a highwayman — not that I had seen one, but I had heard tell of them often enough. I did not believe I had heard of a woman turning to that dangerous way of life, though plenty of women were hanged for robbery of other sorts. A highwayman's life was no life for a young girl: a life of constant danger, as her pistol wound testified. I could not help but want to know more about my strange companion.

And oddly, just for a short moment, I envied her the freedom she must have. She could do as she wished, go where she desired. No one would expect anything of her.

In my wakeful moments, I listened to the sounds of the night: the eerie call of a hunting owl, an occasional distant shout, once a horse's clatter on the rough road, the rustlings and scuttlings of night creatures. Into my fitful dreams floated different sounds: roaring wind and the thunder of cannons and the terrible screams of men dying and my father's scornful words, saying "Coward, boy! You are nothing more than a lily-livered coward. You are no son of mine. I would I had another daughter to mewl and cringe, for you are as useless."

At last, my dreams receded and the small noises outside changed into the sounds of morning, as the ragged moonlight through the window softened slowly into a cold gray dawn.

Painfully, I stood up, hunger clawing at my guts

and my mouth dry as straw. The girl stirred. I felt her brow. It was burning hot still, and yet her whole body shivered. I pushed her shoulder slightly. Her eyes opened. She stared at me without seeming to understand. Frightened, she tried to move but immediately gasped with pain.

I steadied her. "Stay still. You must not move." I offered some water to her lips, and she drank greedily.

"Who are you?" she asked, though not clearly. Her voice sounded distant and strained.

"My name is William. We will talk when I return, but first I must go and fetch physic for you." I did not wish her to know more of me, of my status or my wealth.

She tried to sit again. "My horse!" she said, her voice agitated. "My horse!"

There was still no sign or scent of any horse. It must have long gone. "There is no horse," I said. "I am sorry."

"I fell. I was weakened by this." Her hand flapped toward her injured side. "A day, two days ago. More. I forget." Her words were slurring. "He needs . . . I need him."

That, I could believe. A horse must be the most valuable of all her possessions. It would be the difference between life and death to her. I wished I had my horse. But when I consider that more carefully,

I am forced to admit that if I had had my horse, I almost certainly would not have been there at all. I would have been many miles away. But I could not have taken my horse without being noticed.

She was silent at first, only breathing fast and shallowly. When she spoke, her voice sounded oddly strong. "I know where he will be. He will have gone home." She sank back onto the ground, wincing again as she did so.

"Let me find him. Tell me where and I will fetch him back." Was I mad? Could I take the risk?

"I cannot."

"Why, cannot?"

She said nothing. And then I knew. She did not trust me! She thought I would steal her horse and ride away. Fury flared inside me. Why was I helping her if she did not trust me? Why did I not just leave her here? Better still, why did I not make her tell me where her horse was and then ride away with it, putting many miles between myself and the soldiers?

I almost smiled at this foolish thought. How could I blame the girl for not trusting me when I had just had the very same tempting thought? Would I have trusted a stranger if I had been in her position? Would I have told her where my horse was and given her the opportunity to steal it?

I had no intention of leaving her. It would not have been honorable. Perhaps she did not understand such matters, criminal that she was, but I had been raised always to do the right thing.

The right thing! Was stealing money the right thing?

No. I was a felon, like her, no better and no worse.

—

CHAPTER SIX

"I shall be back as soon as I can," I simply said. "Do not try to move."

Before I left, I made such changes as I could to my appearance, hoping that I would not meet soldiers who might recognize me. With some water, I adjusted my hair, after loosening it from the small pigtail I had worn yesterday. I left my cloak and hat behind. I would be walking fast, so my thick jacket would suffice to keep me warm. And it was dirty enough now that I would look nothing like a rich boy. Besides, it was not my own, but one taken from a stable boy while he slept. He had been smaller than I, and my broad shoulders strained slightly at the coarse material, my thin, bony wrists and large hands hanging too far from the sleeves. I hoped someone would buy him a new one. A kerchief tied around my neck came next, and I imagined that I must look very different from the neat-haired, soft-faced boy who had left his wealthy home days before. I felt different, too. The eyes through which I saw the world had changed.

I took two coins from the purse and left the rest with her. I placed the purse touching her hand, so she would know I was not taking it and disappearing forever.

The pistols lay on the ground. Should I take them? I was much tempted. But if I were caught, it would mean more trouble for me. I checked the priming and left them, half-cocked, by the girl's side, where she could reach them if need be.

Cautiously, I walked through the doorway and looked around. It seemed more than a few hours since I had taken refuge in this place and found myself at the end of a pistol. At that moment I had expected to die, but here I was, still alive several hours later. And I was no less frightened now than I had been then. Then, I had been almost resigned to what would happen, ready for the final sound of the explosion in my head; now, I was facing unknown danger.

I must stop thinking about danger and merely act.

I peered through the misted grayness and set off toward the village, slinging my empty bag over my shoulder. A knife nestled in my pocket, along with the two coins.

As I walked quickly down the sloping road, all my

senses were alert. The hills seemed to be watching me, as though they knew who I was and would pass that information to any searching soldiers if they wished.

I said a prayer, for forgiveness and for protection. Would my prayer be answered? I could not say.

Chapter Seven

After somewhat less than half an hour, I could make out the first houses ahead of me, tombstone shadows on a gray landscape. In the cold, wet light of a winter morning, I came to the village. My heart began to beat a little faster. What if the soldiers were there? What if this were the only village nearby, and they had guessed I would come here? What if they did recognize me despite all my efforts?

Now, I was within sight of windows, some dark, others spilling an orange light onto the street. Although it was early, several people were about, collars turned up, hats squashed down, shoulders hunched, breath like smoke in the white, frosty air. I walked on. The warm, sweet smell of freshly baked bread came over me, and my mouth watered. The bakery was opening, and I bought two loaves, straight from the oven, and held their heat to my chest before putting them in my bag.

"Passing through," I said in answer to the baker's question, roughening my voice as much as I could. "With my master. We 'ave far to go and an early start." It satisfied him, and his lack of curiosity gave me confidence.

Within half an hour, more people were out and about, and I had purchased cheese and a piece of ham as well as the bread. Now I had need of an apothecary.

I found him soon enough, though his angry face when I woke him made me wish I had waited another hour. His nose was purple, his skin streaked with broken red lines. He had the look of someone who has drunk too much, and for too long. My father had a manservant once who had that look. We found him one morning, drowned, face down in the horses' water trough, the gin flagon empty beside him.

"My master is hurt," I said. "A cut, some three days old. He has a fever. I need —" and I was just about to tell him what I needed when he interrupted, swinging the oil lamp so that it hissed and spluttered dangerously.

"It is for me to tell you what you need. I was not roused from my bed before dawn to listen to some puppy pretend he has some knowledge." I decided not to mention that it was, in truth, now well after dawn. I merely said I was sorry and thanked him as well as I could manage.

The man's eyes were gummed with crusted yellow matter. He had little hair and what there was floated like an ancient cobweb behind his skull. God had given him more skin than was necessary and it hung around him in folds, so that when he moved, the creases separated grotesquely, revealing the grime of months or years. He smelled sickly and festering.

Before speaking further, he pressed a finger against one nostril and blew sharply through the other one, sending snot to the floor by my feet. "Has the blood ceased flowing?"

"I think it has. There was fresh blood some hours ago, but there is nothing now."

"Is the flesh blackened? Is the matter exuding from it white, or has it darkened to thick yellow? Does your master sweat? Is he cold, or does he shout and throw his blankets off? Does a rash cover his body? Does his breath reek?"

I answered his questions as well as I could. I knew not if they meant that he had a remedy or if he was trying simply to show that his knowledge was greater than mine.

Casting me a nasty, suspicious look, he stumbled into the room behind the shop and I could see him swigging something from a bottle himself. Would he give me what I needed or some other foul and noxious concoction?

I caught a glimpse of myself in the grimy looking glass, which seemed positioned so that the man could observe his customers. For a fleeting moment I thought it was some other boy I saw there, not this tall, thin, scraggy stranger with dark-ringed eyes and tousled hair. For the first time, it came to me that I looked little like my family. My face was too long, my hair too dark, my mouth too large. My sisters and mother were all fair-haired, my brother and father ginger. Even my dark brown eyes marked me as different. Their eyes were pale, shades of winter sky, weak blues and grays. I felt no part of them.

A splintering crash shattered the air and pieces of glass flew across the floor and through the doorway. The apothecary let forth some vitriolic language before setting to again, pouring liquids from bottles and mashing something in his mortar. I strained my eyes but could not make out the names on the bottles he was using.

The man stumbled back to where I waited. He placed two small, corked brown bottles and a tight-lidded white pottery jar on the table and put the oil lamp beside them. He wrote spidery words onto two labels, tying one around each bottle neck with stubby, fumbling fingers. Finally, he offered me some clean cloths rolled in a bundle, which I gladly took.

He held out his hand and named his price. I knew his price to be unfair. I knew it as well as I know the names of every part of a horse's foot. I opened my mouth to argue, but held my tongue, merely handing over a coin and waiting for the change, my hands large and long, the fingers seeming thinner even than usual, shadowed with dirt and darkness and reddened with cold. They looked, I thought suddenly, like a grown man's hands.

He hesitated, met my stare with his rheumy eyes, and sniffed. He pocketed the coin.

"My master will be waiting," I said, looking back at him.

After only a moment's hesitation more, he gave me the necessary coins. I picked up one bottle and read the label. Southernwood, woundwort, comfrey, turpentine, as I had expected — that would be for the wound. And what for the fever? On the other bottle, the label proclaimed, "Tinct. of feverfew and tansy." There was no label on the white container. I pried open the lid. And put it back down again, firmly, with a grimace. Leeches. Leeches squirming and tangled.

I had seen leeches used on horses. They were often used on humans, but I had been lucky enough to escape their need. People said that there was no pain, only an extraordinary weakness, a floating sensation, and that the fever would disappear within hours. Or not. I did not like seeing a horse weakened until it could not bear its own weight, and I did not like the idea of administering leeches to the girl. But I would do what required to be done.

"Do you advocate cupping?" I asked respectfully, and trying to show that I knew something of such methods.

The apothecary spat on the floor, as with clumsy fingers he tied a piece of string around the pottery jar. "Mere wizardry! Pah! Bleed a fever and save your cups for ale or stronger liquor, I say. Do you know how to administer leeches, boy?"

"Yes," I replied. "I have seen it done on a horse."

But he was continuing anyway. "One leech, applied to an area where a deal of blood resides — ideally, of course, to the wound itself, where it promotes the healing process, though it takes a strong man to withstand such agony. To be administered until extreme weakness occurs. You will see the patient become quieted and the fever reduced."

I made my thanks and left as quickly as I could. Outside, I stowed the bottles and the container of leeches in the bag as safely as I was able, wedging them for protection between the items of food.

I had planned to return immediately to the girl.

That was what I should have done. But fate had other ideas, and very different events took their course.

"As flies to wanton boys are we to the gods. They kill us for their sport." I know my Shakespeare, of course.

A sudden memory came to me — a summer day more than two years past, my portly tutor perspiring in his frock coat and wilting stock as he slouched in a chair; my own neck hot and tight in my stiff indoor collar; my head buzzing like the insects that flapped against the windowpanes, as I recited the passage from Mr. Shakespeare's *King Lear* that I had spent the previous evening learning by rote, understanding little. And all the time I wondered at why I should learn such ancient words that spoke to me of nothing, or of worlds far from my own, when outside were fish to catch and horses to ride and rabbits to shoot. Most of all, I wished to swim in the river — there was a place where a rock stood high above a deep pool. Even my brother would not dare such a thing, but that summer I had spent many an hour with only my horse for company, and in those peaceful hours I had perfected my dive. I should be there now, not here indoors with books and dusty words.

Thinking on this, I paused in my recitation, vowing in a moment of summer madness to question my tutor and to goad him into distraction, dull and dutiful man that he was. I hoped that if I were sufficiently to annoy him he might let me go early. But when I looked up to put my thoughts into action, I saw that his head had fallen onto his chest, and his eyes were closed.

Grinning, I looked outside, at the blue, the deep and empty blue. And looked back to see if he were still asleep. To wonder, perchance, if I could escape and leave him to his dreams while I ran outside where I wished to be.

It was some moments before I wondered that he did not snore, that his chest did not rise and fall, that a chill stillness had crept over the room like a shadow passing the sun, that even the flies had stopped their dizzy humming.

He had died: died while I read aloud. His death shocked me in some way that I could not put words to. For him to have died while only I was there, while only I could have called back his spirit, was . . . strange and disturbing to me, though I had liked him little. Had he thought of me at the moment of his passing and wished to call out? Had his spirit looked down on me as it floated away? I slept little that night, worrying about spirits and ghosts.

I would not forget the words I had read at the time of his dying. "As flies to wanton boys are we to the gods. . . ."

But little good would my learning do me now.

CHAPTER EIGHT

A jar of preserved lemons. That was all it was. You would hardly think harm would come from buying a jar of lemons.

It may sound foolish that at a time of such danger, at a time when a young girl was close to death and I was further from my old life than I could imagine, I was thinking of luxuries. The truth is that I was not. And the truth is, too, that it was not merely buying the jar of lemons that caused the trouble that followed. It was stopping to examine the items on the old woman's barrow, and then remembering that my nurse gave us preserved lemons and oranges in winter to keep away unspecified illness, and being tempted to stop and stare and wonder and remember the delicious tangy taste, and deciding to buy. If none of that had happened, then I would perhaps have heard the soldiers in time. Or I would have been out of sight before they came.

It was as I was handing over the coin, and as the gap-toothed crone was passing me the stone jar, and as I was preparing to put it in my bag, that the sound of their marching and the jangle of chains and the shouts of men came to my ears. At first I did not move, my thoughts confused as to the meaning of this noise. Then I whipped around, dropping the small coins that the woman was handing me.

My staring eyes told her all she needed to know. "Summat to 'ide, 'ave we, chook? Deserter, mebbe?" She grinned, one eye sweeping its gaze madly into the distance, the other fixing itself on my face. The wandering eye skittered like a water drop running across shiny metal.

I shook my head, struck dumb. I looked at the approaching soldiers. At first I could not say if they were militia or the King's army — both wore red coats. But no, they were militia — the militia that my father supported with his money and his fervor, though I saw from their insignia that these were not Northumberland militia and so would not recognize me. Six of them, four on foot and two officers on black horses. They escorted a line of ten men, their ankles linked by clanking chains, heads bowed, shoulders drooping. One man only did not hang his head — he yelled and raved at the soldiers and received whiplashes on his back for his boldness.

It was a press-gang, rounding up men out of work to serve in His Majesty's army. We were still at war, as usual, against France and her allies, and willing men were hard to find. The soldiers would do well from this gang of new recruits — the commanding officer would receive a generous booty and share it, fairly or not, among his men. I could only feel sorry for these poor souls — I at least had my freedom, uncomfortable though it was. They were no more than slaves. Perhaps they deserved no better; perhaps they were felons, lacking in honor. But still I felt for them.

If I could have run, I would have, but my feet were fixed to the ground, and I could not see which way to go.

The old woman held out her hand. "Make it worth summat," she whispered, chewing something sticky, juice dribbling from the corner of her gummy mouth. "Make it good and make it quick, pretty boy."

I snatched up the coins from the ground and put one in her hand, but she held it out still. Another. Her one good eye stared at me; then she looked toward the soldiers and opened her mouth to shout. I put the remaining coins in her hand, pleading with my face.

She closed her yellowed fingers over the coins and

slipped them into her skirt. She paused one moment. And another. Then, grinning, the witch raised her voice and shouted to the soldiers. "Over 'ere! A deserter!"

I ran, dropping the jar of lemons on her table. I do not think they saw my face. I have never found such speed as I found at that moment. And, as I ran, I had only one thought: that if I lived to tell the tale, and if I met her again, I would do to that old woman as she had done to me. And more.

At first I could not tell if I was followed. As I ran, slipping on the slimy cobbles down a narrow, icy street, I heard shouting behind me, but I could not be sure it was for me. But soon I could hear the clattering of a horse's hooves and then I knew.

How might I outrun a horse?

In place of terrible fear, my body was filled with energy, and my head with light, a power and clarity stamping on the flames of any terror. Yes, my heart beat fast and the breath felt painful in my throat, but I almost sang with speed. I knew what I was looking for. I only prayed I would find it quickly.

Darting into a deep doorway, I pressed myself against the stones, making myself as small and thin as I could, and within a few moments the horseman passed, the hooves skidding around the corner, in the direction I would have gone. He was alone —

the others must have taken a different path. I slipped from my hiding place and ran the other way, taking the first turn I came to.

The windowless walls leaned over me. There were no doors, no turns that I could see, just the narrow mouth at the far end. If soldiers came down here now, there was nowhere for me to turn. My face was hot, my breath knife-sharp in my chest, the cold air burning my lungs. Anger drove me on: anger at the treachery of the old woman and her sly, dishonorable theft of my money, anger at the way fate played with my life.

I would escape these soldiers! I would return to the girl! I would live to tell the tale!

At the end of the narrow alleyway, I had a choice: to turn right or left. No soldiers were in sight, though their shouting and the clattering of hooves seemed not far away. A few people were going about their business. A serving girl threw slops out of a doorway into the road. She smiled at me shyly.

The noises came closer. Still, I could not properly judge the direction. "The inn?" I shouted to the girl. "I need the inn. Please!" And I smiled at her, hoping that my dark eyes would work some charm on her.

CHAPTER NINE

She pointed. "Turn left after them trees."

I ran. The noise of hooves clanged closer. Now, I saw two militiamen on foot, some distance ahead of me. Pointing. Running toward me. I swerved into the inn yard, the bottles clanking in my bag.

Here was what I had hoped to find, my reason for searching for an inn. Horses. Four, tied up. Three of them saddled. Their heads hung low as they took their rest. One had his muzzle deep in a bucket of water. This one I avoided — a horse that has recently drunk is not a horse to rely on for speed or stamina. I would need both those things, and more. Good fortune would I need, too, though fortune was not something that seemed to shine on me at that time.

I grabbed the reins of another, unlooping them from the hook in the wall, and leaped into the saddle, sliding my feet into the stirrups. They were too long for me, but I had no time to shorten them. Gripping the saddle with my knees, and hooking the bag over the pommel, I wheeled the horse around and galloped out of that inn yard before anyone could notice.

With my heels digging sharply into the horse's flanks, fast as a hunted hare we veered between the gateposts. In one direction, through blurred vision, I glimpsed the two militiamen. In another direction was the unmistakable figure of the mounted officer, his horse dancing under his cruel spurs. Surprise gave us valuable seconds and, before they could confirm that I was their prey, I had put many yards between myself and them.

"Fire! For God's sake, men, fire!" shouted the mounted officer, and two shots rang out, crashing through the air and sending birds flying in fright. I flinched, though I was not hit. Two more soldiers appeared and more shots rang out. I felt the breath of lead passing my ear. I could do nothing but continue, kicking the horse to its utmost speed, crouching low in the saddle. My face, my cheeks, were taut with effort, as I waited for the terrible impact of a musket ball. I shouted encouragement in the horse's ear and thanked God that I had chosen such a willing mount.

More shots rang out but the men were slow to reload, and their aim was poor. Very soon, I was out of range of the muskets, but I knew I was not safe. An officer of the militia, hoping to brag of his success to his fellow county gentlemen, would not let me escape so easily; sure enough, I could hear his horse's hooves thumping on the road behind me. I could only pray that we went too fast for him to fire his pistol with accuracy.

I did not know my horse, but I knew that he must be used to carrying heavier than me. And I thanked the many hours I had spent in the saddle, riding horses as good as this.

The road was icy, slippery and uneven. Dangerous. Stones rolled and clattered and spun into the air as we passed. It was, as I knew well, the same road that led to the place where the girl had refuge.

By some means, I must leave this road.

Scanning the hedgerows, I looked desperately for a chance to alter my direction. A low hedge ran along to the left. If I did not act now, it would be too late. I veered hard to the right and then twisted sharp left, urging my mount to jump the hedge. Gripping with my knees and leaning forward, I flattened myself along his back as we launched into the air. Sure-footed, he landed on the other side, but I had no time to rejoice: I urged him again across the field, mud splattering from his feet.

Briefly, I looked around to see how closely I was followed. Too closely, too closely by far, the man's coat a scarlet splash against the gray background. A new cold wind whipped across my eyes, bringing an icy rain, almost snow, and I blinked to see clearly. I prayed that my horse would not slip. I wished then that I had not left the pistols behind. If I fell now, I would have nothing with which to fight, no hope at all. I would die. Fear fingered the back of my neck, and I despised myself again. Did everyone feel such skin-crawling terror?

The hill stretched ahead. My earlier strength was failing and my breath now almost burst in my chest. The cold air sliced painfully into my throat. Desperation took hold. Could the horse understand? This was life or death, perhaps for both of us. The horse's withers were frothy with sweat, and I could see the flaring edges of his nostrils, hear his snorting breath. How much longer could he last? I urged him with my body, with every part of me, shouting, "Faster! Faster!" though I knew he tried his best.

Would that be good enough?

CHAPTER TEN

Another hedge threaded the landscape ahead of us. Scanning my eyes along it, I tried to judge the place where it was lowest and veered slightly in that direction.

My head spun with exhaustion. Flecks of sweat flew from my horse's neck.

I could hear the other horse behind me, hear its hollow-barrel breath, hear the slap of its hooves in the mud, its rhythmic grunt each time its front legs hit the ground.

"Common horse thief!" shouted the officer. "I'll have you, I will! I'll not spare you for the gallows! I'll gibbet you myself, by God I will!" His voice sliced the cold air between us, and I shivered. There was nothing to stop him doing exactly as he said. For the second time in one day's span, death sat at my shoulder.

I wanted more time, so much more time. Time to act, to prove my worth. My father thought nothing of me. I thought almost as little of myself. How could fate be so cruel as to pursue me like this and give me no chance to grow into the man I might be? My eyes stung with the unfairness of it.

Sensing the officer closing in on me, I felt my horse near the end of his strength. Yet again I urged him on, asked more of him, even more, as we approached that looming hedge. It looked larger now, huge as it rushed closer to us. Too late, I saw a gate farther along, lower than the hedge. But I could not change my course now.

A few more strides, a few more paces, and with one last effort I gathered the horse up and flew with him as he surged bravely into the air. The bare hawthorn branches tore at his flesh as we passed. But he did not falter! I wanted to shout aloud — we were over!

We landed with a stumbling thud but did not fall, and I turned him sharply to the left, following the line of the hill now, no longer trying to force him upward.

My happiness was short-lived.

Within a moment, a scream and a terrible cry ripped the air behind us. Two noises, merging into each other. I wheeled around, pulling my horse to a halt, and opened my eyes wide with horror. Everything seemed to happen slowly, and in a strange order, an order that did not make sense. Did I hear the screams first or did I see the officer fly through the air and land twisted on his neck? Did the man crumple to his death or did the horse land on its knees first, with that terrible splintering crack that I will remember till my dying breath? Did the man die instantly or did he writhe first, or was the writhing simply part of how he twisted through the air, knowing he was about to die?

And did I leap from my horse before I knew the man was dead or did I sit motionless, struck dumb, for as long as I seem to remember? And did the horse scream in terror and pain and did he bleed and try to rise from those broken front legs? Did I see or did I imagine the eyes wide in shock or was that merely my own horror? And when the horse looked at me, as I ran toward him, ignoring the dead man, did that beautiful creature truly seem to plead with me to do what I already knew I must?

As if in some terrible nightmare, as if directed by some stronger power, I ran to the dead man and pulled a pistol from his belt, not looking at his still-staring eyes. A double-barreled pistol, I noticed. Fully primed. Half-cocked. I ran to the horse, as it lay struggling. I placed my hand on the side of the warm neck, to soothe him, but further than that I did not, could not, hesitate: through my tears, I placed the mouth of the gun against the side of his temple, cocked the hammer, and shot him.

He crumpled instantly. But I shot him again with the other barrel, blindly, angrily, desperately, the force sending me lurching backward. And I wished it was that traitorous, gap-toothed old woman whom I shot. In my anger I wished that more than anything.

A scream was welling up inside me, and I felt a terrible need to collapse, to give up there, even to reload and use the pistol on myself. What sort of life was I leading? Brutal. Lonely, and without control or hope.

But I did not use the pistol on myself. It was not honorable to give up and although many things about my new life were not honorable, that was no reason to sink to the lowest depths. I may have been a coward in my parents' eyes, but I would not yield. I did not know where I was going or what the future held, but I would not give up my life, until life was dragged from me.

I walked slowly to where my own mount stood, its head drooping, its flanks white with sweat, its nostrils wide, all strength spent. I looked at the pistol in my hand. I had a horse and a pistol. I was better placed to survive than I had been only an hour before.

Yet I knew I could not keep them. The soldiers would be looking for a boy with a horse. Stealing a horse was a crime punishable by death. If I were lucky and found myself before a lenient judge, or a corrupt one, I might escape with a lesser punishment, but I had also caused the death of an officer and his horse; add to that the fact that I had stolen money and taken an officer's pistol, and I would be fortunate not to find myself hanging slowly from the gallows after the next court session.

I had seen it happen. I had even seen one gibbeting. My father had made me watch with my brother — he said it was right that a man should watch a hanging, that it was good for a boy's character to see justice done. It seemed that my brother did so with greater pleasure than I could ever feel. As for my father, he had watched without emotion — the victim was a man he had sentenced to death himself, and I marveled at the power my father wielded. It was not a power I would have desired. Could he be sure of the man's guilt? I hoped so. Was he ever unsure? Would he sleep easy in his bed if he was not sure?

I had not believed, until I saw it, that an executioner could be so skillful that the condemned man would survive hanging, castrating, and disemboweling, before losing his senses with the beheading. The cutting into quarters had barely been necessary, except to serve as a horrifying deterrent to those of us who watched.

And what of the pistol? Should I keep it? If I were

caught with it, my punishment would perhaps be the greater than if I went unarmed, not least because I might be tempted to use it. I should leave it in the officer's hand. Then it could be assumed that the officer had shot the horse before succumbing to his own injuries or the cold. I would be nowhere to be found, and it would be viewed as a terrible accident.

I looked once more at the weapon in my hand. To take it or not to take it? I made a decision. Stooping, I placed it in the dead man's hand, closing his gloved fist around it. I had not had cause to touch a dead man before, and I avoided looking at his face. He would have killed me, I reminded myself. He would have done it with pleasure.

Tying my horse's reins so that he would not trip on them, I led him a little way along the track until we came to a gate, which I opened, leading him through. I pointed him in the right direction and gave him a hefty thump on his hindquarters to send him on his way. At first he trotted, before slowing to a walk and then a standstill. He turned his tired head and looked at me. For all his beauty he was a fool: he should have known he would have no life with me. He should have known, and galloped away to his own master.

Wishing I could take him but knowing I could not, I retraced my steps to where the dead man lay next to his broken horse. I had made a new decision. As sleeting snow began to fall from a granite sky, settling on the bodies like a soft, natural blanket, I now took the gun from the man's hand, along with his leather shot bag and his copper powder flask, and the matching pistol from his belt. Sheltering it with my body, I took a measure of powder and placed it in the cup, rammed a paper-wrapped shot down each of the two barrels, replacing the rod in its place under the barrels, all as I had been taught many times. I did the same for the other pistol and then put them both, uncocked for safety, in my belt, covered by my jacket.

Who knew when I might be glad of them?

As I walked away, I turned back once and saw the horse again. He was standing there, head hanging, sniffing at the dead horse's body. I had no choice — I picked up a clod of earth and threw it at him. Bewildered, he looked up and, casting one long look at me, he turned and trotted away.

Never had I felt more lonely than I did then. I did not look again at the dead horse. I could not. I simply walked away with a heart as heavy as it had ever been.

CHAPTER ELEVEN

At last, I came back to the hovel where the girl was. I reckoned I had been away for more than three hours. The dreary February day was now as light as it would become, hung with gray, veiled in a watery gauze that swung between snow and rain.

Fearful about the state in which I would find her, I called out softly as I approached the door. I hoped she had heard me, that she was not waiting with her pistols ready.

I need not have worried. She was lying where I had left her, and her breathing sounded worse than before. The pistols were still on the ground beside her. There was a smell of dankness in the air, and the damp could not have been of benefit to her condition.

Hurrying to where she lay, I touched her shoulder. She jerked awake, and tried to sit up, wincing as she did. Too late, she reached out for a pistol, before realizing who I was.

Grabbing it before she could touch it, I moved them both out of her grasp. "Be calm: it is only Will. I have brought physic for you." I felt her brow. It was no cooler than before. I offered her water.

I will spare the details of her wound and how she suffered when I bathed it in the apothecary's potion. I could only imagine how it must sear her flesh. I bound it in a clean cloth and tied the knots as tightly as I could.

Picking up the other bottle, I raised her head and helped her take a mouthful from it. I could not tell whether she took the right amount, but the time for fretting about such things was over — she needed the remedy and too much would make no difference.

It was time now for the leeches. I would not place them on the wound, even if the apothecary were standing over me.

As I lifted the jar from inside my bag, I knew something had broken. I could feel the crunch of rough-edged pottery. Carefully, I laid it down on the ground. The lid was in several pieces, although the container itself was intact. I had no hope of keeping leeches without a tight-fitting lid, as they could squeeze themselves through even the narrowest cracks, their boneless bodies capable of extraordinary escapes. There was no choice — I must use them now and then dispose of them. Without enthusiasm, I selected the thinnest two of the oozing black creatures, guessing that the thinnest must be the hungriest. They immediately tried to attach themselves to me, sliding wetly up my fingers toward the fleshy parts of my hand. I used my other hand to scrape them back into the container, which I placed on the ground beside the girl. I gently shook her shoulder.

"I am awake," she said with difficulty. Then, after a pause, "Why do you not kill me? I would have killed you."

"Would you? I do not believe so," I said. "Besides, I could not have left you. I could not have left even an injured animal." No, indeed, I thought, recalling how I had helped the horse escape its mortal agony.

"Animal!" she retorted, but cutting short her laughter as she winced. "I am ill," she said after a pause, trying to speak smoothly over her pain. "You should go. Take your money and return to your family. It's clear that you are a gentleman's son."

"I cannot."

"Why?"

"I will not say. You did not see fit to trust me sufficiently to let me fetch your horse. How should I trust you with my story?" She smiled at that and her eyes opened. Black they seemed, deep and black like coal, yet like ice in moonlight. I had a strange sense of her strength: although she lay helpless and sick and in pain, nevertheless she seemed stronger than I. It was as though she cared little what happened to her, and she would meet her fate with that same slight smile. How I wished I might care so little.

"Who are you? Where are you from?"

Her questions seemed small but were more than I wished to answer, and so I did not. Glancing at the leeches crawling up the sides of the container, I spoke firmly. "I must let some blood. For the fever. I have leeches." Her eyes closed again. "I must place them on your arm. Above your elbow."

She said nothing. She was lying on her back, her head on the bare floor, where it had slipped from the makeshift pillow I had made for her. Refashioning the pillow, I lifted her head to make her more comfortable. For a moment I wondered at myself, how I was touching a girl, how I had seen the flesh of her ribs, how she lay in front of me helpless as a kitten.

But none of this seemed to matter. She was nothing more than an injured person, and I the only one who could help her. When, in the daylight now, I saw her well-made jacket, its silver buttons, the lace at her throat, her warm rich cloak, her dark breeches,

I was intrigued by her story, her life, how she came to be armed with pistols, dressed like a man, how she came to steal my money from me by night. I had heard tales of highwaymen, of their bravery and their skill with horse, pistol, and sword. How could a girl be so brave and so strong?

How had she come to choose a robber's life? What evils must lurk in her heart? I had come to felony by accident, through no fault of my own. The victim of circumstance, I had not chosen this way, but she perhaps had? What corruption of mind had brought her to this? Would I come to regret helping her, once she was well again and the evil of her ways became clear? What she did was wrong and unnatural. And very dangerous.

Meanwhile, I would help her, unsure whether I did so because I wanted to or because I had no choice.

Chapter Twelve

I pulled back her sleeve as high as it would go. Her arm was strong and well muscled, quite unlike the soft white flesh of my sisters or my mother. I placed the two leeches on the fleshy part between her elbow and her shoulder, where they quickly settled themselves, wriggling into position and latching on to her.

Within moments they had begun to suck rhythmically. I watched them carefully and with some distrust, while also keeping an eye on the others wriggling in their container. Every now and then it was necessary to push one back to the bottom.

The leeches swelled before my eyes as they gorged on her blood. How long should I leave them there? With a standing horse, it became obvious when it weakened, but the girl was already lying down, already weak and pale.

She spoke, her eyes still closed. "I shall tell you where I live, where my horse will be. I shall draw a map. Later." Were her words slurring? I thought they were. "Water," she said.

I held the leather water bottle to her lips, then drank from it myself.

It was as I placed the bottle on the ground that we both heard it. A noise. Outside. Hooves. Many of them. Men's voices. We looked at each other. I slipped my pistols from my belt, glad now that I had taken them.

"Give mine to me," whispered the girl.

I did not hesitate, not for one moment. We were bound together, this girl and I. If I was wrong, she would shoot me, but what would she gain from that? I reached over and gave her the pistols, first cocking them for her. She gave me a furious look when I did that.

"Perhaps they hunt you?" I whispered, ignoring her look. "The man who fired the shot that injured you, is he not searching still?"

"No," she replied quietly but with certainty. "That was many miles away. Besides, it was a poacher, not a soldier."

I was glad of that. The thought of becoming caught up in her crimes was not one I relished.

We waited — I crouching, she lying on her back but leaning slightly to her uninjured side, each with our weapons pointing toward the door, mine held as steady as possible. I could hear her breathing, hard and fast from pain and fever; her bottom lip was caught in her teeth as she struggled to keep her pistols steady. The noise of hooves changed: no longer was it a rhythmic trotting, but the scuffling and clanking sound of horses stopping, bridles chinking, muskets tapping against metal. Shouted orders. Footsteps, coming closer, the sound now of spurs clacking on stones. Or muskets being primed? Still the footsteps came closer, and I could hear men's voices, too, laughing and joking.

I felt something sliding along my neck. Sweat, I thought at first. I wondered why sweat was sliding sideways, and then upward, creeping toward my ear. A leech! I flung one hand up toward it with a yelp. The girl glared at me, and I could have cursed at my own foolishness. There was silence outside the door. The footsteps had stopped.

We waited — waited for the door to burst open and the redcoats to rush in with their muskets firing. We could hear some voices farther away, and the jumbled clattering of horses shifting position, perhaps still at the road, or perhaps going around to the back to cut off our escape. But whoever was outside the door stayed silent.

A clatter and a shot! A curse. But still the door did not open. The girl looked at me again, the fever giving her eyes a strange light. "Do not fire!" she mouthed. I glared at her — I did not need to be told. No person of good sense wastes a pistol shot, even if his weapon does have two barrels. One shot in each barrel and no time to reload. And how many soldiers outside the door? Too many.

After the shot and the curse, there was only silence. I strained every sense, tensed every muscle, ready to fire my four shots at whoever came through that door. Wait! Now I could hear something. Rustling. Followed by a hiss. And then I realized what it was. And so did the girl. She smiled. I blushed. The stream of piss went on for many moments as we waited there, our pistols still pointing in front of us.

At last, the men finished and soon we heard their footsteps moving away again. Within a minute the horses were all trotting into the distance.

All the girl's strength was spent, and I had to remove the pistols from her hand and uncock them for her. I laid them on the ground nearby. She rested her head on the makeshift pillow and closed her eyes again.

The leeches were still feeding on her arm, now engorged and five or six times bigger than before. Just when I was wondering when to remove them, one fell from her arm, having drunk its fill. Within a few more moments, the other one too had fallen. I picked them up, replaced them in the jar with the others, and tied it up as well as I could with a cloth. I would dispose of them outside. I did not want to share my home with such creatures and decided henceforth to use only the other remedies the apothecary had given me. And to put my faith in God, if God chose to hear me.

Telling the girl I would be back soon, I left the hovel, taking the leeches and a pistol, and hefted the door shut behind me.

Chapter Thirteen

Outside, snow was beginning to fall and the sky was like new steel. I looked around at my new home. It was a bothy — a small hovel standing alone, with a lean-to byre against one side. A pile of split, mildewed logs lay in the lee of the building. Nearby was a pump. I lifted the handle and lowered it. Its rusty squeak was loud in the surrounding silence, but there was no one to hear and I pumped the handle a few times. The water that came from the spout was pure and fresh, for which I was more than thankful. An ancient bucket sat beneath the pump, with black ice at the bottom. I rinsed it out before filling it with fresh water and washing my face in it, gasping at the cold.

We had water, firewood, and enough food for a few days. No other cottages were near, though on a distant, dark hill I could just make out another squat dwelling. The village where I had had my narrow escape was out of sight. If we stayed inside and watched for passing soldiers, we were as safe as we could be.

Until now, I had not liked the harsh landscape of these moors, the vast rolling swathes of rock and heather and dead gorse, the sudden precipices, holes, and deep-cut streams. Everything was coarse and cold, nothing soft, nothing welcoming. The moors stared, uncaring, unknowable. They had frightened me when I heard tell of them as a child: the nursery stories of ghosts and wolves and treacherous marshes and wandering madmen and highway robbery had woven their dark threads through my mind until the moors were a place I had hoped never to pass through. Now, though still afraid of their dangers, I was strangely glad of their loneliness and their emptiness.

I walked a distance from the building and, after removing the cloth, cast the leeches and their jar into a ditch. Returning, I picked up an armful of firewood and pushed open the door, calling out as I did so.

The girl lay where I had left her. There seemed no improvement in her condition, as far as I could say. She was shaking, with cold or ague I did not know. I removed my jacket and laid it on top of her, and spread my cloak upon her, too. She stirred slightly but neither opened her eyes nor spoke.

We needed a fire. There was a risk, I knew, that someone might see the smoke. But the snow was falling outside, and the girl needed warmth.

Collecting tiny dry sticks and pieces of straw from the corners of the room, I began to build the fire. I had seen a flint and steel in her bag, and I did not ask her permission but fetched them now. I was not accustomed to making fire like this — fire had always been available at home, and servants to bring it to me. It took me many strikes before the burning sparks lit the straw. When the first small flames begin to crackle and lick and spit, I smiled.

As the morning passed, the girl mostly slept while I busied myself to make our shelter better protected from the weather. I constructed a means of placing boards across the two small windows, though I left them open now to allow the light in. I filled our water bottles and wrapped our food so that no vermin might reach it. I checked the priming of our pistols and put the powder and shot where I could grasp them easily if I had need of them.

From among the bare trees behind the building, I searched out a fallen branch and used my knife to strip the small twigs from it. With only a small adjustment to its width, it fitted into the slots behind the door, making a sturdy barrier if we should have an unwelcome visitor.

Once, I woke the girl to give her physic but I did not change her dressing, preferring to leave it awhile longer.

In all, I was pleased with my preparations. All that could be done, I had done, and the girl and I would be comfortable here until she was well enough. I had not forgotten about her horse and how I had promised to fetch it. But I did not choose to remind her. Secretly, I did not want to go. It was safer here, and warmer, and I had company. Not, I grant you, that a half-conscious girl was much company, but any company was better than none.

But nor had she forgotten her horse. She woke with a start at around midday, trying to sit up, but quite unable to do so. "I must go!" she gasped. "My horse! I have to fetch him. He needs me." I helped her to sit, and she passed a hand over her forehead, pressing her temples between finger and thumb, closing her eyes for some few moments.

"I said I would go, and I shall," I said, with more confidence than I felt inside.

"No, I must go. Help me up. Hurry!" she snapped.

Well, we would soon discover how strong she was, I thought to myself. I helped her up, supporting most of her weight, and she swayed against me.

Her teeth were clenched as she slowly straightened. "There!" she said. I let go, and she clutched me tight.

"Very well," I said. "Are you ready? You will need to carry your bag."

Her knees crumpled, and she slowly sank to the ground, breathing heavily. "It is better," she insisted. "I will be as good as new. Soon."

"Two or three days. If you do not first worsen," I added for good measure.

She did not reply, and I took her silence for agreement.

"Help me outside," she said. "Please."

"No!" I was exasperated by her stubbornness. "You cannot move from here. You draw a map, and I will fetch your horse. I ride well. And if you still do not know whether you can trust me, remember — I could have killed you, or left you, at any time since yesterday."

"No, you misunderstand," she said, that slight smile again as she looked directly at my eyes. "I need to go outside."

"I . . . oh! Of course!" I realized what she wanted and blushed hotly as I did so. A lady would never . . . but then a lady would not find herself in such a position. I moved over to the door and hoisted it open. A gust of snow blew in, and we both shrank from its chill. I helped her to her feet again, and we made slow, painful progress toward the entrance. I could only admire her fortitude. She made no sound, except the slow, strained noise of her breathing. She seemed to become stronger as she moved and although she was still hunched over, with one hand holding her side, by the time we were in the open air she was walking by herself, though slowly. She turned to look at me, still smiling, though with a white face. "Thank you, kind sir," she mocked. "I can manage on my own now." And, blushing again, I went back into our refuge and busied myself noisily doing nothing in particular.

When she returned, ashen-faced and with a dusting of snow on her hair, I helped her settle down again onto the ground and I shut the door, placing my heavy branch across it. A few more logs on the fire made it burn more warmly, though I did not wish to make too much smoke.

"Clear a space on the floor," she ordered. "So I can draw a map." And she did, using a stick in the dirt. The journey would take perhaps three or four hours, she said. If I did not get lost, or if I did not give up, she added with a contemptuous tilt of her mouth. I wished to tell her then how I had risked death for her that morning, how a horse had died as the price of curing her, the price of her returning strength and sharp tongue. I wished to tell her that, for a coward, I had faced danger more bravely than I had expected.

But I held my tongue. After all, perhaps she would say I had not been so very brave and perhaps she would be right — all I had done was to run away. The horse — well, how brave was it to shoot a horse that would die anyway? No, I had proved nothing except that I did not give up easily.

"I will not get lost. And I will not give up," I said simply, looking straight back at her. She looked down to her map, and she could not know how afraid I felt inside.

I wanted to propose to set off in the morning at first light. But I did not say it — I knew that the horse, if it was not sheltered, might not survive the night if the cold grew too intense. A native pony, thick-haired, stocky, and long-maned, could survive the worst the moors could muster, but her thorough-bred, as I guessed it must be, might not. And even though it was not my horse, I could not take that risk either.

When she was sure that I had understood the map, and when I had packed what I needed in my bag — food, water, and my knife — I slid my two pistols into my belt, and tied the shot bag and powder horn to it. I saw her settled as comfortably as was possible, lean-ing against a wall, everything she needed within easy reach. I placed two more logs on the fire, setting three more beside it, and made ready to leave.

"What is your name?" she asked suddenly. In her fever, she had forgotten that I had already told her.

As I opened my mouth to answer, something prevented me from saying my full name. I had been accustomed to know myself as "William de Lacey, younger son of Sir George de Lacey, High Sheriff and Member for Parliament," but now I said only, "Will. Will." I said it twice to convince myself. I liked the name Will; I liked its simplicity. It was better than William, and better by far than William de Lacey. I did not change my name in order to deceive her. I did it for myself, choosing to be free of William de Lacey, to be plain Will, with no burdens, no expectations.

But I admit, too, that it suited me that she did not know more.

"What is yours?" I asked her.

"Bess," she said.

Will and Bess. Bess and Will. I was glad that she would know me as Will. I knew nothing about her, and she would know nothing about me until such time as I was ready.

Two things only I remember as I went through the door: her black eyes looking at me, deep as a well; and her voice, weakened again by her fever, saying, "I'll look for you by moonlight."

What did she mean? Was it her confused mind, the fever talking? Perhaps that was not what she said. Perhaps her real words had floated away onto the whistling of the wind outside. Who knows?

I did not have time to wonder. I plunged into the thinly swirling snow, pulling my hat down tightly and gathering my cloak around my body. I tried not to think how much I would rather be sheltered and safe in that ruin with her, than out here, alone.

As fast as I could, I marched down the road and away from the village. I knew I must walk some six or seven miles along this road, perhaps for an hour and a half if I kept up a steady speed. Indeed, when I had been walking for what I reckoned must be such a length of time, and with a twilight gloom beginning to fall, I came to a crossroads, with just the signpost Bess had described. I took the left turn and continued up the lane, toward unfamiliar hills.

In the winter afternoon, the ghostly silence of the moors wrapped me up and drew me into their dangers and mysteries. I shivered and hunched my cloak more tightly around me.

Would I find Bess's home, and her horse? Or would a passerby find me some days later, a stiff corpse, and wonder who I might be?

CHAPTER FOURTEEN

Snow starts as something mysterious, something wonderful and magical. On the moors it can quickly turn dangerous. Landmarks disappear and trees change their shape for the approaching traveler. I did not know the landscape even without the snow. With it, I lost my sense of direction.

But Bess's instructions were clearly given, drummed into me in that impatient way of hers. She had told me to follow the lane upward until I came to a row of six poplar trees. These I quickly found. From here I was to leave the lane and continue in the same direction as the trees, always heading upward, until I came to the brow of the hill. There I would find a standing stone, shaped like a cross, and on this cross I would find marked the four points of the compass. Northeast from here, and no more than thirty paces,

I would find a wall with a stile, which I should climb, and then follow the line of the wall, downward and then up the next hill. At some point, I would have to leave the wall, but I should always aim for a hill of a particular shape, which she drew for me in the dirt. Over the brow of this hill, I was to search for the source of a stream, among some large boulders on the very edge of a small pine wood. Bess said it would take not much more than an hour if I made good progress.

Driven by fear of becoming lost, and of being frozen to death, I kept up good speed and, less than an hour later, found myself at the top of the hill, breathless and sweating despite the cold. I looked in all directions, peering through the softly swirling snow. Where was the stone cross?

Which way? Either was possible. A mistake could herald disaster, as the snow was now falling so thickly that my footsteps were covered within minutes of being made.

It was by now late afternoon and the winter light was fading fast, gray gloom shrouding everything. I could see only a few yards ahead of me and the shapes of rocks and trees were like ghosts, staring at me through the veil of snow, waiting to see which way I would go.

I did not have much time if I were to reach the

bottom of the valley before darkness fell completely. Bess's home was over there somewhere, on the other side, but I had to choose the right path down the hillside or I would find myself in a treacherous marsh. Bess had warned me, though I already knew well enough the stories of people walking to their death on these moors, the ground turning to lethal silt without warning to those ignorant or foolish enough to venture into this region unprepared.

I had to choose a direction. Straining my eyes, I thought I could make out the darker shape of something ahead, and I made toward it. I was glad of my thickly woven winter cloak — if it had been thinner, my whole body would have been as wet as my drenched thighs.

Luck was with me once more. There was the stone cross, rising like a stern friar in front of me. I hurried toward it. So thick was it that I could not have put my arms around it, and tall, taller by far than I. I looked up at its cold strength and gave thanks to God for signs and crosses and the men who in early times had placed it there for the sake of travelers.

With my fingers, I traced the marks that depicted the points of the compass and hurried in a northeasterly direction, counting my steps as I went.

Sure enough, there was the wall, the stile. My heart leaped! How could I have been afraid? Almost laughing, I scrambled over the stile and followed the wall as Bess had instructed. Running now, toward the next brow, the cold air sharp in my throat, I hoped against all hope that I should not lose the way. Could I be sure this was the right hill? In this fading light, perhaps the shapes played tricks on my eyes?

At the crest of this hill, I stopped, leaned forward gasping, trying to quiet my breathing so that I could listen for the sound of water, as Bess had told me I must. Nothing. Still nothing. Had I made a mistake? I looked around, desperately. From which direction had I come? Should I retrace my steps and return to the stone cross?

The emptiness was huge, all-encompassing.

And then — suddenly — the unmistakable sound of water ahead of me! Bess had said that beside this spring was the path I was to take down the hillside, starting between two rocks taller than the others. Sure enough, her directions had been good once more — here were the rocks and here the path. I hurried down it, taking care on the slippery stones, all my senses alert. There was no need to worry about soldiers here. My greatest danger was in slipping. I held my arms out for greater balance and to break any fall. But I found that I was sure-footed, and my confidence grew as I sped down the path. Nothing could hurt me! I would reach Bess's home and find her horse. I would ride it back to her and then . . . well, then I would see what might happen. I need not think further than this task. Luck was on my side and God would provide.

Would He not?

Perhaps the spirits of that place heard my boastfulness. Perhaps I forgot that Bess had told me to seek out the turn to the left. Perhaps I simply went with too much haste. Whatever the reason, I missed the fork in the path.

At first, I did not suspect anything was amiss, so keenly did I speed down the hill, so blindly did I follow that path. It was only when I came to the bottom and found no drystone wall that I slowed down. It was only when my feet began to slip and then sink, bringing me to a standstill, that I remembered her instructions and understood my mistake. Stunned, with panic sending a clouding rain over my vision, I stood stock-still. The wind slapped icy water at my face.

The marshes! I had come to the marshes. I should be nowhere near them. I turned, or tried to. I pulled one foot from the mud, bringing my boot only with difficulty. My left leg was deeper in the mud beneath the snow. The more I tried to move, the more it sank. I fell forward onto the ground, digging my hands into the gray slime. A flurry of wind blew fresh snow into my face. Lying as flat as I could, I very slowly began to pull my leg from the mud. It would not come. The harder I pulled, the more the mud sucked it back.

Fear and loneliness threatened to overcome me.

With every jot of strength, and anger at the weather, which seemed to shriek its laughter in my face, I fought my fear and forced myself to be calm, and at last, with a horrible sucking sound, my leg came free. I was safe.

But I would not be safe if I stayed much longer. Weeks or months later, I would be found, a ragged skeleton and no one to say who I might have been. I must move. I must go backward — I could only be a pace or two from safe ground, I reasoned with myself. I slowly raised my body onto my hands and knees and crawled backward. When I thought I was surely safe, I stood up, carefully, feeling the ground firm beneath me as I straightened. Now, all I had to do was turn and walk back the way I had come. Inch by inch, I turned until I judged myself to be facing in the right direction. The blizzard now was swirling so thickly that there was nothing my eyes could tell me.

I took a step forward . . . and sank once again to my ankles. Heart thumping, I slowly dragged my heavy foot out, and placed it but a short distance to the right. It sank again. Which direction was I facing? Which way had I come? Which way was safety?

CHAPTER FIFTEEN

I stood, motionless, desperately trying to judge which way I must be facing, to decide what to do. I was shivering now, not only from the cold. My father was right — I was a coward. I knew this because my mind was crying out to be led to safety. I was desperately clinging to life, whatever that life might hold. I wished that anyone were here instead of me.

I think I shouted. I shouted to the wind, to God, to no one at all, for I knew no one could hear. I screamed out my fear and my fury and my prayers.

It was at this moment that I saw it — though even now I cannot be sure. I blinked. Could I have imagined it? A light. Far ahead of me, moving slightly, swaying in the wind, like a lantern held at shoulder height.

I blinked again. The light disappeared. But no! There it was again. Swinging. Moving away from me slowly. I peered into the growing darkness, my wide eyes stinging in the whipping snow. Wiping my hand across my vision, I strained to see. Yes! It *was* a light.

But then again, perhaps it was not. I still could not be sure what I saw. I am still not sure now.

I had a choice: I could ignore the light, or I could follow it. Something drew me on, something that I will never understand. It was not bravery. It was something deeper. We are drawn to light as moths to a flame, even if the flame may singe our wings.

The light seemed to move in one direction. And disappeared. Now it appeared again, swinging in the same direction, and disappeared once more. The next time this occurred, I thought perchance that whoever held the lantern meant me to move in the same direction as he had moved the light. Tugging my foot, I took one step. The ground was firm. The light moved again. I stepped again in the direction indicated. Firm ground once more. Could I be rescued? I began to dare hope so.

I stepped forward.

Firm ground was beneath me at every step now, as I followed the swinging direction of the light. I hurried forward, trying to get closer to whoever held the lantern, or whatever it was. Sometimes the light disappeared completely, and I would stand and wonder if I had imagined it, as I peered into the darkness and the swirling blizzard. Perhaps I did? But each time I glimpsed it again, I believed it, and followed it eagerly.

As I hurried, the light moved faster away from me. But then, in a sudden lull of the wind, the snow thinned and I could see a dark shape — a horse, surely a horse! A rider on a horse. I could even observe the outline of his cloak. And then, as suddenly, the snow swirled again, and I could see nothing but the faint swinging of the distant light.

I do not know how much time passed as I followed the light across the marsh. I forgot my tiredness, my soaking clothes, my icy skin; I almost forgot my fear, fixing my mind only on the light and the occasional flimsy glimpse of the shape of a horse and rider. If that was what I saw. Each time I saw it, I thought I was certain, but within moments I was equally sure that my memory was playing tricks.

The light disappeared. Now I could not see it at all. I stood still again. "Where are you?" I shouted. My voice was as weak as smoke, blown away on the wind. No reply came back, only another swirl of snow.

I walked forward. What choice did I have? I walked on and the ground was firm beneath the snow. But where was the lantern, the horse, the rider?

Whom might I thank? There was nothing to be seen, merely motionless shadows and shapes disappearing deep into the night.

I looked at the ground in front of me. The snow was covering everything quickly, large flakes settling with increasing thickness. But surely . . . I stepped forward, bent down to see more clearly. Surely these were hoof prints? I ran forward, following them as fast as I could, before they could be covered completely.

After a few moments, I could see them no more. They had simply disappeared. When I looked behind me, there were the ones I had followed, still just visible. But there were none in front. Perhaps the snow had been shallower here? Perhaps the horse had begun to gallop, and its prints were farther from where I was looking? Perhaps I had lost my sense of direction again?

At that moment, just when I was wondering which way to turn, I heard a sound. The unmistakable whinny of a horse. I listened again. Once more it came, muffled, from my right. That was the direction I took, caring nothing if it might be dangerous, wanting only to find the person who had helped me. I needed his help still. I did not know where I was or what to look for. Bess's instructions would be useless now that I was far from her path.

A few yards farther on, a little way up the slope, I could make out the shape of a building in front of me. I halted, hesitant once more. There were no lights, no smoke, just the dark shadows of the walls and the outline of a roof against the night sky. I heard the horse again, the soft noise of its feet moving. It seemed to come from the black hole of an open doorway — a wide doorway — of a stable or barn.

As I walked toward it, the snow began to fall less heavily. I looked around, but could see no movement, of horse or human. No danger. Apart from the black doorway. Anything could be in there, anyone, waiting for me to come in, ready for me. But of whom was I afraid? Who could be lying in wait, and why? If someone had guided me in safety across the marsh, why would he do so if he then meant me harm?

Although reason told me there was little danger, my beating heart said otherwise. I walked forward as strongly as I could, looking behind me as often as I looked ahead and pulling both pistols from my belt. There was no time to check their priming, and I knew there was a strong chance that the powder had not stayed dry. I put one pistol back and took the knife from my bag in place of it. Pistol in one hand, knife in the other fist, blade pointing upward, I walked firmly on. And as I came to the doorway, I sprang forward with a shout that sounded braver than I felt.

CHAPTER SIXTEEN

No one leaped back at me. No one shouted. I peered into the darkness. I could see nothing. I strained my eyes and ears. But it was my nose that told me what the barn contained. Horse. The unmistakable smell of warm horse.

As I stood there, slightly away from the open doorway, waiting for my eyes to become used to the deeper blackness, I heard a sound, footsteps, slow footsteps, coming toward me. But not human, I knew. Horse. What I did not know was whether there was a rider. I held my knife out in front of me.

It was only the horse, riderless. He came toward me and put his head over the top of his stall as if I were an old friend, trusting me, or perhaps sensing that I was no danger to him. Horses know such things, I believe. He put his muzzle in my hand.

I could tell little of his appearance or breeding in the darkness, only sense his size and power.

Reassured by his friendliness, I went into the stall with him. Now, I could tell he was well-bred, muscled, strong in his tall withers, his mane finely groomed. I felt his flanks. They were dry. He could not have been the horse I had seen out on the marsh. So, where was his master? There were no lights in the dwelling, no sign of human life.

He could not be Bess's horse. Bess's horse would still be saddled and bridled from when she had fallen, and this horse was not. He simply had a rope halter with which to guide or tether him.

So whose was he? And where was his owner? I was still in danger, I knew, but I needed shelter. If I did not take the shelter offered here, I would be a frozen corpse by morning.

Through instinct, I did as I would have done with any horse: I ran my hand down his legs to check for soundness. It comforted me as much as it might the horse. It was while doing this that I could just make out the white coronets around both front feet. Could he be Bess's horse after all? She had told me of his markings, so that I would know him if I found him wandering. She also told me of a ridged scar on his near fore knee. I ran my hand around this knee — and there it was. He must be Bess's horse!

So, where were his saddle and bridle? Did Bess ride without tack? Was she so skilled? I put the thought aside: the important thing was that I had found Bess's horse, and, I assumed, her home.

How had I had such good fortune? How had I lost my way so severely and then found my destination in so unlikely a fashion? It was as though the mysterious horse and its rider had led me there. What a foolish thought! How could the rider have known where I wanted to go? It must, after all, have been luck.

Already I was doubting my memory. Perhaps I had *not* seen a horse and rider. Perhaps the light had been in my imagination, the thoughts of a wishful mind. Surely I had found my way here by chance alone? And why not? I had been dogged by misfortune thus far — surely my luck must change at some time and perhaps that time was now.

The horse must be hungry — he could not have been fed since Bess fell from him perhaps three days ago. He might have found some scraggy winter grass before the snow fell, but I knew he should be hungry now. As I stumbled past him, I kicked over a bucket and heard the water splash across the ground. The horse was lucky there had been any left — no doubt the water trough outside would be frozen.

I was in sore need of dry clothes, and a fire, and

shelter for the night, but the horse must come first. I had been taught that, but I felt it in my heart, too.

I searched around, my eyes seeking shapes in the darkness. It was not long before I found a large rack with stored hay, and a box with meal that was only slightly damp. A scuttling in the corner spoke of mice, or rats, but they could do me no harm.

Having given the horse his feed, I scraped the snow from his trough outside and broke the ice, before carrying a fresh bucket of water to him. He drank only a little and ate nothing. It crossed my mind fleetingly to wonder why. He should be hungry. But I did not stop to think for longer than a moment.

Shivering again, suddenly noticing how deeply the chill had settled into my bones, and how wet my clothes were, I made my way over to the small dwelling, my feet crunching in the thin snow. There were no lights. It did not occur to me to consider that there might be someone there. This was Bess's home and Bess lived alone. How might anyone be there?

I should have considered.

I should have had my pistol in front of me. Or my knife. I should have been prepared.

I knew this the moment I opened the door and stepped over the threshold. But by that time, it was too late.

Chapter Seventeen

For the second time in less than the space of two days, a gun was pointing toward me. This time, however, it was a full-size musket. Worse, a deadly bayonet was attached. True, it wavered slightly, but a wavering musket is as deadly as a steady one at such close quarters.

I could not, at first, see the shadowed man who held it. I looked only at the barrel and the steel blade. My mouth felt dry, and my knees began to quiver like petals in the wind. I told myself it was the bitter cold and wet, but I knew it was not. I forced my knees to be steady.

A dim lantern on a table sent an eerie light around the dwelling. The thick curtain draped over the window had prevented me seeing this from outside.

How could I have been so heedless? I cursed my lack of caution.

I backed away. "Stay! Put your hands in front of you!" cried a voice, surprisingly young and light. Surely this was not another girl? Surely I was not destined to have my life twice threatened by a girl? But as soon as I looked at him fully, I saw the dirty red of a soldier's coat, the white of his breeches. I saw, too, his small size, his thin legs, and as my eyes traveled slowly upward, I realized that this was no more than a boy. Younger, probably, than myself.

Nevertheless, if he was dressed in His Majesty's uniform, he was deadly and well trained. Yet, I reasoned at the same time, my thoughts working fast, if he was in His Majesty's uniform, what was he doing here? Was he a deserter?

If a deserter, then he was on the wrong side of the law. As was I. Yet if he was a deserter, he was the more dangerous — because he knew that if he was caught he would be killed, shot without reaching the gallows. So, he had little to lose, and would not spare my life for small reason.

How should I talk to him? Or should I rush him and hope to cross that small space before he fired? But no, the bayonet would halt me, and I could not assume I was stronger than he.

Another thought brought a new concern. Were

the soldiers pursuing him? If they found him here, it would mean discovery, and perhaps death for Bess. And for me.

"I heard the soldiers," I lied. "They are coming this way. They will find you here. If you shoot me, they will hear. If you leave now, you have a chance. You could escape, if you make haste."

His face was clear to me now. I have never seen a face hold such pale terror. His eyes were wide and his lips open, the jaw rigid. He looked like a small boy waking from a terrifying dream, but this was no dream and he knew it.

I took a step toward him.

"No!" he almost whispered. "No! Please!"

A soldier does not say please before he shoots, but I did not wish to frighten him further. I stopped, holding out my hands, palms facing upward to show that I held nothing. "I will not harm you," I said. "Only let me make a fire and change my clothes. You can leave, and I will say nothing."

"Why wouldst thou say nothing? Why wouldst thou not give me away? They would reward thee." His voice sounded thin, pitiful, close to the edge of madness.

I gambled. "I would not risk it," I said. "I am running from the soldiers, too." It was the only way I could convince him that it was safe for him to leave. I knew it to be a risk but I could think of nothing else.

He kept the musket pointing toward me as he edged toward the door. I turned slowly, keeping him in my sight, holding my hands steady in front of me. If he would simply go, that was all I wished for. Exhaustion began to take over, as I waited for him to leave, thinking of the fire I would soon make, the dry bed I would soon sleep in. For a moment I felt dizzy, just thinking about resting my aching limbs.

He made his way to the open door and through it, out into the veil of snow. The blizzard had eased, and only a few flakes fell now. The yard was almost silent as he hurried away.

I turned into the room, breathing hard, and closed the door firmly behind me. I adjusted the lantern to burn more brightly. Holding it up, I looked around. The room was surprisingly well furnished, with two large chairs, a solid table, and several well-made chests. An open door to the right revealed a deep box bed with many blankets piled on it. Ahead, to the right of the cold fireplace, a narrow staircase led upward. On the table in front of me, a tankard and plate held the remains of —

No! I heard the sounds outside, moments before I understood what they were. How could I have been so foolish? I crashed the lantern onto the table, flung open the door, and ran outside.

The lantern sent its orange glow pooling across the snowy yard.

The boy was there, one hand on the horse's saddle, the other steadying a stirrup as he placed his foot in it. I hurled myself toward him, yelling, "No!" and grasped him from behind. His musket was slung over his shoulder, and he had no time to take it in his hands before I had pulled him away from the horse. The animal reared in fright, and I grabbed the reins as I kicked out at the boy, catching him on his shin with a loud crack. Uttering a cry of fury or fear or pain, he fell, grabbing my foot as he did so, his musket falling in the snow. With a surprising strength, he pulled my foot toward him, and I too fell to the ground, letting go of the horse's reins.

The boy leaped onto my chest and sat there heavily, his left hand pushing my forehead down, the right hand reaching for his belt to draw his pistol. My arms were pinioned by his legs but with the mighty effort of someone in mortal danger, I wrenched one arm free. I gripped his wrist as hard as I could, trying to hurt him, trying to force him to do anything other than get that pistol. I could hardly breathe and already black spots of dizziness swam across my vision. Fury, terror, anger, desperation, all of these rose up inside me. This boy would not overcome me! He could not!

Chapter Eighteen

It was the sound of Bess's horse galloping away in fright that gave me the strength I needed. With my free arm, I grasped the hand that held my head, dragged the wrist toward me, and sank my teeth into the flesh below his thumb. The boy screamed and pulled both hands away, the half-dislodged pistol falling from his belt. Taking advantage of his pain, I whipped around, twisting my body underneath his, onto my side and then onto my front, and thrust myself upward onto all fours, hurling him violently backward. His head hit the stony earth where the snow had been swept away by our fight and for a moment he lay stunned.

Only for a moment. With a snarl of fury, almost like a wild animal, he scrambled to his feet. Seeing that he was about to attack me again, I snatched the pistol from where it lay, twisting my body around again, so that although I lay on my back, I had the pistol firmly in my hands. Pointing directly at him.

By then, I had faced death often enough. It would not overcome me now, and I knew that if I had to fire a shot then I would do so without hesitation. I would kill him if I wished. It was a good feeling. A feeling of power.

I wanted him to come at me. With a sudden, horrible urge, I wished him to come at me and then I would shoot him. He had tried to kill me! He would have stolen Bess's horse. He was a deserter from His Majesty's army. I would do my country a service if I shot him, would I not? I was exhausted, frightened, angry, and I held a gun in my hand.

I cocked it with my thumb. I was ready. *Come at me! I challenge you!* The words were silent in my head, but I willed them to reach him. *Come on! Deserter! Coward!*

But he stood there. He did not move at all. I could see his wide eyes staring, frightened. And exhausted, as I was myself. How could I shoot him?

But if I did not, I would not be safe. Bess would not be safe. And she would lose the horse, which it was my duty to save.

I tensed my finger on the trigger. It softened and prepared to spring beneath my touch. Still he stood there. His chest rose and fell, his breath smoky in the cold, dark air.

I did not know if he had another pistol in his belt. I could see nothing beneath his red coat but that meant little. If he so much as moved one hand a fraction toward his belt — if he perchance seemed as though he were going to — then I would shoot him. I would not wait to be sure.

Yes! A movement! A faint flicker. Perhaps I had imagined it. But whether I had or not, my own finger had moved.

I fired. Straight at him. Only a few feet away, at point-blank range. He did not stand a chance. I could not miss him. The flash from my gun spread sideways, and the hollow crack shattered the air.

He crumpled to the ground.

Chapter Nineteen

What had I done? My first thought was to wish I had not fired the gun. He had not been reaching for his pistol — suddenly I knew that. It was merely an excuse I had sought. What a coward I was! The gun had made me feel brave. Brave? I had been facing an unarmed boy who had only been fighting me because I was trying to stop his terrified escape.

Who had been the more frightened? He or I? Was I any better than he? Would *I* have been brave enough to stay in the army? He must have been brave to run from the soldiers, knowing that capture meant shame and certain death. I had not even dared to join them.

Scrambling to my feet, I went to him where he crouched on the ground, his head hanging down limply. I flung the pistol aside. With its single barrel, it was useless now. When I touched his shoulder, he looked up. Tears were pouring down his face. I saw this with distaste.

But as he raised his head, I saw that there was no blood on him. Had I missed? I could not have done at such short range. The bullet must not have fired. It was then that I remembered: there had been a sideways flash from the pan — a noise and a flash but no effect, no deadly bullet fired, no harm done. It was a common happening, I knew. In those conditions, and with a pistol loaded by an inexperienced boy in a blind panic, it was not surprising. His own lack of competence had saved his life. I could have made the same error myself.

I held out my hand to help him to his feet but he took it in both his hands and shook it, up and down and up and down, as if he would never stop. My hand felt enormous inside his smaller ones. He looked as though he would fling his arms around me in gratitude. Disliking his tears and because he little knew how much I had wanted him dead — and for no honorable reason — I stepped away from him.

"We must find the horse," I said to cover my confusion.

The horse could be a mile away by now, though it was much more likely that he had not gone far from his own shelter.

"I am sorry." His voice was shaking and weak.

"No matter," I said hurriedly. For I was the more sorry. And ashamed again of my cowardice. "Fetch the lantern," I ordered. And a few moments later the boy came back with the lantern, which he handed to me. I understood then that he must think this was my home. It would do no harm for him to continue thinking so. My home, my horse, my hospitality that he had abused. I knew then, too, that it was he who had unsaddled Bess's horse and fed him.

As we trudged around, calling the horse's name, Merlin, I felt weariness wash over me. How I longed to be warm and dry and safe again. When would I be able to sink into a soft bed, sure in the knowledge that no man was hunting me? How far away seemed my own home now. I could barely remember the smell of it, scarcely recall the feeling of crisp linen sheets or the taste of a venison stew and apple dumplings and a glass of my father's claret from France.

It was the boy who found Merlin, a little distance away under some trees. He grabbed the reins but the horse was startled, stamping around with the boy hanging foolishly on to him. I took the reins myself, speaking softly, stroking the horse's nose and muzzle. Turning away from his eyes — for frightened horses will not come if you stare at them — I led him toward the stable, with the boy trotting along behind like a silly puppy.

"Don't walk where he cannot see you, fool," I snapped, and the boy rushed around to the front, ridiculously keen to please.

Back in the cottage, he vexed me further, trying to please me by clearing his small possessions away. He dropped something on the floor, uttering a frightened cry of apology. I was too tired to speak to him, but I admit that the fire he soon had roaring up the chimney was worth praising. I stripped off my wet clothes in front of it and wrapped myself in the blanket he held out for me.

Bread, cheese, and ale appeared before me. The boy was a conjurer. Tiresome, but a conjurer all the same.

But before I could eat, I knew I must strip my pistols down, and I moved well away from the fire to do so, first emptying the powder onto the ground outside. Only a fool would sit naked, in the dangerous circumstances that we were in, without pistols primed with dry powder and shot and ready for firing. And as I did all this, I marveled at how much I had learned about self-preservation in a short time. A hovering death is a harsh taskmaster, but an effective one.

Now the boy spoke. "Shall I fetch you some dry clothes?" When I nodded, he ran eagerly up the stairs.

Soon, he came down again with some items that smelled faintly of mildew and disuse. Near-white breeches, stockings, a white shirt, dark plum or brown jacket — I could not tell in the dim orange light. Everything was somewhat loose on me but the fit was passable, and better than the too-tight jacket I had been wearing. Now at least I could move with freedom. Whose were they, I wondered? Why did the girl have them? They would be too large for her.

Better dressed now than I had been for several days, I ate and drank my fill, watching my wet clothes steam in front of the crackling fire. Tiredness swept over me like wind in a storm, and the strength seemed to float from my body as I slumped in the chair. My cheeks began to burn in the bright heat from the fire.

The boy stood there. What was he waiting for? He was behaving like a servant. I understood that I was probably treating him as such. It was what I was accustomed to doing. But what did that mean? Where were the things I was accustomed to? Did being accustomed to something matter one jot?

Chapter Twenty

"Sit down," I said. "Eat some food. And drink."

He did not wait to be asked again and fell on the food as though he had not eaten for a long time. Then he stopped, with a piece of bread almost in his mouth. He dropped his hand to his platter, put the bread down, sat back. His eyes were worried again. What was wrong now? "I mustn't. I cannot."

"Why not?" I asked. "It is my food, and I offer it to you. Eat."

"My mother an' my sister are starving. I am on my way to find 'em, to give 'em food, and I 'ad wanted to give 'em money but . . ."

"You would have been better waiting to be paid before running off," I said with some contempt. "How will it help your mother and your sister when you are shot for desertion?" My parents had always spoken with such disdain for deserters, and I heard an echo of their sharp words in my own voice now.

The boy leaped to his feet. I lurched to mine.

"No!" His voice was shocking in the small room. The fire hissed and crackled as we stood there. How dare he speak to me like that? The fact that I had not been wearing my gentleman's clothes should make no difference — he must know I was worth more than him. Was I not? Without the badges of my status — the long coat, the embroidery, the soft leather of my shoes — was I nothing more than him? Surely my soul was more valuable to God than his?

My thoughts were strange, and I could not grasp my new position. I had lost all that I had known. I had thrown it away the moment I stole that purse. Or the moment I decided I could no longer bear my father's sneers, my brother's contempt. And when I ran from my home during the night, leaving it all behind.

But I did not have to respect this boy. "Well, what are you then, if not a deserter? Look at you! Wearing the King's uniform, running away, hiding, and sniveling in fear! What are you then?"

The boy was silent for a moment, standing there with his shoulders heaving and his fists clenched tight as grapeshot. Then he moved quickly toward a corner of the room. I moved my hand closer to a pistol, ready to snatch it. But I did not need to.

He rummaged behind a chest and pulled out a canvas bag, which he carried over to the table where I sat. He ripped it open, fumbling in his haste, and pulled out three smaller bags from inside and placed them in front of me, glaring, his eyes shining in the firelight — with anger or tears, I could not tell.

"What is in them?" I asked. They were shapeless, each the size of a small ham.

"Open 'em, and thou shall see," said the boy.

I undid one of the bags, each of which was tied with string at the top. White powder. Gunpowder? Surely not? Surely he would not be so foolish as to place gunpowder close to a fire? I took a pinch between thumb and finger and put it to my nose. Flour. Just flour, unusually white and finely milled.

He spoke again, anger giving his voice strength and a bitterness I had not heard from him. "Flour. Three small bags. For my mother an' my sister. They're starving — I told thee. The army 'as so many bags o' flour they need not miss 'em. But they did."

"The army must eat, too," I said, thinking of the circumstances I knew the soldiers often faced. We were always hearing of the difficulty of provisioning troops on the march and how an army cannot march hungry. Though, I admit, I could not see how three small bags of flour would make much difference.

But it was the principle. Stealing was wrong and the punishment should be severe, to prevent others doing the same.

Yet, I too had stolen. But from a rich man, a man who would not miss his purse of gold, who would quickly recoup its value from his land or his tenants. It was not the same. Stealing from the army was stealing from the King. So I told myself. My ancestors had supported the King against Cromwell, and royalist blood ran unquestioned in my veins.

"Eat?" The boy almost laughed, his eyes afire. "They were not going to *eat* this flour. This flour's too good for eating! This flour's special — set aside for whitening the 'air of us soldiers. For a soldier must 'ave whitened 'air. How can an army fight with undressed 'air?" His anger quickened. "Ay, that were the flour I took an' now they are looking for me an' they will never give up till they find me." His voice began to crack and break into pieces. "An' they will kill me, an' all because I need to feed my mother an' my sister."

I said nothing. Often had I heard of the suffering of the poor, but I had never given much thought to it. My father's servants and tenants had little but he would not let them starve, would he? As long as they worked hard, of course. And did not the church also help the poor of the parish? I had heard tell of people starving but was it not their fault for not working hard? Stealing was not the answer, was it? My own guilt settled like a bitter worm in my stomach.

I had never encountered someone with such a life, such a choice: steal or starve. Such an *absence* of choice. And when I had stolen, it had not felt like temptation; it had not felt low or shameful, though afterward I had regretted it — but that was because of the consequences. It had simply felt like something that needed to be done. To save my own life. Was this what it felt like for him?

Was I no better than he? Did I have a greater right to survive than he? Because I had been more highly born? Because I knew what was right and wrong? Because I went to church on Sunday? Because I had been baptized by a bishop, no less?

"Let me stay," he said now. I could not look at him. I did not want to see his pleading eyes, his wet, thin cheeks, his frightened face. If he went down on his knees, I did not think I could stomach it. My father hated to see a man beg.

Yet this was a boy, not a man. And when would I stop echoing my father's thoughts?

I rose to my feet, moved away from him. I stood facing the fire, in pretense of warming myself.

"This is not my home," I said at last. "This is a young girl's home. You would not wish to place her in danger by leading the soldiers to her, would you? She is injured — I have merely come to fetch her horse and as soon as morning comes, I shall go to her." I paused. "You may stay until I leave but then you must go, as fast and as far as you can. And here, take this — for your sister and your mother." I took the food from my bag and placed it in his hands. It had been bought with the money I had stolen, and in many ways I was glad to be rid of it. Did that make me less guilty? As he began to stutter his thanks, I silenced him. "Do not thank me. I would have killed you earlier and you would have killed me, too."

He took the food and wrapped it all up inside his bag, along with his stolen flour. Although his cowering still irked me, I suddenly felt sorry for him, truly sorry. He was alone and I was not. By now the soldiers had perhaps stopped searching for me, probably would not recognize me if they saw me, but they would not stop searching for him, not while he still wore the redcoat uniform, not while they knew his name. Deserters were fair game. Deserters who were also thieves were very fair game indeed. I did not like to think of what would happen if they caught him.

I looked at him then and spoke from the heart, though awkwardly. "I hope the soldiers do not catch you, and I hope you reach your mother and your sister."

After this, I made it clear that I wished to sleep. I would not sleep in Bess's bed — it did not seem proper — so I made myself a pillow by the fire and lay down, with a blanket from Bess's bed over me. I could hear the boy rustling in a corner somewhere.

I wished he did not think he had to sleep far from the fire, just because I was there. Perhaps he was afraid of me. But I did not think that was his reason. I knew that in truth he felt himself lower than me, by instinct, by my educated voice, by the way I held myself, by my sharpness when I spoke to him. Even by my face and skin. I had been born different from him. It was the way it was.

He was like a weak puppy that knows his master and cowers. I did not find the thought comfortable. I wondered if, beneath my skin and my clothes and the sound of my voice, I was perhaps no better than he. I too had stolen. And for myself, not for someone else. I too had run away and felt terrible fear. I felt fear now, as I thought of the journey back to Bess, and wondered at the dangers which would face me in my new life.

But one thing was certain. I could not go back to my home. Perhaps not ever. A lump formed in my throat, and, ashamed, I pushed the tears away.

"My name is Will," I said a few moments later, my voice loud in the near darkness. "What is yours?"

"'Tis better thou dost not know," came the thin voice. "If thou knowst nothing about me, thou can give nothing away under force."

"I will give nothing away," I said. "Even under force. You can trust me." I did not like to think of what force they might use.

After a short pause, during which I suppose he weighed how far he could trust me, I heard him say, strongly, proudly, as though challenging fate to remember his name, "My name is Henry. Henry Parish."

It was a name I would come to remember. With fear. And anger. And with sadness.

Chapter Twenty-one

It was soon after dawn when I awoke, stiff with cold, my shoulder cramped where it had pressed on the hard ground. My mouth was dry and foul with hunger.

The boy, Henry, was up already, busying himself making the fire again. I stumbled to my feet, wrapped myself in my cloak, pulled on my boots, and went outside. The wind was bitter, but the sky was clear. There would be no more snow, though what there was had partly frozen during the small hours of the morning. It crunched beneath my feet, loud in the stillness.

After using the latrine at the back of the cottage, I broke the ice on the horse's trough and drew fresh water from the pump into a bucket. Back in the dwelling, Henry was beginning to put food on the table while waiting for water to boil.

"I am not hungry," I lied. I would not look at him. I was disturbed by the way he irked me. Why did his goodness set my teeth on edge so? I pitied him, but could not like him. He did nothing wrong, yet I could not warm to him. It was like having pieces of grass seed or grit inside a shirt — harmless, but unpleasant.

He put the food away, without eating. I did not mean for him to refuse food as well. My own hollow hunger only increased my anger, and I snapped at him to put the fire out. "There is no time for that," I said angrily, drinking some of the warm water and handing him the rest without looking at him. "I shall leave soon and you must leave first. I told you that the girl who lives here was injured. Do you want her to suffer longer?"

He looked afraid again. His hands almost flapped beside him, as though he did not know where to put them. But I hardened my heart. What else could I do? He was not my concern. His troubles were his own. Yes, I pitied him, but I could not endanger myself and Bess for him. The longer he stayed here, the greater the chances of the soldiers finding him. They could even now be searching nearby.

I watched him hurry into the nearby woods. He was not strongly built and his arms drooped as he trotted off, his thin shoulders lower on one side than the other, one arm hanging more loosely. He looked around and raised his hand in a hesitant farewell, but I did not return his gesture. I despised myself as I watched his small frame disappear into the cold darkness of the trees.

I tried to put him from my mind.

As quickly as possible, I made ready to leave, putting my newly borrowed clothes back where they came from and dressing once more in the ones I had arrived in. I saddled Merlin and fitted his bridle. He let me do it, sensing my expertise.

The boy would have held me back, I told myself. He did not have a way with horses. I could not risk Bess's horse, or Bess, or myself, for sake of a deserter. And perhaps he would escape. Perhaps he would take the food to his mother and sister. Perhaps . . . But I would not think of him again.

Merlin was strong, but responsive. He had been well-handled. You can judge a rider from the behavior of his horse, and Bess, I could tell, was a skilled rider.

I retraced the directions that Bess had given me and before long I was at the place where I had mistaken my way before. This time, in daylight, I avoided the dangers of the marshland, though I could see it not far away, where the wet ground had sucked the snow into its soft mud. I stopped for a few moments, to rest Merlin, and as I did, as I breathed warm mist into the gray air, I looked over to where I had been trapped and where I had been led to safety. By what? By whom? Had it been nothing but a figment of a frightened mind on a dark night?

Perhaps I would never know.

After missing my way only once, and after stopping to buy a cheese and bread from a small farm, and to drink a cup of warm new milk, I came to our hiding place less than two hours after leaving Bess's home.

The yard was in silence. The door hung open, swinging on the wind.

At that moment, I heard it. A single shot, ringing out over the moors. It came from behind the bothy, to the right. With sudden squawks and frightened flapping, a flock of pigeons flew up from the naked trees, as the sound of the shot echoed over the hillsides.

CHAPTER TWENTY-TWO

Leaping from the horse, I hurried with him to the byre at the side of the hovel, where I roughly tied him. With both pistols drawn and half-cocked, I ran back to the door, darted inside and flattened myself against the wall behind the opening. Stilling my heavy breathing, I cocked both weapons, and waited.

Footsteps, slow footsteps, soft padding on the ground outside. Still I waited. Silently. The figure came through the doorway. I waited till the person had come right in, and smiled as I stepped forward with a cry of "Halt!" She did not move as I held both pistols to the back of her head, behind the ears, where she had held me at gunpoint only two days before.

"Don't be foolish!" she said. But she did not turn around.

I kept the pistols there, just to show that I could, to show her that *she* had been foolish to walk through the doorway without care. "You should have ensured there was no one here before you came in," I said reprovingly.

There was a slight pause, a silence in which I waited for her to answer. Her answer was not what I expected. In an instant, she flashed her hands upward, knocking my pistols clear out of my grip, whipping around and grabbing both my wrists before I even had time to exclaim. In another movement she had twisted one of my arms behind my back, forcing it upward until I almost screamed.

She held me there for several moments, enough to tell me that she could have held me longer. When she released my arm, I scarcely managed to keep upright. I cannot describe the humiliation I felt at being bettered by a girl. I had wrestled with boys of my age, and I knew myself to be strong, yet her wiry strength contained a determination and cunning that I could only wonder at.

A freshly killed hare hung by its feet from her belt, its head wrapped in sacking to soak up the blood and prevent it dripping.

Only as she walked away, turning her back on me as though to prove that she need not fear me, did I see that she still did not walk entirely straight. Her breathing was labored. She was still in pain — and certainly the more so after her actions — but she was not going to show it.

Well, I would not show it either. "I brought your horse. He is a fine animal."

"Yes," was all she said at first. Then, as she walked stiffly to the door, discreetly holding her side, she added, "I thank you for bringing him." She continued out to the byre where the horse stood. Running her hand over his shoulders and down his nose, she examined him thoroughly, before nodding approvingly, finding nothing amiss. "Did you feed him?"

"I did. Hay and meal."

She unfastened the buckle under the saddle and reached up to heft it from his back, but I saw her stifle a gasp. She could not bear its weight.

Before she had to ask me for help, I moved to do it for her.

"I can do it!" she snapped.

"I believe you can. But you should not. You might open your wound again, and if you do that I will have to fetch more remedies, perhaps even an apothecary." She said nothing to that. "How is your fever?" I asked.

"It is passing. I am strong. It would take more than a fever to finish me." But she shivered in the wind which now flung icy rain at our faces. She led the horse through the door into our shelter, and I closed it behind us. Taking him over to a far corner, she removed the bridle and stroked his neck. The horse stood there, unknowing of any human fears or worries. His raw, warm smell was a comfort to me.

I stoked the fire and soon it crackled and spat, lifting the gloom. Then I made her bed more comfortable and shook out her cloak. "You should rest," I said as she watched me. "And dose yourself with physic. And your dressing should be changed."

"I do not need your help," she said, beginning to skin the hare expertly with a knife.

I was stung by her rudeness and hostility. More than that, I was afraid that in truth she did *not* need me. It hurt me to confess this, but I needed her company. More, obviously, than she needed mine.

But I would not show it. I would not stoop so low. I would not stay if I was not wanted.

I stood up, straightening my back so that I was as tall as I could be. Staring at her for a long moment, I spoke. "You are right — you do not need my help. In that case, I will go. But, if you recollect, you were the one who first stopped me with your pistol." I stooped to pick up my bag, gathering my few belongings into it, and moved toward the door. Opening it, I simply said, "Farewell," and left the place.

I pulled my hat well down onto my head and walked away without looking back. Feeling her eyes burning into me, I desperately willed her to change her mind, to call me to return. I did not know where I was going, and life seemed empty without another human soul with whom to share it.

I did not know her. I did not even much like her. She made me feel small and foolish. Yet, there was no one other.

The thought of dying on my own, with no one to know or care, was more than I could bear.

Yet, bravely now, I walked away. Bravely? I had no choice. Is that bravery? Is it actions that count as bravery, or how you feel inside?

I did not know. I knew only that what I felt was coldness and misery, and these did not feel in the least like bravery.

CHAPTER TWENTY-THREE

Wearily, I trudged away. Perhaps I went slowly because I hoped she would call me back.

She did not. I continued. Could I put thoughts of her from me? I must.

Very soon, I heard hooves ahead of me on the stony road. I stopped to listen. Should I hide? My heart began to beat a little faster. It sounded like one horse only. I was right — he was coming around the corner in the distance. Dark, stepping high, trotting proudly.

Ridden by a redcoat.

Although I could not be sure I had anything to fear, the last time I'd seen a mounted redcoat he had died because of me. This one might be searching for me. I did not believe he would know who I was as the soldiers had barely glimpsed me, and I was now wearing a hat and a cloak, which I had not worn when I was at the village. But I could take no chances. I darted into a gap in the hedge and crept around to the other side.

A few moments later, he trotted past. He did not seem to be searching for anyone. He looked ill, slouching in the saddle, his large body drooping. I saw his face as he passed, noticed the redness about the nose, the half-closed eyes set above fat, greasy cheeks, the wet, lolling lips. His pigtail was whitened, the flour clotted in the wet air. The boy, Henry, came unwillingly into my mind. I stood and watched the man, uneasy for no reason I could name, except that Bess was alone.

But Bess had said she did not need me.

The soldier stopped his horse and slid off. He stumbled, tottered slightly as he walked to the edge of the road and unbuttoned his breeches to pass water. A loud belch reached my ears. He was drunk.

With some difficulty, he clambered back onto his horse and continued along the road, an ugly dead weight upon his mount. I watched him. I was glad that I did, for I saw him stop at the turning to the hovel where Bess was. I watched him direct his horse into the turning and disappear.

Goaded by fear now, I ran back in the same direction, thinking only of what he would do if he found

Bess. It was well known how drunken soldiers behaved if they found a girl or woman on her own. Bess was strong, but it would not be enough against the full weight of this soldier.

I reached the turning to see the redcoat sitting on his horse in the middle of the yard. Peering from behind a tree, I could see that the door was shut. Did I see a movement at the unboarded window? I do not know. Perhaps I only thought so as I later tried to piece together the events that followed.

I do know that the redcoat slid off his horse; that he walked slowly toward the door; that he did not take his pistols from his belt. I remember that he stopped at the door, for a moment, a moment during which I neither moved nor breathed, and that he turned aside. I watched him turn and move away. He did not open it. I do not know why he did not open it, why he walked away, but I am saying only what he did, what I remember.

But I heard the door creak as it opened.

And then, as he walked away from the door, as he turned slightly, I remember, in a terrible blur, his chest exploding into a shocking mess. He flew into the air and crumpled instantly to the ground, where he lay like a mangled scarecrow. But scarecrows do not pour bright blood onto the ground.

I ran toward him. Bess stood in the doorway, her

hair tumbling around her shoulders, her eyes wide with something that was not quite fear, or shock, but something more unexpected.

Later, I would come to know that it was pure hatred.

"What have you done?" I shouted, looking briefly at the body and then turning away. "What have you done?"

She stood there, her lips curled back in a strange grimace, without making a sound. Smoke still breathed from the ugly mouth of the gun. "Is he dead?" she said at last.

"How might he not be dead? And now there will be a price on your head. You did not have to kill him! He was walking away. You did not have to! Why? Why did you?" Shock increased my anger.

Her voice was almost calm, though if you listened carefully you would have heard its tension, tight as the spring on a new musket. "I did have to. Because of what they did. Because I know what they did." She walked away, dully, back into the hovel.

I followed her and found her crouched on the floor, her back hunched, breathing hard. I went to her and touched her shoulder then and she did not move. I did not ask her what she meant — there was not time. I knew that we must leave that place. And with all speed. I would discover later what turned her from the calm and reasoning person I had thought she was to the weak and unguarded one I now saw before me. She was crying, and she did not even try to hide it.

"We must go, Bess," I said. "They will search for him and find him, and they will find you here, too. We must go. Now." She let me lead her horse out to her. She watched, with blank expression, while I saddled and bridled him. I had to help her mount, partly because her wound still hurt her, partly because I do not think she knew what she was doing. I told her to wait while I collected our possessions. We did not have much. A bag each, our pistols, some scraps of food, our cloaks, hats. The dead hare I left, skinned and disemboweled — a feast for rats and scavengers.

Quickly, I glanced around the bothy, making sure we had left nothing behind, and sparing a brief thought for this place where my life had changed once more. What would happen now? How far might I control my fate? Little enough. Little enough.

Outside again, the icy drizzle falling around us, I swung up behind her and together we trotted away, leaving the soldier's body. His horse stood over it, patiently, without understanding.

Bess did not need to tell me the route — I would

not make the same mistake again. She said nothing as we traveled, holding the reins loosely in her hands, trusting her horse, and trusting me, too.

Was it her lingering fever that had made her behave thus? She had not needed to kill the soldier. He had done nothing, was walking away. What manner of girl had I become involved with? So unpredictable: one moment laughing, the next scornful; one moment brave and strong, the next unable to control her actions. Could I trust her? Why did I stay with her?

How could I not?

Chapter Twenty-four

Later that night she told me her story. And then, everything made sense. Or one sort of sense. An uncommon sense. Now I understood her and trusted her.

It was beside the fire in her cottage that she told me. We had arrived as the afternoon gloom drifted into twilight. By now composed, though nearly silent, she had begun to groom and feed the horse, but when I had offered to do it, she had agreed, to my surprise. She had lit some oil lamps and made up the fire, slowly, still in some pain and stopping frequently to take deep breaths. I said nothing about the boy who had used her home, and she noticed nothing amiss. I wanted to forget him, though every time I looked at the fire, the table, the mugs of ale she put out, I thought of him and could not help but wonder if he were still alive.

I had made her let me dress her wound again. That apothecary was skilled, I had to admit, and she was strong — the wound was clean and knitting together well.

We had then begun to eat and drink, silently still, our faces becoming red in the fire. And then, at last, she had begun to speak, her eyes dark above her pinked cheeks, her voice fatigued by her passing fever. "I thank you for helping me today. I am glad you came back."

Although my heart swelled, I chose not to respond. Instead, before the moment disappeared, I risked her anger again by asking what I most wanted to know. "What was your meaning when you said the redcoat had done something? He had done nothing. He was walking away."

She answered at once. "I hate the redcoats. Were you a redcoat, I would have killed you when I met you. I have been waiting for the chance to kill one. Today, I had that chance, and I took it. He deserved to die. I am more than glad." Her voice was level but I saw her eyes inflamed with anger and hatred, her mouth tight.

"Why, Bess? What have the redcoats done?" I knew from the way she spoke that she must have her reasons.

She was leaning back in her chair. She bent

forward now, placed her elbows on the table, and stared into her mug of ale before speaking. "I have never told anyone this story before, and I do not know if I can. It has been told to me, many times, but I have never had anyone to tell it to." She wiped the back of her hand across her eyes.

And then, she told her story. By the end, I knew why she had killed the redcoat. I believed she would do the same again, and I could hardly blame her if she did. It was a tale that would catch and trap even the coldest heart and melt it. She spun me into her life with the words of her story, a story of bravery and love, of heartbreak and fury, of honor and dishonor.

This was Bess's story.

"My father was a highwayman, the best there was. He chose his victims for their wealth and their corruption. He said that stealing from them was like lancing a boil — their money was poisoning them. He kept only what we needed and gave the rest to the poor. I was seven years old when he met his end. But he had already schooled me in horsemanship, and to use a pistol, even to use a sword — he had one fashioned especially for me.

"You may wonder what my mother said to this: but I never knew my mother. He took me to her several times, at night, but I was too young to remember. When I was some three years old, he stopped taking me, at her insistence. She said she could not bear to see me and yet not have me with her. He continued to visit her, and he would tell me how she loved me.

"My mother had been fourteen years old when I was born. Her father came close to killing her when he discovered that she was to bear a child out of wedlock. He was the landlord of a tavern, nothing more, but he had hoped my mother would marry above her station. When I was born, he took me from her and gave me to a servant. "Take it far away," he said. "Let me never see it or hear of it again." The servant gave me to someone who knew where my father was. Folk knew my father and trusted him to take good care of me. They knew he was honorable. He did care for me, with the help of a local woman, and it is that woman who recounted the story of my grandfather's terrible anger and all that followed. Aggie was her name.

"It was Aggie whom I was with the night my father died. She kept alive for me the story of his death, and my mother's, too, telling me the tale again and again over the following years. My mother was never wedded, though many tried to woo her. She refused their advances, always making excuses, feigning madness, or illness, or sullenness. Her father, the landlord, did not forgive her for that.

"Aggie put the pieces of the story together after that terrible night, the night my parents died. Many saw part of what happened, and guessed the rest. Another man died the next day, too, to pay a price for what followed. Or to begin to pay. That man deserved to die."

Bess paused now, gathering her strength for the rest of the story. She took a mouthful of ale and set the tankard down slowly. I saw her thin fingers on the handle, tight and white as though no flesh sat between the skin and the bones. I said nothing, waiting for what was to come.

CHAPTER TWENTY-FIVE

"It was a fierce night when my father left our lodgings for the last time. The equinoctial storms of spring were stripping dead twigs from the trees, and a full moon scudded between the clouds. My father was after a prize that night — he had heard that Sir John Sowerby's coach was taking his ill-gotten wealth to Scarborough. On his way, he rode to see my mother, to snatch a kiss, and, perhaps, to taunt her father with a glimpse of him. He took pleasure from such risks. Aggie was often angry: 'Think on t' child,' she would say. 'Thou hast a child. Bess's child.' And he would tilt my chin toward his face and smile and place a kiss on my forehead before leaping onto his horse and galloping off into the night. And I was never afraid for him. Never."

She closed her eyes, as if conjuring up his image.

"I remember what he wore that night. I remember it as if he were standing here now. I remember the fawn-colored breeches, unwrinkled above his long, black boots with their laces up the sides. I remember his velvet coat the color of wine, at his chin the bunched lace that I had washed myself that morning. I remember how hard I had tried to make it look just so and how vexed I was when one edge would not settle neatly. Everything gleamed, sparkling in the lamplight as he stood inside the door and checked the powder in his pistols."

Opening her eyes, Bess touched one of the pistols lying on the table in front of her. I looked at them as she spoke, imagining him as he left her that night.

"He wore his sword, too, as he always did, but I fancied it twinkled more brightly than ever. He saw me watch as the light bounced from the jewels on it and danced over the ceiling, and he twisted the hilt to make the light play across my face. His hat was in the French style, the brim turned up and with a cockade of lace at the top. And, as he blew me a kiss, I did not for one moment think that I should not see him again. Aggie worried every time he went after a prize, but I knew that he would always return. I thought he was like a god — immortal. He might be away for a day or two, if the redcoats harried him, but he told me never to be afraid, and so I was not.

"I wear his ring around my neck — in a locket, which is the only thing he has from his own mother. She gave it to him in secret when he left home." She touched a chain beneath her collar and fingered it as she continued.

"Bess, my mother, was sitting at her casement, waiting for him. He had sent word to her, through those he could trust. To tell her he would come to her. And as she waited, she plaited a dark red love knot through her long black hair.

"They were watched. Bess's sister, Annette, watched, worrying for Bess. Annette knew about the baby that Bess had borne, and remembered how their father had raged. She had seen him hit her sister across the face, until her mouth was bloody and swollen. Annette loved her sister. And so she worried when she heard my father say to her, 'I'm after a prize tonight. But I shall be back with the yellow gold before the morning light. If there is danger, if they hunt me, then I will come tomorrow night, so look for me by moonlight. Watch for me by moonlight.'"

The words were familiar, but I could not at first place them. Then I recollected: they were the words Bess had spoken during her fever, as I left her.

"But Annette was not the only one who heard my father promise to return. She was not the only one who saw him press his face in Bess's hair before galloping away to the west.

"Tim, the idiot stable boy, listened, too. In the crazy darkness of his mind, he thought Bess was his. Ugly Tim, Mad Dog Tim, Scarecrow Tim, Hollow-Head, and Rat Boy, those were some of the names they called him. He lived in the darkness, hating the light, blinking with white and empty eyes if he came out into the light of day. How could he think Bess would love him in return? I hate him. I hate him. If he lived now, I would hunt him down. I would shoot him dead, dead like a rat in a gutter. How could he think . . . ?"

Her knuckles were white, her lips tight in the firelight, her face pale against her tumbling black hair. Again her hand went to the chain around her neck.

"My mother watched the winding road through her window, the road where he would come. He did not come at dawn. He did not come in the cold March noon. He did not come in the afternoon, even when the sun sank into the russet sky, and Bess must have been beside herself with worry now. He had told her that he would return, but this time perhaps she did not believe him. Then at twilight, finally, a redcoat troop came marching, marching along the very road that he would take.

"Annette knew Bess waited for him, knew why her face was white as she served the hungry soldiers their meat and ale downstairs, silent as she tried to ignore their mauling, pawing hands, their crude, coarse jibes. Annette saw whey-faced Tim, the idiot stable boy, go crawling to them like a cringing dog, but she did not hear his words. Later, when it was too late, a terrible regret haunted Annette, as she tormented herself with thoughts of how she could have silenced Tim, somehow, or warned Bess.

"Perhaps she could have prevented it; perhaps not. But at the time, she did not understand. So she listened helplessly as the soldiers went into her sister's chamber. She could only hope they would not harm her. Little did she know . . .

"Then Annette, fearful now, tried to send word to someone who could warn my father, the highwayman, but the landlord saw what she planned. He locked her in her room, pleased at the thought that the man who had taken his other daughter's virtue would now meet a fitting end.

"No one knows what those soldiers did to my mother. No one will ever know. But some things we know. We know that they tied her to the end of her bed, gagging her viciously, so viciously that, when her parents found her later, the sides of her mouth were lacerated. We know that they tied a musket to her, the muzzle digging into her breast, tied it so tightly that the shape of the barrel made a long, ugly bruise on her flesh.

"She must have struggled in silence as the soldiers watched for her lover through the windows. She must have twisted her fingers desperately until one rested on the trigger. What thoughts went through her mind as she waited and as she watched the ribboning road in the moonlight, the road that he would take? How brave she was! What terrible fear must have filled her heart as she waited there, with no one knowing what she planned?

"Did she think then of his words? I think she did: 'Watch for me by moonlight. I'll come to thee by moonlight, though Hell should bar the way.'

"The moonlight lit the bare and winding road that night. Annette watched from her window, too. She stared at the moors, eyes wide, thinking of her sister, wondering what was in her mind, not knowing what was in her heart. She heard the horse's footsteps ringing through the ghostly air. She wanted to scream. Afterward, she wished she had, though perhaps it would have done no good.

"There he was! Galloping toward them. When would they shoot? He was perhaps out of range; Annette could not tell, did not know of such things. She held her breath, shut her eyes, could not bear to watch. She heard the shot, one shot only, shattering the moonlit air, and opened her eyes to see the crows fly up with a fearsome noise. But the highwayman did not fall. Clattering to a halt, he paused for a mere moment and then wheeled around and was gone, galloping away, waving his rapier defiantly at the wind. Safe! He was safe. Annette's heart sang, and she wanted to shout her joy to the moon.

"Something stopped her. Some premonition perhaps.

"Why was there only one shot? Why did only one soldier shoot?

"Moments later, a terrible scream tore the air. And another. Annette's body froze, her blood turning to ice, a strange moan creeping from her throat. Her face grew gray, and she sank to her knees as she listened to the noise from Bess's room. Rousing herself, needing to know what awful event had caused her mother's screams — why the continued wailing, why her father's anguished yell, and the shouting and confusion — she scrambled to her feet. Her door was flung open by a wide-eyed servant.

"Numbly, she ran down the corridor toward her sister's room."

CHAPTER TWENTY-SIX

Bess took another drink of ale from her mug and continued her tale.

"The door was open, the room crowded with people. Moonlight slanted still through the casement window and onto a terrible, terrible sight. My mother, her black hair cascading down, her head bowed, was slumped over the scarlet mess that was now her breast. There was the gun, still strapped to her, its barrel pressing into her blood-drenched flesh. The soldiers stood foolishly, away from the bed, some by the window, some still watching vainly for their intended victim, others gripping their muskets, looking at each other as though wondering what they should do. What could they do? Everything had been done. Everything they could ever do, they had done.

"Not till dawn did my father hear what had happened, and they said his face grew gray when he heard how Bess, his beautiful Bess, Bess the landlord's black-eyed daughter, had watched for her love in the moonlight and died in the darkness there. And when he heard, when he understood that she had paid with her life to warn him of the redcoats' presence, he roared his curse to the sky. Then my father turned his horse and galloped blindly, madly, for many miles and many hours, until in the cold noon he reached once more the end of the road that ribboned the moors. And there he shouted his defiance as he rode toward them, brandishing only his sword, and at the last moment they shot him, shot him at last, shot him down on the highway. They shot him down like a dog on the highway, and they laughed as he lay dying in his scarlet blood on the highway."

Bess looked at me, and when she saw the tears in my eyes she smiled. "The story is not quite finished. Annette, and others who saw him as he lay dying there, with the soldiers running toward him, said he shouted his love to the sky, his love for Bess, his black-eyed Bess, the landlord's red-lipped daughter. But before he died, they also say he whispered his curse again into the dusty road. With his last gasping breaths, he cursed the men who had done this and he vowed to haunt them. Folk say he does. They say a highwayman haunts these moors and that if you have evil in your heart he will find you and settle his curse on your head, too."

I shivered at that, thinking of the ghostly figure I thought I had seen on the moors.

Bess continued, "Don't be afraid. I do not believe it myself. And besides, they have said such things for much longer than the seven years since my father died."

What should I say to her story? Perhaps I need say nothing. I looked at her. Telling the story had seemed to compose her. She looked strong once more, her eyes bright but dry, her lips red now in the warmth of the fire. Then she spoke again. "They killed Tim, the mad stable boy."

"The redcoats?"

"No. Friends of Bess and Annette. Perhaps Annette set them to do it. They tied him up and hung him by his neck from a tree. He was two hours in the dying, they did it so carefully." There was raw spite in her voice.

I stared into the flames, taking this in, and I knew I was glad that he had died in such a way. What is justice if it does not feel right, if it does not echo the evil? Justice should be passionate and hard and fiery. There must be balance, a sense of rightness. The stable boy had acted without honor, and he had caused two deaths. It was proper that he should pay.

But would my father, if he had been sitting in judgment over him in his court, have sentenced the boy to hang? No, the law would say that the stable boy had been right. And my father was on the side of the law. What was right? Was it what *felt* right or what the law said was right? Was the law always right? Even if it did not feel right? I did not know. It was too confusing and too new a thought.

I pushed such difficult matters away. "Did you live here with your father?" I wanted to think of them here.

"At first we lived in Scarborough, in lodgings. Aggie lived with us. She cared for me, believing that I needed a woman's attentions. But he cared for me, too, and taught me to read and write, even to read Latin and Greek and to know the paths of the planets. He taught me music and dancing, too, though I confess that dancing was not my favorite pastime. My father was highborn, the youngest son of a Scottish landowner, educated at Edinburgh University, destined for the church, but he had turned away from all that and come south for a life of adventure. He had not thought to stay here for long before traveling farther south, but he fell in love with my mother. Then he would not leave. And, of course, I was born. And so, we stayed.

"He was also a dancing master, entering all the wealthy houses in the area under the guise of teaching the young ladies and gentlemen to dance. They had no notion of how many secrets he learned about their lives. Certainly, they did not suspect that their elegant dancing master by day was the man who robbed their carriages by night.

"Perhaps a year before he died, he rented this cottage and a small piece of land. The landowner asked no questions. My father did him a service — he kept footpads and common thieves away. Many folk knew what my father did, how he put food on our table, how he paid for my clothing. They kept their silence because they respected him. He defended the weak, the poor, and the downtrodden. Always he stood for what he believed to be right, and he taught me to do so, too. And now, people know that they will receive the same from me. They know I can handle a pistol and a horse. Perhaps they suspect that I have followed in my father's footsteps. That I am a highwayman. But if anyone were to ask, I have a different story."

She paused, and although I knew she was going to tell me whether I said anything or not, I asked her what her story was. How did people think she had money for food or for shoeing her horse, or for any of the other necessities of life?

"I say I am a ballad seller. And indeed, I have sold many ballads," she said with a degree of pride. "There is a printer in Scarborough who buys them from me willingly. I have even sung them myself, on occasion, to earn the more."

I had heard of such things, although I had never had cause to listen to one sung. I knew that uneducated folk were willing to pay to hear the ditties and rhymes of the ballad sellers. A happening such as a hanging provided rich material. Once, I had heard my father sneering to one of his friends that no one who could not write in the languages of Homer and Cicero should be allowed to pen anything in the English language.

"It is a way of passing a winter's night when I have gold in my purse and no need to ride after a prize."

"May I hear one?"

"No, you may not. No doubt you have been schooled to look down on the ill-written ditties of the ballad sellers." She looked at me, and I did not need to answer.

I turned my eyes away.

"I was telling you how I came to be here. My father came to this place when he wanted to be alone, when he needed to lie low. I came to live here with Aggie after my parents died. But Aggie did not like the moors — she considered them lonely places fit only for bogles and ghosts. But she stayed for me. And for my mother and father, because she promised me she would. She died a year ago."

Bess's face toughened as she said this, her jaw rigid as she struggled to keep her voice level. I marveled at how strong she must be: to bear what she had borne, to live on her own, still to smile sometimes, to fight for her survival, and not to sink into the weakened torpor of the poor.

Even though she was from highborn blood, she had lost her status now. She was destined to be forever either poor or a felon. There would be no way back to gracious society. I pitied her, denied her rightful station in life. But then I thought: she would no more wish to be gilding the ballrooms of gentlefolk or keeping high company than I would wish to be a swineherd. Perhaps even less so. She was as happy with her lot as my brother and sisters were with theirs.

I tried to imagine them here, in this simple smoke-filled room. My brother would look around in sneering contempt, while making some trite comment on the weather. My sisters would hold their breath as they wondered how to place their smelling salts in front of their noses at the same time as holding high their skirts, in unfeigned horror at the dirt on the rough, stone-flagged floor. No, I thought with a smile, my sisters would likely be swooning.

How easy their lives were. How easy mine had been. How little they knew.

I did not know what to say. I had suffered nothing by comparison to her. Yet she was stronger by far than I. Or perhaps it was her suffering that had made her strong?

Perhaps it is what we endure that shapes us for the better?

CHAPTER TWENTY-SEVEN

"I am sorry," I said. "You have had a hard life and . . ." But she brushed aside my silly words with a flick of her wrist. I fell silent. Anything I might say would seem empty, though there were many thoughts that I could not voice. Confusing thoughts.

She stood up, stretching slowly, carefully. "I am going outside to wash. Then we should sleep. There is much to do in the morning. We must cut logs and we need food, in case the weather worsens again. And then, perhaps, we should get you a horse."

My face gave no sign that I had understood. Had I understood? Did she mean me to stay? Or did she think she could be rid of me only if I had a horse on which to make my departure?

"A horse?" I said, sounding foolish, but then I never did know for certain what to say with Bess.

She was too unpredictable, too different from any person I had known. And even though she was more lowly born than I, I felt that somehow she knew far more. She had an air about her, a knowingness that seemed almost like wisdom. But how could she know more than I? Only a girl, and brought up by a villain and a woman of low birth — how could she know more, even if her father had once been from a family of wealth? How could she make me feel as though she was in some way above me, when she was not above me in status? Status is something we are born with, is it not? Is it not given to us as part of God's natural order?

"Yes, a horse. You will be of little use without a horse. I know you can handle horses — I have watched you. You have been well taught." I did not need her to tell me that. But I was glad this had not slipped her attention.

"And where shall we find a horse?" I asked. "Do you intend to steal one?"

"I would not steal horses," she said harshly. "It is too risky. And it is wrong. We will go to Scarborough — I know a man who will find us a horse."

Right to steal money, wrong to steal a horse; right to kill a redcoat; right to kill a crazy idiot; wrong to kill a highwayman. Right or wrong to steal flour from the army? Right or wrong to steal a purse of gold from a rich man? Wrong to steal but right if the thief gives the money to the poor?

These thoughts spun in my mind, and I suddenly became aware that Bess was asking me a question.

"Well?" She stood in front of me, a rough cloth in her hand and a bowl to carry water in.

"What?"

"Well, do you wish to stay?"

I struggled to keep the smile from my face, to maintain my composure. "I thought you did not require my help."

"Did I say I required your help? I do not recall it. I asked if you wished to stay. I can manage very well on my own. I have done so for the past year."

"I would be pleased to stay," I said as calmly as I could. This was not the moment to make a clever comment or to argue with her. Inside, my heart was singing. For the first time since I had left my home, I could grasp the future, though weakly. I could not know what would happen, but if I was not alone I believed that I could face it. Bess knew what she was doing; I did not. But I could learn. And I thought that a life with Bess, confusing as she was, was better by far than a life on my own, on the run, always afraid, always hungry.

I felt as though I was on the edge of something, something exciting. I had thrown away my old life and comforts, and I was more than willing to learn new ways.

"As a companion," she said bluntly. "You shall not share my bed."

The heat rose from my neck to my temples, and I could think of nothing to say except to splutter, "Of course. Of course not." Before I turned away, I saw her face. A thin shiver of a smile, which was almost not a smile at all, disappeared as fast as it had come.

That night, when eventually we lay on our beds — or her in her bed and I on the floor by the fire on a blanket that did little to soften the flagstones beneath — with the embers of the fire spitting and crackling gently, I had a strange new feeling: that I had never been so happy as I was that moment. I thought that nothing could ever make me frightened again.

How foolish we are sometimes.

CHAPTER TWENTY-EIGHT

Early the next morning, we argued about who was to ride her horse. It pleases me to say that I won, though I would not show my pleasure in front of her. She was clearly not well, pale and tight-mouthed when she arose stiffly from her bed, wincing as she lit the fire to boil water for an oatmeal gruel. I guessed that her head pained her, for she kept pressing her fingers to her temples. My suggestion that we wait till the following day met with her firm refusal, however. In truth, her fever had passed, but she was weak from it. This weakness was the first reason I would not ride the horse.

And she was a girl. That was the other very strong reason.

I could not comprehend her argument. She seemed to think that if I walked then it must be because I thought her weaker and more delicate. Well, she was correct: that was indeed what I was thinking, although I was struggling to continue thinking so in the face of her spirit. I had been taught to believe that the fairer sex is the weaker sex. The fact that I had seen women, serving women, carry burdens that would have felled me, and that I had seen their sturdy muscles as they scrubbed floors or beat rugs or kneaded dough in the kitchens, did not stop me thinking that in essence women are fragile.

For certain, she had held me at gunpoint, but was that not merely because she had a gun and had taken me by surprise? Yes, she had insisted on holding a pair of pistols when we thought the redcoats were about to breach our refuge, but was that not merely because she would have been more afraid without the pistols in her hand? Surely it was so?

Besides, even if I had to admit that she had an uncommon strength, it was still not proper for me to ride while she walked. Only if she had been my servant could I have done so. And she was not.

However, I won the argument by persisting until she snapped in exasperation. "You had better walk fast, as I shall be setting a good pace. I trust you have sufficient strength." And she threw the sidesaddle onto Merlin's back with an angry heave, trying to prevent me from seeing how much it hurt her injury.

I omitted to mention: Bess was not dressed in man's attire now. She wore a good dress, with the skirt of some fine, dark blue, woolen material, very full, tightly belted, and the top part of the same material but with wide lace cuffs, all covered by a short dark cape, allowing her arms to move freely. I noticed her leather gloves and riding boots, polished to a shine and well made, even moderately expensive once. Her face was clean — though certainly with the signs of illness etched in the dark circles beneath her eyes — and her hair brushed and twisted neatly into some clever arrangement mostly hidden by her wide hat, tied beneath her chin with a dark blue sash to prevent it blowing away in the wind.

I felt ragged by comparison. And out of place. You would have thought me to be her servant. And when, after some three hours of her purposeful speed, stopping only to rest and water the horse once or to pay the toll at a turnpike, we could see Scarborough in the distance, with the castle to the left and the shimmering German Ocean in front of us, I understood that that was exactly what she planned.

Just outside the town walls, Bess stopped the horse. We were beside an inn, graced by a hanging picture of an enormously muscled bull. Surely she was not going within? It would not be proper. Or safe. She would be thought a loose woman. There were a number of persons about, all making toward Scarborough, though none seemed to give us more than a slight glance. Nevertheless, I was worried among these crowds; I could not say why — only that, since my recent escapes, too many strangers made me wary. I found my heart beating faster, though I knew there was no good reason. Surely no one might recognize me here?

I simply did not know what was going to happen, or what Bess was doing. Could we not just buy what we needed from the town, then go to the horse market, or wherever Bess planned to buy a horse, and return to safety?

"Bess," I said urgently. "You are not . . ."

"Come with me," she said, kicking Merlin to a trot so that I was obliged to run to keep pace. We went through the courtyard to the back, where she slipped gracefully from her saddle and passed the reins to me without looking. If she was still in some pain, she did not show it. "Wait for me here," she said with irksome authority. It did not seem to occur to her that I would not do exactly as she said. How dare she treat me so?

But she was already striding across the yard toward the back door, holding her skirts high. The door was slightly open, and I could hear loud voices from within. I could even see blurred figures through the thick glass windows, men with heads thrown back and laughing. As she came to the door, she stopped, turned, shot me a smile, before turning sharply away and walking to a door farther along, a small closed door.

She was teasing me. She had never intended to go into the main part of the inn. She knew exactly what I had been thinking. When would I learn to hold my thoughts inside me? Would I ever be as sure as Bess? I was torn between vexation and admiration. Envy was what I truly felt, if I were honest.

I watched her knock on the door. A few moments later, it opened, and a woman, short and stout and somewhat elderly, came out. With a cry of surprise, she embraced Bess. I could not hear what was said. Bess must have mentioned me because the woman cast her eyes in my direction and seemed to examine me before nodding. Bess disappeared through the door with the woman, without so much as a wave or even a glance.

Chapter Twenty-nine

I stood in the cold. I was hungry. My legs and feet hurt, and I ached to sit down. But I would not sit on the ground. It would not be right.

Instead, I stood and my anger grew.

So, a servant was I to Bess? I need not stand for it. I could leave as soon as I wanted. Could I not? If she was determined to make me feel inferior, then I did not have to bear it. Not from a girl. Not from someone who was more lowly born than I. I was William de Lacey, son of . . .

But I was not, was I? Not anymore. I had put that behind me. And did I regret it? No, not for one moment did I regret leaving behind my father's expectations and his sneering disdain. I had decided to embark upon a new life, a life of unaccustomed choices, and to prove my worth. To myself, even if my father were not there to know.

So, I could not — would not — leave Bess, however much I might be irked by her manner and the way she made me feel weak. Not yet, at least. Because, whether I liked it or not, my life had more certainty and more reward if I stayed with her. I had shelter and company. Surely she, too, would find some advantage in my presence? I could ride as well as she could. I could cut logs, learn to help with the many things she must need to do to look after a cottage by herself. Surely she needed human company as much as I did?

I would have to show her that I was not merely some spoiled, wealthy boy who knew nothing of the real world.

I had to admit, too, that her life, her story, interested me. She was from a different world, and if that was the world I had found myself in, then I wished to know more of it. Had I not been taught to think, to seek after wisdom, as Socrates did? Socrates took nothing for granted, questioned everything.

But Socrates did not have a god. And I did. Of course, I would not doubt God. But God had made this girl and her world, too. If God made everything, then it was my duty to try to understand His world, not only the small part that I knew.

I would have to cast off my father and my old life.

It was not enough to leave the comforts of my home. I must leave his influence behind, start afresh and open my eyes to the world. A different world from the one I knew.

A world where a girl could seem to know more than I and to be as strong. A world where right and wrong were not as clear as I had surmised. A world where suffering was raw and real. A world where fair and foul merged into fog, a fog in which I would either fall or find a light to guide me through.

Therefore, I would put my trust in God — as my Bible classes had taught me. God would provide and He would surely look more kindly on me if I strove to discover what was right.

I would find my own way to true honor.

All this I thought as I waited for Bess to come out of the tavern. And even if there were any traces of my earlier annoyance, her smile, when she came through the door again, soon put an end to them.

"Help me mount," she said as she took the reins from me. I knew it to be impossible to mount a sidesaddle without help, if there were no mounting block. I did nothing. She waited but not once did she look at me. "Help me, Will," she said again.

Still I kept my silence.

"If you please," she said. Grinning inwardly, I placed my hands into position and she stepped onto them, pushing down harder than she needed, perhaps, and I hefted her into the saddle. She looked at me, knowing very well what was in my mind, and said, politely enough but with that slight smile, "I thank you, kind sir."

It was enough: I had made myself clear and perhaps she would now behave with greater civility.

"I have good news," she said as we departed from the inn yard.

"I do not suppose you have any food?" I said. My stomach was painfully empty, and glimpsing those men eating and drinking in the inn had only increased my hunger.

"The news I have will bring food to last till next winter!" she exclaimed. Her eyes shone with an excitement I had not seen in her. All weakness from her illness seemed to have vanished, although she was still pale and her lips were dry.

I could not but admire her resilience. My sisters would stay in a fragile state for weeks after recovering from the mildest ague. One of them, Eliza, would have a fainting fit if a small pain passed through her head. And when Caroline, the youngest, had been stung by a wasp, she had screamed until she had fainted, too; a doctor had been called, who had pronounced her so prostrated that she must remain in her bed for at least a week — but this had not been enough for Caroline, who had declared that she would surely die if she were required to rise from it before a month was up. As for Annabelle and her behavior at the mere sight of a spot of blood . . .

Bess continued. "I was meeting with an acquaintance. A friend of my father's. He can no longer ride but he helps me. He gives me information. He had some news for me today. There will be a rich purse for us if his intelligence is correct. I will tell you more later but first, you need a horse. And my friend was able to help me there, too. Follow me."

We set off toward the town again.

CHAPTER THIRTY

Passing over the old moat, now little more than a dried-up riverbed, we came through the town walls under the New Brough Barr, pausing to let a carriage pass before us. I could smell the sea, see and hear the gulls twisting and turning overhead. It was as though I was aware of the world, and its dwellers, for the first time. They did not look at me — I was as nothing to them — but they were everything to me, as I began to see the world in all its strange detail.

But Bess did not leave me much time for deep thoughts. I must keep pace with her. She knew what she was about, and I did not. I must keep my wits about me.

Soon, we came to the center of the town, after walking through the busy marketplace. This was a

Thursday and persons of all descriptions traded their products, spreading onto the cobbles and gutters. The noise of rumbling wheels and the screams of gulls and the singsong calls of the criers merged into one, along with the smells of fish and horses and coffee and something burned. A sudden meaty warmth rolled from a chophouse as we passed, and noise surged as a door opened and two men stumbled out arm-in-arm.

When I heard and then saw a carriage swing past, saw the gleaming silver on the harnesses of the high-trotting horses, and when I glimpsed the feathers fluttering inside, the fur-trimmed cloaks and thick woolen blankets over the knees of the occupants, I thought how far away their world already seemed. Briefly, I wondered who they were.

Did they wonder about us? Did they know any-thing about the world beneath their feet? For my part, I had not known, and little enough did I know now, but at least I could see that it was there.

As we hurried along in the cold, I noticed the crowded buildings, the ancient timbers tottering in ramshackle fashion among the newer and more gracious façades. We passed men and women shout-ing their wares: cherry jams and treacle, damson cheese and muscle-plum cheese, codling jelly, maca-roons, ratafias and cracknels, pistachios, hot saloop, kegs of brandy, sheep's tongues, neats' tongues, pullets, peafowl, ducks, and turkeys. Old women sold hot eel pies at a roadside stove; a woman roasted lobster claws and smashed them open for customers to pry out the sweet meat; I saw serving girls buying saffron cakes for their mistresses, French loaves, muffins, and other breads I recognized from home, my earlier home. We passed a man carrying a pole over his shoulder, strung with dangling hams, pigs' ears, and sausage links, and I could only imagine the aroma of them as they sizzled over the fire at Bess's cottage.

I kept my hand over my pocket, guarding my purse. Who knew what villains and pickpockets might be waiting to slip their fingers inside?

My earlier fears of being recognized had gone: Scarborough was very many miles from my birthplace, and no one would know me. Besides, although Scarborough was fashionable, my parents and their acquaintances would no more be seen there in February than they would have eaten their meals with the servants. The wintry weather would discourage such a journey, and it was my mother's considered opinion that only the height of summer was fitting for exposure to the cold spa waters, and then only with great care and modesty. As for the sea, she had always had a horror of the bathing machines that women used to preserve their modesty, ever since hearing that an acquaintance of hers had had an unfortunate but unspecified accident in one.

In addition, my father was contemptuous of the modern fashion for spa resorts, believing them to be the playground of those who aspired to higher rank but who would never achieve it simply by spending their money on fashion and frippery. "These people of the middling sort cannot disguise their lack of breeding by silks and satins," he would sneer, sipping a large glass of port wine with the Lord Lieutenant of the county and discussing which fine young gentlemen should be promoted to higher rank in their militia.

No one of my acquaintance would be in Scarborough. I had nothing to fear on that score.

As for the soldiers who had pursued me, and the militia whose job it was to apprehend me after I had stolen the purse, I was now certain that they had moved on to more interesting quarry. Thinking on all this, breathing in the sights and sounds and smells, I enjoyed being merely one among many. I believed that I would not be noticed.

Imagine, then, my shock when I saw someone whom I, myself, recognized. I stopped, slipping behind a man selling thrushes, dozens of them, tied by their feet and hanging dead from a stick, their little beady eyes still bright. My heart thumping, my eyes narrowed, my mind spinning, I looked more closely.

There was no mistake. It was the woman who had been selling her jams and preserves, the one who treacherously gave me away to the redcoats, naming me for a deserter, keener to claim her reward than to protect the honesty of her soul. Now she had set out her wares on a small cart at the end of the market street. My hatred returned, burning my throat. I wanted to spit out the taste in my mouth.

Bess had noticed my hesitation, and she pulled Merlin to a halt. "Will?" she was saying sharply. "What are you doing?"

I hurried to her, keeping my face away from the woman's gaze in case perchance she should look up. "I have just seen . . . I have just seen a person who almost caused my death." My voice was calm, but inside me anger burned. The crone had wished me dead, knowing and caring nothing about me, thinking only of her own reward.

"Where is he?" said Bess, straining her eyes in the direction we had come.

"She," I said. "She is selling wares at the corner of the square. She is knitting — do you see? Hunched, wearing a black shawl?" Bess looked, catching sight of the woman easily from her position on Merlin.

"I shall remember her," she said. "And now, let us proceed. I have a plan for that old woman, but she can wait."

I knew the old woman had not seen me, perhaps would not recognize me, but still I felt a shiver crawl down my neck as I remembered that day. That horse! How close I had come to death. I hated her and her careless attempt to have me shot for desertion.

We moved briskly on, taking a turn to the left, followed by one to the right and perhaps another to the left — I do not recollect clearly, except that we were moving toward the castle. It was clear to me that Bess knew where we were going. If she were not going to tell me, I would not ask.

CHAPTER THIRTY-ONE

We came to a street less crowded. All the houses were older in this place, for the most part with the black beams of much earlier times, and some upper stories perched on top like drunken old men. No grand façades rose here. Bess was examining each house, searching for whichever one she had been instructed to come to. She stopped at a building with the sign of an anvil hanging from a leaning post. A smithy.

"This is the place," she said, and I followed her through an archway to the back.

Over the normal stench of a town, of people and their detritus piled in the gutters, and the dry, salty scent of the sea, I could smell, suddenly, the wonderful aroma of horse. I could even hear a gentle whinnying, the soft harrumph of contented animal.

As we came around the corner, I saw a row of stable doors, with three horses' heads peering over. Would one of these soon be mine? The feeling of excitement brushed aside my earlier unease at seeing the gap-toothed old woman.

Once more, Bess slid down from Merlin's back and tied his reins to a hook in the wall. We walked toward the forge, where we could hear the clanging of hammer on iron. A thin man of perhaps thirty years bent his long body over his anvil, red faced and shining. He was, I am sure, the tallest man I had ever seen so close. With a wide arc of his arm, he swung his hammer, holding the horseshoe between tongs in his other hand. We watched the sparks fly for some moments before he saw us.

He looked up, stopped what he was doing, wondering perhaps why a neatly dressed young woman and a more crudely attired young man were standing at the entrance of his forge. He turned back to his anvil and brought the hammer down once more with an enormous clang.

Bess spoke up. "Sir Jack sent us," she said.

He seemed not to hear, clanged his hammer again, and then dropped the horseshoe into a bucket of water, where it hissed violently.

Bess raised her voice. "We have come from Sir Jack. One-Legged Jack."

"I 'eard," said the blacksmith gruffly. "And who art thou?" His thin face tapered to a point at the end of a jutting jaw, and his eyes were narrow as he inspected us. His cheeks looked as though they had been chiseled from granite, so angular were they. I was minded to tell him to take care of his manners, that he was speaking to a young woman of good blood and a man of better. But I held my tongue. I think I was beginning to understand that I no longer had the badges of my rank to protect me.

Bess spoke confidently, looking directly at the blacksmith. "I am Bess. Bess Irvine, John Irvine's daughter."

The man looked up once more then, looked properly at Bess, and a smile lit up his leathered face. "Indeed? Then I be pleased to make thine acquaintance. What brings thee 'ere? Wouldst thou take of beer and victuals? My missus'll . . ."

"I thank you, but we are here to buy a horse. My companion"—and at this the blacksmith looked at me with open curiosity, his eyebrows rising when I murmured something in greeting — "is in need of a good mount. Sir Jack said that you have an animal to sell. The horse fair is many months away and I can give you a good price now. I can save you the cost of feeding him."

"Aye, mebbe thou can." The man nodded thoughtfully, wiping the sweat from his brow and then drying his hands on his apron. I noticed the marks from many years of burns.

"Do you have a horse to sell?" asked Bess, somehow managing to sound polite and yet demanding. "Shall we look?" She did not delay. I noticed, too, that she had not accepted the blacksmith's offer of food. *She* may have had no appetite, I thought, but I was still hungry. I wondered when Bess would have a mind for anyone other than herself.

The blacksmith wiped his hands again and walked out of the forge toward the stables, with us following his sticklike frame. His legs were bowed and he walked with a noticeable limp, his arms gangling beside him. He had two horses to show us, a bay gelding and a chestnut mare with a white flash. As he began to speak to Bess, she interrupted. "No, my friend will choose. He knows what to look for as well as I do."

The blacksmith looked at me with obvious doubt. Perchance he could not get the measure of me. Perchance he wondered at my silence, at my clothes, my youth, the manner in which I spoke. Well, I would show him what I knew. I hoped I would make the right choice.

He showed me both horses, speaking of their value, their soundness, their speed and trustworthiness. It seemed to me that he wanted me to buy the bay. Perhaps not, but I had the sense that he kept looking at this one quite deliberately, as though drawing me toward that purchase. Indeed, the bay was a perfect age, four years old, strong and steady, with an intelligent face. The mare was younger, three years old according to the man, and looked skittish, perhaps even nervous, jumping slightly when he moved to bridle her.

I would not be hurried. I wished to know why the blacksmith preferred me to buy the bay. Taking my time, I looked at the bay's teeth, his eyes, walked around behind him warily in case he kicked. I ran my hand down his legs, over his withers, feeling the muscles there, pausing over the joints. Then I did the same for the mare, soothing her with my hand on her nose and not looking at her eyes until she was ready. I stood slightly to the side so she could see me as much as she wanted. She settled immediately under my touch, and I felt a small rush of pride as I heard the blacksmith make a noise of surprise.

"I should like the mare," I said decisively, after examining both animals.

"How so?" said the blacksmith, narrowing his eyes. "This gelding now, 'e be a good 'un. The mare, she be of . . . unsteady disposition."

"The gelding has spavins," I said. "I need a fast

horse, and sound. I prefer the mare. The gelding will not be fit until the summer is well on its way, perhaps not even then. He will be better for gentle use."

The blacksmith smiled, straightening his long, rickety body. Standing so close to him, I now saw just how tall he was — he must have been more than six foot, by my reckoning. "Well done, lad!" He turned to Bess. "Thou'll be right with this 'un. A daughter o' John Irvine deserves good friends. He passed my test. And now, will ye both eat?"

CHAPTER THIRTY-TWO

I am glad to recount that Bess accepted this invitation, and we followed the blacksmith inside.

I was used to strong smells in public places — all the more so during those last few days since leaving my home with its flowers and lavender water to keep unpleasant smells at bay — and have never considered myself to be faint of stomach, but the stench of that place assailed my throat and made my insides shrink. I tried to breathe as little as I might, fearing some sickness from the noxious air. If Bess noticed, she gave no sign. I did not know what the smell came from but it was bitter and gasping, sticking in the throat like the juice from one's stomach after vomiting.

In the room, I counted three children of different ages and a small, thin woman. She came to greet us, dragging one leg as she walked, curtsying awkwardly to both of us, or perhaps more to Bess than to me. There were deep lines on her face, a furrow between her eyes, and her skin was flaky and blotched with raw pink patches. A child with a crusted nose sat on her hip, his curly locks framing a pale, quiet face. The other children, aged perhaps four and six or seven years, hung about her. They wore the usual garb of a tradesman's children, with the oldest boy proud in his breeches, but I thought his jacket sleeves too short and noticed that his feet were bare. The woman's dress was voluminous enough — near drowning her thin body, in fact — and the apron clean and nearly white, but worn and patched.

A sound of coughing came from a corner of the room, and only then did I notice another child lying on the bed. I could not tell if it was a boy or a girl, or of what age, but the child moaned weakly after it had finished its paroxysm. Surely there was bad poison in the air here? I could not help but cover my mouth with my hand.

The woman smiled widely, saying nothing but pointing to some rough sheets hanging from lines above the fire. I could not see what I was to look at or what she meant to say. She grinned again, nodding and opening her mouth but still saying not a word.

The blacksmith spoke for her. "T' missus 'as no

tongue. She says she be sorry for t' stench. Cow dung — it be cheaper 'n soap what wi' tax, an' all." He seemed about to say more, but held his words back.

I had never thought much about the soap I used at home. I knew there was a tax on it, and I supposed that some people could not afford it. But cow dung? Perhaps one would become accustomed to it. I did not wish to try.

The blacksmith bade us sit down, and he and his wife bustled around to bring ale and deep bowls of hot pease pudding, with bread to mop it up. The thick sauce slid easily down my throat, and I thought then that I had never enjoyed any dish so much as I did that simple fare. It was as much as I could do not to fall upon it greedily. But, just in time, I realized that I must not: the blacksmith and his wife had not expected guests and, as far as I could see, there was little enough to go around.

But why did the blacksmith and his family seem so poor? He had a trade, a business, two horses to sell, a forge, a home. Over some ale, which the woman poured generously for us, the blacksmith told us more of their story. And I did not like what I heard. I confess I was happier before I knew.

The blacksmith and his wife had been childhood sweethearts — at this, he placed his hand over hers, and she smiled and nodded. The first child had been born less than a year after they wedded. There followed a second child a year later. At this time, the blacksmith's father had died, and the forge passed to his son. Everything seemed set fair for a thriving business. A third child was born. All the children were healthy, strong, more than could be expected. God smiled on them, and they were happy.

Then the wife had been with child again, a fourth time. Shortly before her time to give birth, she had crossed the path of a fortune-telling hag from a traveling fair. She had no coin with her that day, but the gypsy did not believe her and so put a hex on her. Shortly afterward the woman had given birth. The baby was healthy but when the woman tried to stand, she found that she had lost the power of one leg and arm and her voice had been taken from her.

They knew then that this was the curse of the gypsy woman.

The blacksmith had paid every quack and healer thereabouts to find a cure for his wife. Eventually, she had regained the use of her arm and leg, at least for the most part, but her voice never returned. Meanwhile, money had been spent on physic, spells, trickery, as well as a wet nurse for the new baby and then a servant to help. The forge had begun to fail, with the blacksmith preoccupied with his wife and children, neglecting his work. Another blacksmith took their customers.

But around a year ago, their fortunes had begun to change for the better. The blacksmith, with the support of his wife — who would not see him fail on her account — had begun to bring customers back to the forge, working all the hours that God gave. Once more, they clasped hands and she smiled at her husband.

Four months ago, two events had occurred. First, one of the children had become ill. Very ill. A feverous cough with a fearful whooping sound. The child could barely breathe. An apothecary had been called and only his skill, good fortune, and a very great amount of money had prevented death from coming to their door. The child was now left weakened and with a perpetual cough. More money had gone to apothecaries and quacks.

And then, the blacksmith had been named in the ballot to join the militia. But how could he leave his mute and weak-limbed wife and four children, with one of them very sick, and no income to provide for their needs?

So, he had done what everyone did who wanted — or needed — to avoid serving in the militia. He had paid a substitute to take his place. And with the war against France, Russia, and Spain draining the army of many men every week, and the army, in turn, draining the militia, there were precious few men left to act as substitutes. And so a high price must be paid — the fearful sum of forty guineas. The money had to be borrowed, and his wife's wedding ring pawned, and now he must scrimp to repay it.

Even Bess was silenced by this story. I had known, of course, that some people were poor. But I had thought it was through their own fecklessness or through God's punishment for their sins — but this blacksmith's state of affairs did not seem to be caused by either. It seemed caused by man, and not the sufferer himself. Did my father know the hardship of those he drafted into his militia? I had heard him speak harshly of the unwillingness of some of the men, but did he think about what happened to the women and children left at home? I do not know if he did.

These were painful truths to learn. Was this how God ordered the world? Or how mankind disordered it? Where did my father stand in this world? And where did I?

CHAPTER THIRTY-THREE

While we ate and drank, we reached agreement on the price for the horse. It was difficult: the man refused to take more than the horse was worth. His face reddened when we tried to offer more. But I found my own answer to this: as Bess helped the woman take the dirty platters outside to the pump, I slipped a coin under the sick child's pillow.

I have never been more pleased with any action of mine than I was with that. I wished I could make the child live, but that would be in God's hands.

As we rode away from the blacksmith's home, with his wife smiling and nodding and the children hanging on her skirts, I breathed deeply in the fresher air. I was riding without a saddle — Bess had said there was one at her cottage. She did not say, but I guessed she must mean her father's saddle. I wondered how it would feel to ride it.

The mare — whose name, I omitted to mention, was Sapphire — felt skittish beneath me, and it required all my skill to keep her riding straight. But she soon settled under my touch. She had, I thought, been ridden little. But I was well pleased with her. I hoped she would be mine for a long time. I had not forgotten my own horse, Blackfoot — how could I? But I tried not to think of him overmuch. No good could it do to dwell on what I might not have.

Bess said she had some small purchases to make — vinegar, lump sugar, flour, yeast, and hogs' lard, she said, ticking each one off on her fingers as she made sure to remember, and a few more items that I do not now recall. When we came to the busier streets again, with barrows being wheeled, and wares being shouted, we dismounted and led our horses to a water trough. I waited with both animals while Bess went to buy what she needed.

As she made her way through the crowds, lifting her skirts to keep them from the sludge underfoot, I watched her, though not closely. I confess my mind was elsewhere. I was thinking of my discomfort because I had let her pay most of the money for my horse. We had discussed — if you can call any conversation with Bess a discussion — the necessity for this. But that did not prevent me from feeling discomforted.

She had said again that I would be of no use to her without a horse, and that if it was my pride that held me back then I could repay her from my share of our booty when we next captured some of the excess wealth of our county's corrupt masters.

That, too, discomforted me. It would take more than a few determined words and resolutions to change what I had so often been taught: that stealing was wrong. Was that not true, whether the victim was rich or poor? "Thou shalt not steal." I had already asked forgiveness for yielding to temptation. What would that forgiveness mean if I merely did the same again?

But we must put bread on our table, must we not? By some means. And for certain I did not know of any other skill I had that might bring us money. Nor could I, in truth, see Bess sitting composing her ditties for the rest of her days.

Too much thinking is a dangerous pastime. It was because I was thinking in this way that I failed to notice the boy robbing Bess.

All I can say is that from the depths of my wandering thoughts I heard her cry, "Stop! Thief!" I whipped my head in her direction: she was some thirty yards away or more, beginning to run. But she could not do so easily in her heavy skirts.

Where was the thief? There! A boy with thick yellow hair was speeding away from her, darting through the crowds. Toward me. Just before he reached me, he slipped down a nearby street. Passersby turned their heads, but no one moved to help. Perhaps they could not see what had happened; perhaps they did not care.

"Stop that boy!" she shouted. "Stop him, Will! He has my money!"

"Take the horses!" I cried to her, and flung the reins from me as she approached.

I set off, slipping at first on the damp stones. Where had the thief gone? He kept disappearing but I could see the thin crowds parting in startled fashion as he sped through. I had to catch him! This was one thing I could do, after all Bess had done in buying the horse. If I could not retrieve her money, what use was I?

Darting through the crowds, shouting at them to move, I raced after the splash of yellow hair. I was so angry at his theft that I did not spare a thought for how I too had stolen a purse only a few days before. I knew only that I wanted to retrieve it. For Bess. And for my pride.

The boy must not escape! He must not!

Chapter Thirty-four

"Stop!" I continued to shout. "He stole from a lady!" I added. "He hit a lady!" I lied.

I was fast. I was sturdy and strong. And I was furious. The crowds parted for me and, even though I lost sight of him every now and then, his yellow hair kept reappearing. Closer and closer. Blood was pounding in my head now. My whole body jarred with the shock of my feet hitting the cobbled ground.

Now he darted across the road. He leaped to one side to avoid a passing carriage, stumbling as he slipped in the slime of the gutter. As the carriage passed, he dashed down a narrow street. I sped after him, not caring where this led, caring for nothing more than catching him.

Swerving left, he ran up an alley narrower than the first. The buildings loomed over our heads, almost cutting out the wintry light. The ground was slimy and uneven here, but he was sure-footed. Agile, too, and thin. And very fast. But no faster than I. Fear may have lent him strength, but I was spurred on by fury. And I was better than he — I would not be beaten by a common thief!

No people walked here in these darker streets. If I caught him, what would I do? Or was he perchance leading me to his gang, if he had one? Footpads often did, I had heard. And once there, I would find no mercy, I knew that, too. But I tried not to think on it.

Left again. Surely now we were near the street where we had started? I could hear the crowds, the market, the whinnying of horses, even see spreading light at the end of this alleyway. But the boy had turned again.

I was gaining on him now, slowly but surely. I could hear his panting, the guttering breaths choking him. With a burst of extra strength, of desperation, I surged forward.

It was then that I heard the noise behind me. Clattering hooves. Approaching fast. I could not turn around — there was no time. I cannot describe my fear, how it hit me with a force that almost took the breath from my lungs. But I pushed the thought away. I would not be beaten by terror this time. I was on the side of right. This boy had stolen, and I was going to retrieve what he had stolen. God would watch over me because I had not done wrong.

I had nearly reached the boy now. The noise of hooves grew louder. I shut my ears to it. When I reached out with my hand, I could almost touch him, almost, so nearly. And then, with one huge effort, I had grasped his jacket. But he was spurred on by fear and he ducked away, slipping from my clutches.

I dived at him, wrapping my arms around his legs, and we fell together. A sharp pain shot through my neck as it was forced backward, my jaw against his thighs. My elbow hit the ground hard, and I yelled.

"Will, it is I!" Relief surged through me as I heard Bess's voice and then her footsteps as she slipped from the horse and ran to retrieve the purse. "Well done!" she said, her eyes gleaming with excitement. "Come, we can both ride Merlin. Hurry!"

The boy kicked like a wild thing, and it was all I could do to hold on to his legs. Desperate situations require desperate measures: I hit him hard on the thigh with my fist. Still he struggled. Out of the corner of my eye, I saw a stone. Reaching out quickly, I picked it up and hit him again, harder, on his bony hip this time, with the sharp edge of the stone. He screamed.

"Be still!" I shouted. He did so, falling silent, apart from his labored breathing, which came in suffocating sobs. His face was buried in the dirt, and I knew very well what that felt like. I ought perhaps to show mercy — now that we had reclaimed the purse, there was no need to take vengeance further.

Once I was sure that he would not try to struggle free, I carefully lifted myself from his legs and rose to my feet, dusting myself down and feeling a degree of pleasure at my success. I rubbed my bruised elbow.

Bess was smiling at me as she put the purse back in her skirts. I smiled back at her. For the first time, perhaps, it seemed that she accepted me as her equal.

Her equal! Was I not above *her* in station? And she a girl, too!

"We shall leave him here," she said. "If you would be so good, gentle sir, as to help me into the saddle, then we . . ." She stopped. She was looking over my shoulder, and what she saw turned her white. I twisted around.

Two figures stood there. Their arms hung loosely at their sides, their huge hands open. Two men. Large men.

Grinning.

CHAPTER THIRTY-FIVE

Bess moved by instinct toward her horse.

"Leave it!" barked one man. "It is ours."

Bess obeyed, even moving farther away than she had been before. At that moment, I knew not why she did so.

I had need of a weapon. The stone still sat in my hand, but that would not suffice. Not against two large men who looked as strong as bulls. And the boy to help them.

Still the men stood there. They were some twenty yards away. I tried to judge whether I would have time to pick up a piece of wood I could spy a few feet from me. But what would Bess do? I was still trying to decide my next action when I heard a noise behind me. I swung around. The boy had climbed to his feet.

And he was not alone. Another older boy stood by him now, with a nasty grin and a mouth entirely empty of teeth. His eyes were white and rheumy, his skin badly marked by pox, and he had the appearance of something from the other side of the grave. I shuddered. He held a thick wooden club, a piece of jagged metal sticking from it.

My mouth was dry. I could not swallow. Thoughts spun like a storm in my head. This could not be happening! How had we allowed ourselves to be trapped? How could we possibly escape?

Bess was whispering from the side of her mouth, so that only I could hear. "Be ready. Watch me."

Oddly, through my near panic, a voice of calm came to me. It was not Bess's voice, though hers, too, sounded steady. It was a voice from deep inside me. And it said, "Be brave. And you shall succeed."

And so, barely breathing, but thinking, thinking fast, controlling my thoughts, I waited, watching her. I would not let Bess down.

I was ready.

"Now!" she shouted and, without thinking what she wanted me to do, I dived for the piece of wood. As I did, I saw the men move toward us. And from the corner of my vision, I saw Bess pick up her skirts and run, fast as a hunted hare, toward the horse. In astonishment, I saw her crouch and then spring through the air, twisting as she did and landing in the sidesaddle. I had never seen that done — I could not imagine how any lady would even think of trying, and if I *had* thought about it I would never have thought it possible. But there Bess was, sitting in the saddle, apparently without pain from her injury, gathering the reins and urging Merlin to a gallop.

Straight at the two huge men.

On some instinct, I twisted around, just in time to swing my piece of wood at the yellow-haired boy as he leaped at me. It hit him around the side of the head with a terrible crunch, and he crumpled to his knees on the ground, clutching his ear, blood trickling from his fingers.

The toothless boy hesitated, but only briefly, before a grin split his pockmarked face again and he came toward me, moving jerkily, with the club held in front of him. I was about to raise my stick to hit him, too, when Bess shouted, "No!" and I whipped around.

I saw a knife blade rise and begin to fall. I did not have time to raise my arm high enough — all I could do was hurl myself desperately to one side. The knife slashed through my sleeve, but I felt nothing else.

Scrambling to my feet, I saw Bess jerk the reins upward, making her horse rear up. How could she not fall? But she did not, and I felt a thrill of ugly pleasure as I saw one of the men trip as he tried to dodge the horse's legs. He was felled with a terrible cry and lay groaning on the ground, blood pouring from a wound in his head.

There were still two assailants left, though they had less spirit for the fight. Even the thickset man hesitated, his black eyes darting from side to side as he judged his next move. I kept the young one in my sights, swinging the stick in front of me, ready for him, waiting for the moment when he might leap toward me.

"Go now!" I shouted at them. "While you still have a chance!"

"Give us t' money," snarled the larger man, his voice ugly with menace.

"Not while there is breath in my body!" I retorted. I do not know where such fury came from. Perhaps the exhilaration of fighting back, the thought that, with two of them disposed of, Bess and I had a chance. A small chance, but nevertheless a chance.

But two things happened at the same moment. One was that my mind flitted for no good reason to thoughts of my horse, Sapphire — where was she? What had Bess done with her? And while I was distracted so, the injured man pushed himself to his hands and knees and then, in one swift movement, his feet. He stood there briefly, shaking his huge head and making a noise which was something between a groan and a bellow. Blood covered one half of his face. He wiped his eyes.

And began to move.

CHAPTER THIRTY-SIX

The injured man lurched toward Bess and Merlin. The other man hurled himself toward me with a cry, his knife slashing downward as I ducked again. Bess's horse was rearing but now the boy was running toward her, too, hitting the horse from behind. Landing on the ground again, Merlin lashed out in fear with a well-aimed back foot, and the lad collapsed once more, screaming and clutching his leg.

Surely someone would hear us? Surely someone would come to our aid?

Everything was happening too quickly. I did not know if I had been cut with the knife, but if not then I could not say how not. I lashed out in every direction with my stick, the sounds of blows hitting their mark mixed with the sounds of our grunts and yells. Merlin reared again and whinnied in panic.

A shout from somewhere above us was followed by the liquid contents of a bucket landing on one of the men, plastering his hair to his head and producing a maddened roar.

One of the men went down again — I do not know if I hit him. The thin one soon stopped his grinning when Bess whipped him across the face with her reins. One man only was left, seeming undamaged, still holding his knife. I lashed out frantically, swinging my long stick wildly in front of me, just managing to keep him at bay because my stick was longer than his arm. Every time he lunged, I parried him, as I had often been taught by my fencing master — though I had never fought for my life in any rapier lesson.

Suddenly, he lunged forward again, his eyes wide. Wielding my stick, and trying to dodge to one side, I hit him on the side of the head, but weakly now. My strength was fast fading, and there seemed no power in my arms. Black spots rushed across my vision and red rain poured down. I wiped my hand across my eyes — blood, bright, horrible. I had not even felt the blade against my skin.

But worse was to come.

My breath escaped in a weak moan. I sank to my knees, all strength leaving my legs. Roaring in delight, my assailant came at me again with his knife. I rolled to the side, sending him tumbling, and caught sight as I did of the thin boy on his feet once more, his trousers torn and blood coming from a gash in his leg. With a furious face, he leaped toward Bess, from the side, where she could not see him.

That was all I needed to urge me to desperate action — summoning my ebbing strength, rolling away from my opponent, I lashed out at the boy's legs with my stick. He turned, but he did not fall. I leaped to my feet and hurled myself at the boy, hating his snarling pockmarked face.

"No! Behind you!" yelled Bess and, without looking around, I threw myself to one side. The man's knife came flashing down, passing the place where I had been only a moment before.

The knife slashed across the boy's eye and a thin red line appeared slanting across that side of his face. He collapsed screaming, his hands covering his eyes.

"Here!" shouted Bess.

I ran toward her, grasped her outstretched hand, and leaped up behind her, landing half on and half off the horse's rump.

It was enough. She did not wait for me to right myself before urging Merlin on. We left that terrible place as fast as our horse could take us, with me hanging off his back. The screams of that boy echoed through the narrow streets, almost drowning the angry shouts of one of the men as he argued with somebody at a window.

Once out of danger, Bess pulled Merlin to a walk and I slid off the back. She dismounted and came to me, concern in her face. I wiped the blood from my eyes again, feeling my legs begin to tremble like butterflies with exhaustion and relief at our escape.

She pulled a cloth from a saddlebag and made a pad, which she pressed on my head. I felt no pain.

She removed the pad to examine the cut. "It is not deep," she said. "Wounds to the scalp always bleed richly." She pressed it again.

Now my bruises began to make themselves known. I did not know how much I had been hurt, but I knew nothing was broken. My sleeve was torn, but that would mend.

And, of course, I had retrieved her purse, for which she was profuse in her thanks. All my aches and pains seemed as nothing if I had proved myself not entirely useless.

"Where is Sapphire?" I asked.

"A tea seller has her. Do not worry for her. I know whom to trust."

And I, too, knew enough to trust Bess by now.

At the square we found a pump, and I washed the blood from my face. The cut had stopped bleeding, but I did not tempt it to open again by washing the blood from my hair. I made such improvement as

I could to my appearance, though I could only guess at the result. Wearily, I walked beside Bess, who rode her horse, without question this time, and we slowly made our way to where she had left mine.

Horses know things, if you are minded to listen to them. I would swear Sapphire knew me when I came to her, and that she knew I needed her now. She nickered as she nuzzled my ear. I wished I had something to give her.

A muffin man was passing, shouting his wares. His cheeks, pink in the cold air, were round as muffins themselves. I bought three from him and gave one to Sapphire before giving another to Bess. Eating that simple muffin and drinking the hot, milky tea that we bought from the kindly faced tea seller, I felt a wave of pleasure wash through me.

There were persons to trust, I told myself. One had merely to learn who they were. There was good to be found in every level of life. And bad. And sometimes one looked very much like the other.

It was as much as I could do to find the strength to mount my horse. But somehow, and soon, I was riding beside Bess, exhausted, bruised, but strangely happy, as we made our way back home. We talked little, each buried in thought, or in tiredness, or both.

We could not know that we would require more strength before the day was out.

Chapter Thirty-seven

Darkness was falling fast as we rode up to Bess's home, not far from the foot of the valley. Behind, dark forest cloaked the hillside, sheltering the cottage, and I could hear a stream, unusually loud in the still, frosty air.

We dismounted in silence and led the horses to the stable, where we did what must be done for their comfort. They had served us well. As we walked across the small yard toward the black-windowed cottage, my limbs were stiffening. I wanted nothing more than to fall onto a bed and sleep till morning came.

But it was not to be.

Perhaps we were too tired to notice anything amiss. Perhaps our heads were too full of the events of that day. But, whatever the reason, we noticed nothing at all. Nothing out of place.

Bess had built the fire and lit it expertly with flint and steel. The flames were beginning to catch and their welcome warmth and comfort had started to soften my limbs. I had paused to stare at them for a few moments, but roused myself before I could fall asleep. She had lit two oil lamps from the flames. I had brought water from the pump, which was soon heating in an enormous pot over the fire. We planned to wash in warm water, a pleasant thought after days of discomfort.

She had allowed me to dress her wound again, and I was glad to see how well it was healing, with barely any inflammation now. It had bled a little more, but that was only to be expected after her exertion of the day. She made no sound as I bound it tightly once more. As for her fever, it was entirely gone, though her face was still pale and tired-looking. But she brushed aside my concern, wishing me not to know if she was in any discomfort. I wondered at her stoicism.

We had taken our purchases, and Bess had put them away on shelves or in cupboards. We talked little as we did this, save for my occasional questions to ask where something should go.

"I shall change now," she had said when everything was done. "But first, let me bring some clean clothes for you. You look as though somebody has attempted to kill you!" And she had walked toward the narrow staircase to the upper room.

She had smiled, black eyes glimmering, and I returned her smile. We both knew how close we had been to death. I tried not to think about the boy whose face had been so terribly cut. I could not view my part in that with shame — they had tried to kill us. We had wanted only to retrieve what was ours. And I had not wielded the knife. God could not judge me harshly.

She ascended the stairs, carrying a lighted candle, and her skirts disappeared into the flickering half-light. I was just turning away, just bending down stiffly to remove my boots, when suddenly my heart jumped. I had heard a noise.

Two noises, and I cannot say which came first: Bess crying out or the small thud from the upper room.

No light came from up the stairs now.

Chapter Thirty-eight

I leaped to my feet, grabbed an oil lamp, and hurled myself up the stairs, shocked into action once more. What would I find? My thoughts raced, tumbling over each other as I tried to make sense of this new danger.

Taking the stairs three at a time, I reached the top. There stood Bess. The candle smoked on the floor, the holder rolling backward and forward as it settled. She was frozen, still as stone, though there was fire in her staring eyes.

Henry Parish. The runaway redcoat. The flour thief. Standing wet eyed, wide mouthed, his musket held in front of him at shoulder height. Finger on the trigger.

His eyes slid between the two of us, the musket moving unsteadily from one to the other. He swallowed and licked his lips. Red were his eyes in the lamplight, his dirty streaked cheeks telling of tears.

I did not know how much more I could bear, how many more times I must face danger. I was tired, my head ached, my vision was blurring. And then anger ripped through me, surging in my stomach. How dare he? I had given him food! I had told him never to return. How dare he break into Bess's house again, abuse its hospitality, sully its air with his sniveling? The traitor, the cowardly worm!

"What do you want?" I said, anger making my voice sound bold.

Bess spoke. "Do you know this boy?" I could hear venom in her voice, and then I remembered. This was a hated redcoat. If she could have attacked him with her bare hands she would have. Henry would do well to be careful, musket or no musket.

"He was here when I came to fetch Merlin. I bade him go, never to come back."

"He is a redcoat, Will!" she snapped. "He is a deserter, too! Dishonorable on two counts. You ought not to have trusted him. You should have killed him."

I said nothing. I knew how nearly I *had* killed him, but it would help no one to say so now. I knew, too, that he was not only a deserter and a redcoat but also a thief. Now was not the time for explanations. I placed the lamp on the ground. Our shadows leaped up the wall.

"What do you intend to do with that musket?" Bess snapped at the boy contemptuously. "Your hands are shaking. You could not shoot a giant at two paces with your hands shaking like that!" She took a step forward.

"No!" breathed Henry, his voice almost inaudible. "I will shoot! I will!" And he turned the musket toward me, preferring no doubt to shoot me instead of Bess. His finger moved almost unnoticeably, tightening slightly on the trigger. The gun, I could see, was cocked, ready to fire.

I would not stand and wait for the shot to come. Had I fought today for nothing? Had I ridden desperately from the militia officer, and seen him die, for nothing? Had I been guided across the marsh by a mysterious rider, and all for no reason?

Instead, I simply spoke, my wits sharpened by fear. "Your flint is worn," I said. "Your musket will not fire."

For an instant, Henry looked at the flint on his musket, hesitating, and in that moment I dived toward him and slightly to one side, grabbing his musket with my right hand as he swung it toward me.

He gave up. I should wish to say that I overcame

him, but it would not be true. He simply sank to his knees in fear or exhaustion, utterly defeated. I twisted the musket from his hands and threw it to Bess.

She leveled it at him, and he looked up. "No, Bess," I said quickly.

Her eyes gleamed in a way I had seen twice before, when she shot and killed the redcoat, and when she told the story of Mad Dog Tim's hanging. Her finger tightened on the trigger.

"The flint is done for," I reminded her.

"The flint is perfect, as you very well know," she replied, her words squeezing through tightened lips.

"Bess, you do not know what you are doing. He is no ordinary deserter. He has good reason to hate the redcoats as well. Let us talk. We can decide downstairs."

Henry knelt there, shoulders heaving in silent sobs. How I wished he would stop his sniveling, that he would stand up and be a man!

"Get up," I said, pushing him with my foot. "Go down the stairs."

We followed him down. He looked to me to know where he should go. I pointed to the floor, near the fire but not too close.

"Sit. And listen. Do not speak. And do not move." He pulled his knees up to his chest and hugged them, sniffing frequently. I had never seen such a miserable face. But what did he have to be anything other than miserable about? What choices or chances did he ever have?

I acquainted Bess with all that I knew about him. As I did so, I avoided looking at him. He repelled me. I detested his thinness, his crawling poverty, his driveling weakness. I hated the way he had crept back here like a mole driven into its hole at the first sign of light.

How I wished, above all, that he would go and that I did not have to think about him.

Once Bess had heard his story, why he was running from the redcoats, how desperate he was to take meager flour to his mother and sister, even though it would not remedy their poverty, she burned with a different fervor. She forgot how close she had been to shooting Henry Parish dead, and in her desire to wreak vengeance on the redcoats she would do anything, however dangerous, however misguided. I suppose, too, she recognized his poverty and would not stand by while richer men made it worse. No doubt, her father would have felt the same, and burned with equal fervor.

"We will help you!" she said. "We will help you escape. Tonight you must stay here and tomorrow . . . tomorrow we shall make a plan."

She thought that by aiding Henry, she would be

fighting against the redcoats, I could see that. What they wanted, she wanted to take from them. And so, foolishly, thinking nothing of herself — or of me — she was prepared to risk everything for a boy who should mean nothing to her.

And yet, I knew that she was right. We had to help Henry Parish. It was the honorable thing to do.

Bess, though a girl of low station, was as brave and as honorable as any gentleman I had met. Braver and more honorable than many.

CHAPTER THIRTY-NINE

Tired though I was, at first I could
not sleep. My head throbbed and my bones ached in
places where they had not before. And I did not
know what would happen the next day, how we
could help Henry escape. I confess I hoped he would
escape far away from here, and never return. His
home was many miles away, he told us, to the northwest, by Carlisle. Almost in Scotland. He named the
place but I did not know it. I hoped that once there,
he would never find his way back here.

I was considering only myself, I admit that.

I did not know for certain why he deserved our
help. His troubles were not ours. He could indeed
bring danger upon us, great danger. And he had done
little enough to show bravery or honor. Running
away for the sake of a few pounds of flour? How

might that have helped his mother and sister? They would have eaten it within days and then where would they be? Still hungry and their son and brother with a price on his head.

He was foolish. He was foolish, cowardly, and weak.

We made him sleep in the small room up the stairs, under the eaves. It was colder up there, without the fire, and probably damp, but safer. Safer for us, that is. Nor did I wish him to be able to slip out during the night and steal one of the horses. Bess slept in her bed in the smaller of the two downstairs rooms, after taking the chill off the mattress by use of a warming pan filled with embers from the fire. I was content with a horsehair bolster and a pile of blankets on the floor by the hearth.

Before Bess had gone to her bed, we had briefly talked about the next day, while she stitched the tear in my sleeve. My head was heavy with exhaustion, and I contributed little. After her recent illness, I do not know where Bess found the strength to talk so late.

She had some idea of using the horses and taking Henry to the nearest staging post, giving him some clothes, disposing of his redcoat's uniform, and sending him on his way home. As far as I was concerned, whether he reached home or not, I would perhaps never discover, and would care little to know. As long as I never saw him again.

I am not proud of such thoughts, but I could not warm my heart to Henry Parish. He had brought nothing but trouble until now, and I believed that he would bring nothing but trouble in the future.

But Bess's plan was the only one we had. Little was I to know that she had wasted her breath in speaking of it.

Eventually, I slept, though when I woke I did not feel refreshed. I woke in the stygian gloom of that February morning. No, I realized, the day was the first of March. A new month. Spring would be on its way soon. Light and warmth would return to the land, new life. A new life for me, too.

But why had I awoken so early? Nothing stirred in the cottage. I strained my ears. It seemed that something had woken me, but what?

Carefully, pushing back the blankets and forcing my stiffened joints to move, I began to stand up. A sound. Outside. Horses! Many horses. I leaped to my feet, wide awake now. Stumbling in the darkness, I dragged on the clothes Bess had given me, tugging on the woolen stockings and fumbling with the buttons on the unfamiliar breeches, slipping my feet into the well-worn shoes that were only a little too big, pulling on the jacket.

The sound of hoofbeats came closer. What were they doing here at this time, so early in the morning?

Perhaps they would go past the cottage; perhaps they were not minded to come here. But, indeed, I could not think where they might be going if not here.

With my heart pounding, I hurried to the room where Bess slept. "Bess! Bess!" I whispered urgently. "Hurry! You must rise. Now!"

At once, she grasped the urgency of the situation. We could both hear the horses now, and the shouts of men, orders being given. I left Bess to dress herself and ran back into the other room, where I stood, unable to decide what to do. There was not sufficient time to warn Henry — I could only pray he had heard. But how would that help? He could not escape now.

Should I light a lamp or not? Would it be better if I could see, or better if they came into near darkness? But before I could act, a loud banging shook the door. Hurrying to it, I slid the bolts open. What else could I do? If we did not open it, they would merely force it.

Redcoats, not militia. I knew immediately that they were looking for Henry. Why else could they be here? Suddenly the full enormity of our danger hit me like a fist in the chest. Henry was upstairs. What if they searched? And, of course, they would. And when they did, they must find him.

What would they do with him then? What would they do with us?

Chapter Forty

Six men had burst into the cottage just as Bess came into the room, wrapping a cloak tightly around her crumpled dress, her hair a tangled mass tumbling about her face and shoulders. I saw her teeth clench, her jaw tighten, as she saw the red-coats. I hoped she would do nothing foolish.

"What is your business here?" I demanded, trying to sound strong and innocent. Two of them carried storm lanterns, which swung their orange glow, sending shadows flitting around the room like giant ghosts. The cold air rushed in, bringing fresh snow. I shivered.

They filled the room, huge and loud with their bright jackets, their white-edged tricorne hats scattering water as they shook them. Their muscles bulged like ships' ropes in their tight white breeches.

Some — four at least — carried muskets, ugly bayonets fixed at the end.

One of the men — an officer from his markings, cruel from his arrogant sneer — spoke, after a pause in which he seemed to be deciding whether I was worth regarding. Did he not know? Did he not recognize that I was no journeyman, no person of the lowest order?

"Where is your father? Where is the householder?" Water dripped from his orange moustache.

"This is our home," I said boldly. I had no time to think. I could only react to whatever came to pass. But I tried desperately to think, to form a plan. I did not look at Bess. She was silent, for which I was thankful.

The officer laughed. "Two children! What age are you, lad?"

"Sixteen," I lied. "We are brother and sister. Our father is at sea. With His Majesty's ships." I had no plan to tell such lies. Did I blush as I did so? Did they see my trembling?

"Brother and sister? This is your sister, eh? By gad, what a sister!" And the officer walked over to Bess, slowly, knowing he could take as much time as he wished. He stood in front of her, his chest puffed out and his mouth slightly open, looked at her face, let his eyes wander down her body. As he put out his hand and with a finger touched her hair, I began to leap forward, but I was held, grabbed by two of the soldiers. I could smell their sweat and the doughy scent of their hair, caked in damp flour as it was. I thought of Henry and why we were all here.

Was it all for this? Was the appearance of a soldier's hair more important than a starving family?

"Do not move, boy!" snarled one.

"Not while a gentleman is examining your wares," sneered the other. Two of the other soldiers started picking objects up and dropping them. They opened every cupboard door, sweeping contents aside as if what they sought could be hiding in there. Or as if it mattered nothing, as long as they caused as much damage as possible.

I could not watch all of them, could not tell where to keep my eyes.

One picked up a keg of beer, opened the bung with his teeth, and drank from it noisily, tipping his throat far back, so that the muscles in his neck moved like a caterpillar. His skin was covered in ugly red spots. I said not a word. I wanted only to protect Bess, and I cared nothing about the beer. A taste of the bitterest anger flooded my mouth. I could almost smell it, almost sense blood on my tongue as I struggled to hold myself back. But if the worst came to the worst, then I *would* fight. Even if it meant pain or death —

because I could not honorably let them harm Bess. And I could not have borne to watch that myself.

The officer's finger curled around a tress of Bess's cascading black hair and played with it, one side of his mouth turned upward in a smile. I could not bear it. I strained against my captors' arms, but the more I struggled the more they laughed and the more they dug their iron-strong fingers into my flesh.

Still she looked down and said nothing, but I could see her shoulders heaving as she gathered breath to speak. She must not! She would only make it worse.

"What do you want?" I asked. "What do you want from us?"

"We are searching for a deserter," said the officer, still playing with Bess's hair. "But I warrant the deserter will wait. We are in no hurry. We know he cannot be far away. Perhaps he is here even now? Perhaps, at this very moment, he crouches upstairs, cringing like some frightened cur. We have the cottage surrounded. He cannot go far." The officer looked toward the stairs as he said this.

"There is no one here!" I said. "We would not harbor a deserter! Our father fights for the King! If a deserter came here, we would turn him in."

"What about you, girl? Would you turn in a poor young boy? Or would your woman's heart soften and take him to your . . . breast?" And as he said this,

his finger traced softly the edge of her jaw, slipping down her neck and slowly sliding around her throat.

The other men laughed, urging him on with lewd gestures and sounds. One man walked past Bess and dropped something at her feet.

"Oh, how foolish of me!" he said, looking at the others for encouragement. And he bent down, slowly, until he was on his hands and knees behind her. He stretched his hand underneath her skirt, reached until he could touch her ankle. Bess raised her knee — I saw her skirts move — and stamped down hard on his hand. She was wearing her pattens, and his cry of pain as the sharp edge caught the bones of his hand was satisfying in the extreme.

Furious, the man stood up, shaking his hand. Another man laughed. The officer spoke again, his mustache trembling. "She has spirit, your sister. She should be doing her part to serve His Majesty's army. Soldiers have their needs, and a girl of such spirit as this would be of great service indeed."

The man's finger was now at the very edge of her cloak, where she held it wrapped around her body. A moment more and his fingers would be sliding inside her garment. I struggled and strained, trying to kick my captors, but their strength was too great.

Still she did not look up.

Then the officer's finger slipped beneath her cloak. And in one fluid movement, Bess gathered her breath, raised her head, stared into his gaze, and spat. Her spittle hit him between the eyes and dripped down his nose. Everything froze, silent and still, Bess's fury matched only by the officer's menacing quiet.

I could not blame her. But I wished she had not done it.

Chapter Forty-one

Now a soft noise rose from the men, a sort of thrill, the thrill of men who are about to strike, whose blood is up, who are ready to kill.

Into the waiting air, the officer spoke, softly, oozing menace. And yet, beneath the softness was the strength of an iron chain: "You will be sorry for that. When we find the deserter, you will be sorry. Do you know the penalty for helping a deserter? For being a traitor? I can shoot you. I can say that I shot you while you protected the deserter. But before I do that, I can do with you whatever I wish. No one will know or care. And my fellow soldiers may have their turn with you, too. We have been long away from our women, and we may use you as we wish. In the name of the King's army. For the good of our country. You will, at least, know you played your part. And your brother will be witness."

Bess stood, her shoulders heaving with anger. But she dropped not her gaze. Her black eyes blazed.

She spat again. This time he hit her, his hand lashing out against her cheek, flicking her face aside as though it were a wasp. She whipped her head back again and stared at him defiantly, her eyes wild.

"I have never hit a lady," he said, his voice shrill now, sharp as a rapier, "but then, you are no lady." Turning on his heel, he barked orders to the men: "You two, remain with them. Let them move not one step. The rest of you — search the place. Leave no corner unturned. And when you find him, it is my right to shoot him."

A soldier grabbed Bess. Another held me, locking my arms behind me so that I could not move without wrenching the muscles in my shoulders. The men dispersed, loudly throwing items aside, once more smashing objects needlessly on the ground.

The officer cried, "No, leave the girl's sleeping place to me. It would be of no surprise were we to find the wretch sniveling in her bed, keeping it warm for her." And he strode into the other room, where I watched the bedclothes being hurled aside.

It did not take long to search the two rooms downstairs. Now, only the room under the roof was left.

What could we do? I know I felt little for Henry Parish, but these men had insulted Bess, had used me like a child or a dog, had treated Bess's home as though it were no better than a cowshed. I had begun to grow my own hatred of them and their cruelty, their arrogance, their unconcern for others.

And now, I would do anything for them not to catch Henry Parish.

But what could I do? I looked at Bess. She did not look at me. Was she trying to devise a plan? Did she fear for herself, or me, or Henry Parish? Or was her hatred of the redcoats raging so furiously that she could make no plan at all?

Two men began to climb the stairs, one behind the other in the narrow space, their bayonets held fixed in front of them.

"Stop!" ordered the officer.

What now? Surely they must search upstairs! He walked over to us, his sword swinging against his thick thigh. I stared at his chest. I noticed a stain on it, of grease or gravy perhaps, and I had a sudden picture of him laughing and drinking and burying his face in a piece of roast venison, dripping a thick port sauce from his chin before wiping his mouth on the tablecloth. And he cared about the theft of some flour by a poor boy whose mother was starving? The injustice of it came to me suddenly, like a full moon appearing unexpectedly from behind a cloud, lighting up the darkness in a strange glow.

This is not right, I thought. Surely this was not what God intended? Surely this was human error and greed? "Blessed are the meek. Blessed are the poor. It is easier for a camel to go through the eye of a needle, than for a rich man to enter the Kingdom of Heaven." I had heard these things many times; never had their true meaning come to me as it did now.

And as these new thoughts occurred to me, my hatred grew further. And I prayed, as I had never prayed before, that somehow, somehow, Henry Parish would be saved.

The officer was standing in front of me still, looking at me, not at Bess. Perhaps he sensed that he would get nothing from her, no show of fear. Well, he would get no show of fear from me either, however I felt inside.

He spoke. "We know the boy is here. We found a vagrant, who informed us. After some . . . persuasion. Of the harsher variety. He would have us believe that the girl knew nothing about it. Clearly, she has a way with men, that he would choose to endure pain rather than blame her." He looked briefly at Bess, his lips parted slightly, a sneer on his face, then back at me. "When we find him, as you know we shall, your sister's charms will help her not one jot." And he barked his order, "Men! Do your duty! And remember, I want him alive."

I held my breath, tried to show nothing on my face. Bess and I did not look at each other, though I could sense her anguish, too.

Two men held us. I could smell them, their sweat and their foul breath. One soldier stood at the door, his shadow from the flickering lantern larger than life, stretching the height of the wall. The officer watched us, smiling not at all now, contempt in his eyes, and determination. He would take delight in killing Henry Parish in front of us. And then what would he do with us?

The other two men rushed up the stairs, two steps at a time, their bayonets held eagerly in front of them. They turned the corner. We heard them reach the top; the sound of the door being forced open; footsteps, crashes, a few moments while we did not breathe, while we held our hearts still in our breasts as we waited for the sounds that would tell us that Henry had been caught.

But no such sound came. The men said something that we could not hear. Then we heard footsteps again, and the two soldiers came running down the stairs. "'E's not 'ere!" said one, confusion and anger on his face.

I struggled to maintain my composure, to show

not one single sign of the joy I felt inside. How could he not be there? The cottage, they said, was surrounded. They would have ensured that before they came to the door. He could not have escaped from the window, not with the soldiers watching there.

With a cry of fury, the officer shouted at me. "Where have you hidden him?"

"I told you," I replied, trying to keep my voice steady — there was no point in annoying them further with some clever remark. "Our father fights for the King. We would not harbor a deserter. We have not seen him."

He turned to Bess. I prayed she would not endanger us with her fury. He placed his face close to hers, so that she must smell his breath, see the veins under his swarthy skin. "And you?" he said. "Are you so sure? Have you not had him in your bed, warming him perhaps?"

"No, sir," answered Bess, with exquisite softness. "I have not." And she smiled, which she should not have done. But she was lucky. The soldiers wanted their deserter, and their reward, more than they wished to waste time on us. We were beneath them.

They left, as suddenly as they had come, leaving the door hanging wide and snow blowing in on a sharp wind.

Chapter Forty-two

For a few moments, we stood there, Bess and I, staring at each other but daring to speak not a word, as we listened to the sounds of them mounting their horses and galloping away. Then, still not speaking, we ran up the stairs.

They were right. Henry Parish was not there.

Through the open shutters, glimmers of dawn lightened the gloom, and we looked around. Not a single sign showed that he had been there. The blanket that we had given him was, we found on inspection, folded neatly in a wooden chest. Some objects — tools and a frayed basket awaiting repair, an old lantern, a small pile of yellowed papers, and a silver-trimmed tricorne hat — all sat, dust covered and untouched, as I think they had been before. The dust on the floor was disturbed by the soldiers' feet, and if Henry had been there, one could not have said for sure.

It was as though we had dreamed of his visit. Henry Parish was nowhere to be seen.

I hurried to the casement. It was closed, but not latched. Henry could have left through here — indeed, he must have done. But he must have pushed it shut as he jumped. He could only have done that if he was making every effort not to leave a sign of his exit. I marveled suddenly at such honorable behavior, at how frightened he must have been and yet how mindful of our safety.

But what about footprints in the snow? We peered into the dingy light. Footprints there certainly were — of horses. If Henry had in truth jumped from the window, all traces of his fall and his escape would have disappeared by now. It had been snowing when the men arrived, though it was not now — perchance his marks had already been covered, or the soldiers had not looked, so confident were they of finding him in this room.

Henry must have left long before the soldiers came. He must have decided for himself that he wished to put us in no danger.

I felt a new respect for Henry Parish. He was brave, far braver than I had thought. And honorable. Now my hatred of the redcoats and their arrogance blazed red. Six strong men on horses against one poor, thin boy who desired only to feed his family. It was not right!

"We have to help him, Bess," I said as we stared out of the window, searching for signs, for anything to give us hope.

She turned to me. "He cannot have gone far. With the horses we should find him soon. I know those woods."

We hurried downstairs. The room was cold and damp, wet wind rushing through the open door. I hurried to close it. We had no time to build a fire or make tea, but we knew we must eat. The contents of the cold cupboard were strewn on the floor, so we recovered what we could and quickly ate bread and some ham, washing it down with water. We did not pick up all that the soldiers had left on the floor — there was no time, and our thoughts were on more important matters.

We had a plan, of sorts, but first we must find Henry. Dressing as warmly as was possible in a short time, we hurried outside, into the grim, gray morning. Bess wore man's clothing again, with her hair hastily wound in tight coils and stuffed inside her hat, and, although I still found this strange and discomforting, I knew it was the more prudent way and I did not question her. Bess was not as others are, I was coming to see, and she minded nothing what any might think. She did what must be done, what she thought was right and necessary, rather than what was right and proper.

As we saddled the horses, I calmed Sapphire, and she responded well to my voice, though I think some of my fear and anger must have been plain to her, for she skitted and sidestepped as I mounted her. But I soon brought her under control, and was glad of her strength and spirit. The last thing I wanted was a sluggish horse, and that indeed I did not have.

Bess led the way and soon we were entering the woods behind the house. We knew the soldiers had not gone there — we had heard them ride away along the road, and the snow would have told us if so many feet had passed this way of late. We peered at the ground, looking for any sign. But if Henry had passed this way, his marks were covered.

Into the gray silence of the trees, we called his name. Only the occasional fluttering patter of snow falling from sloping branches answered our call. Every now and then, the scuttle of some small animal came from the undergrowth, and then the snow slithered faster from the trees above.

The path took us deeper into the forest. We trotted, knowing that if we were to catch up with Henry we must make good speed. I shivered as a gust of wind threw wet air at my face and down my neck. How must he be feeling — cold and very alone? Bess and I had each other for company, and a fire to return to, but Henry Parish had nothing.

Now the trees were closer set and the snow on the path was thinner. The most recent light snow had had no chance to reach the ground here. If there were footprints, we should see them. We peered downward as we trotted. It was Bess who found what we were looking for. I was expending more effort controlling Sapphire, who had skittered sideways again, frightened by some innocent noise behind her, when Bess called out, "Stop!" and pulled Merlin to a halt.

She was pointing to the ground, where I could just make out footprints, a single set. It must be Henry. We called his name again. But once more all that came back were the soft noises of a hushed forest.

Carefully, we followed the footprints. After a while, they led away from the path. We looked at each other, but continued. More slowly now, pushing branches away from us before they could scratch our faces and tear our hair, we moved deeper into the forest. The ground underfoot was uneven, pitted with treacherous dips and crisscrossed with fallen branches.

"Henry! Let us help you!" we called at intervals.

And, at last, came an answering call, and Henry appeared before us, small, frightened, and wet. His hair hung like the thin tails of rats, clinging to the sides of his face, plastered down onto his forehead. His eyes stared, large and wide and tired.

"I thought — I thought — I thought —" he stuttered.

"You did well," said Bess, smiling at him to reassure him. She dismounted and walked toward him. "How did you escape in time? You must have fled before the soldiers came."

"The man," replied Henry. "'E called to me from outside. 'E told me soldiers were coming and I should follow 'im. But I lost 'im." His teeth were chattering, and his lips were gray with cold.

"What man?" I asked. Though, with a chill crawling over my skin, I knew.

Chapter Forty-three

"I 'ad a dream," replied Henry. "'E 'eld a lantern, and sat on a black 'orse. And when I woke, I was that confused. I looked from t' window and I thought I saw 'im. I thought 'e was calling me. But then, 'e disappeared and I saw it was only a dream. I was that afeard, an' I thought . . . I thought . . ."

Bess and I looked at each other. "It was a dream," said Bess firmly, as much to me as to Henry, and perhaps to herself.

"I know," said Henry. "But I was that afeard and I thought . . ."

"A dream," said Bess again. "But you were fortunate, Henry, for the soldiers did come. But they have gone now and all is well."

I knew she must be right but I shivered for all that. The men of the church tell us not to put our faith in ghouls and witchcraft, but on the moors this is easier said than done. The mists rise and wreathe the landscape and breathe into the night air and anything is possible.

We wasted no further time in musings, but quickly outlined our plan as Henry listened. Several times, he shook his head. Once he said, "No, I cannot. It is too dangerous for ye." But we bade him not think on that. He shook his head but continued listening. At another point he looked into my eyes, and opened his mouth to say more, but I would not let him speak. There was nothing we needed to hear.

Henry Parish and I removed our jackets in the cold air and exchanged them with each other. He seemed to take mine with as much reluctance as I took his, though for different reasons perhaps. He knew the danger I would face but he could also sense our determination. Henry's jacket was tight on my shoulders, and short of arm, but it would suffice.

"Your breeches, too," said Bess. I looked at her. "Yours are too dark," she explained. "Henry's may be dirty, but they still look as though they once were white. You must change them."

She was right, but we would not do it in front of her gaze. Henry and I looked pointedly at her. With a click of irritation, she turned away, folding her arms as she avoided looking on us. But I was taller than Henry and broader of thigh, and I could not pull his breeches on. Even Bess agreed when I allowed her to look. We must hope that the red jacket would be sufficient to fool them, from a distance. Besides, I hoped not to be too close to them. I pulled my breeches back on, and felt glad of them, I confess. They were more in keeping with what I was accustomed to, even if they were not my own.

Taking the soft, unshapely hat from my pocket, I thought briefly of the servant at my father's house from whom I had taken it, and handed it to Henry. In my turn, I took his soldier's hat and pulled it firmly onto my head. It felt odd to be so dressed, to wear the uniform I had never wished to wear. I tried not to think on it too much.

Bess gave Henry some money, which he took reluctantly. Then, with the knife from my belt, between us we cut Henry's hair short, Bess holding the hair straight while I hacked it off. We stepped back and looked at him, and he stood there, limply, his arms hanging by his sides, enveloped in Bess's father's clothes, still shivering, his lips now blue.

He held out his hand to shake mine and I took his, unwillingly at first. I did not want his gratitude. I wished him well, from my heart, and tried not to think too hard about what I was going to do.

But he gripped my hand. "I . . . thank thee," said

Henry Parish then. "Thou'rt braver 'n I could ever be. And if . . ." He stopped. Tears were in his eyes. "If I do not . . ."

"Think not on it," I said quickly.

"No," he said, fighting to control his voice. "If I do not reach 'em, tell my mother and my sister how I tried. Tell 'em I did not desert for cowardice. Tell 'em that."

I could only nod. I was holding back emotion myself. With one final look at Henry Parish, and then at Bess, I mounted Sapphire's back, settling comfortably in the saddle, thinking again of Bess's father who had sat in it before. Could I be as brave as he?

"Be safe and take good care," I said to Bess. She nodded, and smiled at me so that I knew she thought well of me, as she too mounted her horse. Henry swung himself up behind her, using her stirrup before settling with his legs dangling free. We cantered away — Bess taking Henry through the forest and to the road going northwest, and I proceeding along the valley and toward the southeast. Toward the nearest village, where I hoped the redcoats would see me.

The plan was that they should chase me, seeing my red coat and thinking that I was Henry Parish. The plan was that by the time the soldiers might perceive that I was not Henry, he would have escaped.

Meanwhile, I had a spare jacket in a bag attached to my saddle and could dispose of the red coat when the time came, once I judged that we were both safe.

It was a dangerous plan, but it was the only one we had.

CHAPTER FORTY-FOUR

Bess had told me where the soldiers were billeted. The town was near the road to Scarborough, and at once I rode toward it, knowing the direction well enough by now, the landmark shapes of hills and woods.

I admit to fear, to feeling cold, to smelling the sweat from my body. But I vowed to do what I could, to fight for what seemed right.

Back through the trees we cantered, Sapphire and I, back the way we had come, down the hillside. We passed Bess's cottage and found the lane, following it as I remembered from my journey with her only the day before, out of the valley and toward the next hillside. I did not canter now — it was better to save my horse's strength. I rose and fell to her elegant trot, settling into her gait, coming to know her better.

Though the snow had stopped, and indeed was thawing underfoot, a biting March wind buffeted my face and neck. Yet a thin sun brightened the grayness to the east, silvering the air, lightening the heartbeat. Spring would be here soon. Would I live to see it?

We came to the top of a hill and found ourselves looking down into the next valley. Here the snow lay only in patches, more thinly. There was the road twisting downward to the left. As we proceeded toward it along a narrow path, I kept my eyes scanning the horizon on all sides. Where were the redcoats? Were any of them still searching, or had they returned to their billets near the town? They must see me, but not at too close quarters. I must stay out of musket range and be able to outrun them. I must keep my eyes open — I must not be surprised.

The countryside was bleak and wild, some slopes thinly covered with snow, others mottled with dull shades of browns and grays, where trees or rocks or sheltered areas protruded through the wintry landscape. Lonely groups of trees dotted the glowering hillsides. Lines of low stone walls dipped and wove along the contours like wrinkles, but most was open space, scarred by patches of rock or dead vegetation. Where there was little snow, sheep grazed on coarse grass between clumps of gorse, their thick coats whipped by the wind. Tracks led from place to place, and in the crooked elbows of hills there rushed fast streams and gushing waterfalls.

My red coat would be visible for miles, if anyone should care to look.

I wondered where Henry and Bess were now. Bess was to take Henry to where he would catch the stagecoach west and then north. From there, he was on his own, as safe as we could make him from the redcoats' clutches. As I pondered this, I could not stop myself thinking of my own home between Hexham and Durham. I wondered what my father and mother thought of me now. Or what they would say if they could see me. If they knew that I was helping a deserter?

Would they believe that I could be risking my life for another? In the name of justice? I thought not.

A shot! Another! I twisted in my saddle. Redcoats! Horsemen riding toward me from some trees. Other men kneeling and firing. I cursed inwardly. How could I have been so foolish? They must have been waiting!

I dug my heels sharply into Sapphire's sides and she began to gallop. I felt her fear, but fear is no bad thing when a horse must summon extra strength and speed. We left the track and headed diagonally uphill. I kept a light touch on the reins — she needed to use her own judgment to avoid stumbling on the uneven ground.

I snatched a glance behind me. Four mounted men were following me. I could see their swords glinting as they slapped against their horses' sides. Some hundred yards distant, perhaps less.

Two more shots rang out. Why did they fire when I was out of their range? I had left the kneeling soldiers far behind by now, so why did shots still ring out? And then I saw, out of the corner of my eye, the glint of steel in the distance, flashes of red jackets, the sparks of flames from a shepherd's hut. Instinctively, I ducked, offering the smallest target possible, and panic rushed once again through my body. We had not foreseen this! That so many soldiers would chase Henry Parish, that they would split into groups and hunt him down relentlessly. And all for some flour!

Full of fear now — though mostly fury at the injustice of it — I urged Sapphire onward. Up the hillside. The hill curved around, and I could not be sure what direction I was now taking. Perhaps I was riding toward Bess's cottage? I must not do that. I veered slightly.

We leaped a stream, scrambling up the bank. A little farther on, we flew over a low stone wall. Sapphire stumbled as she landed, and I almost fell, sliding around her shoulder. With great effort, I righted myself, thanking the well-made saddle that let me grip it without slipping.

I knew in my heart that the stories of a ghostly highwayman were just that — stories, but I confess I prayed that, if there were anything in the stories, Bess's father would look kindly on me now. Or that any spirits of the place might look with favor on a boy who only did what he thought to be right.

How alone I felt on those moors! How helpless! I could not know where the soldiers were now. I knew that the horsemen still pursued me — I could hear the thunder of hooves, the clanking of metal, the occasional shout. But were more soldiers awaiting me farther on?

If I could only find a place to hide and throw off my red jacket, I might escape. If I could only summon some extra speed, mayhap I could round a corner, or find some trees, or take a turn that they did not see. The soldiers' horses were built for strength, not speed — I could perchance outpace them.

Again, I pushed Sapphire on, pressing her hard with my legs. I spoke to her, praising her, urging her, asking everything of her. My fingers gripped her mane tightly, and I could smell her rich scent as she galloped, giving every bit of her strength.

But how long could she keep this up? Sweat flecked her shoulders and her breathing was heavy now, labored and gasping.

I could hear a bugle in the distance. I did not

know what it meant. Were they coming from another direction? I tried to look around, searching for movement, looking for the telltale red splashes of their jackets. But in the snatched moment I could tell nothing useful. Everything was blurred, like raindrops scattering across a window in a storm.

We were approaching a hedge. Knowing not what was on the other side, I had no choice — we must jump. I held my breath and squeezed shut my eyes as we rose into the air, flying over the bare winter branches. Sapphire stumbled, catching her foot on something in the hedge. It was only a slight stumble, but it was enough — with horror, I felt myself spinning helplessly in the air, flying, falling, and landing on my back with a thump that shook the breath from my body. Desperately, I rolled over, back toward the hedge: when the other horses jumped, I had no wish to be beneath their pounding feet.

My arms clasped over my head, my eyes screwed shut, my body tensing for the pain, I lay there, waiting. A small pat of melting snow slid off a branch and dropped on the back of my neck.

Still I waited. Perhaps they would not see me? Perhaps they would charge on before they even knew I was there? Sapphire had galloped onward. Or so I thought.

But after some few moments, when I dared look up from my position face down in the wetness, I saw her standing not far off, holding her front leg awkwardly. With fear, I saw how her fetlock swelled already and her head hung down in pain.

Poor Sapphire would be no help to me now.

CHAPTER FORTY-FIVE

Nothing could save me. I could only wait for the redcoats to come. When they discovered that I was not Henry Parish, I might expect no mercy. I clenched my fists and breathed the mud and snow beneath my face. The wetness was seeping into my clothes.

Moments passed and stretched into a time I could not measure. And still I could hear no approaching hoofbeats. Nothing except the haunting sounds of that bugle. And, when I listened more carefully, the distant rattle of a drummer. What was happening?

After a few moments more, I rolled over and began to get to my feet. Buzzards wheeled overhead, floating, waiting.

With caution, I peered over the hedge. No horsemen approached. But farther away, two groups of men, redcoats, were riding toward each other. One group, I guessed from its direction, was the same one that had been pursuing me. I saw other men, on foot, at various points along the brow of a hill, to the left.

I was looking almost south — this much I could tell by the pale glow of the sun behind the clouds a little to my left. To the west, thick mist hung mysteriously low, hiding the landscape. One group of riders came from there. From the direction Bess and Henry had taken.

Sapphire stood behind me, blowing vapor into the air. I went to her and stroked her nose. Neither one of us could know more than the other what was about to happen.

And then I simply stood behind the hedge. Uncertain what else to do, I watched and waited. I knew not what to think — whether to fear or to be relieved, whether danger was past or only waiting for me. My heartbeat settled, my body became calm, but I still could not know what to do.

Now the two groups of horsemen, together, had wheeled around and were galloping to the west.

And then . . . no! I strained my eyes, trying to see as clearly as I might. Two figures on horseback, coming slowly from that same direction. One in a red coat, the other in some darker color. But . . . surely it could not be? I narrowed my eyes further. It was! It was Bess. But if this was Bess, where then was Henry? And why was she here? With a redcoat riding beside her? Why was she riding into danger?

The redcoat with her did not seem to hold her prisoner. She appeared to ride slightly ahead of him.

She was riding toward the mounted soldiers. Her horse was no more than trotting, as though she was in no hurry. I could not say if the men she approached were those who had entered her house so roughly and treated her with such contempt, but if they were, might they not recognize her?

Fear came rushing back now, and I wished that Sapphire was not lame. But what could I have done even had she been sound?

The horsemen slowed and stopped when they came to Bess and the other rider, who both stopped, too. Some conversation took place, and I saw Bess point in the direction from which she had come. I did not understand. That must be where Henry was. Why was she pointing in his direction?

My jaw was clenched tight as a poacher's trap as I waited for her to walk on, for them to let her pass. Several times, I thought I saw them shift, moving to let her through, but each time, she moved not onward and I could only hope and pray.

When, at last, they parted and she walked through

alone, I found that my fingernails had dug so hard into my palms that blood formed in crescent shapes. My knuckles were white.

I watched her closely, still watched them, too, for any sign of trouble, of more danger. But she seemed only to walk on as though nothing had happened. They, meanwhile, galloped away in the direction she had indicated.

I wished I could call out to her. I must speak to her, must ask what had happened. Where was Henry, and why had our plan gone so awry? And what should we do now?

The mournful sound of the bugle came again, and I saw the men on foot reassemble. I saw them stand and wait. What were they waiting for?

Bess was now moving across the hillside to my left, riding east. I watched her stop. She looked back at the disappearing riders, glanced casually at the soldiers, appearing to have no fear. What was in her mind? I surmised that she knew they did not want her. To them, she was just a passing lad, adequately well dressed and mounted on a good horse with a high-quality saddle. They did not know she was in fact a young woman, that tumbling black hair was coiled beneath her tricorne hat. How could they know?

But no matter how I tried to read her mind, I could not know why she was there.

I watched her begin to move again, walking, sometimes trotting, but not appearing to hurry. She parted from the track and veered farther to her left, until, eventually, she was riding up the hill, almost toward where I was. Did she know I was there?

I looked down the hillside. Another bugle call trailed through the air like music from a watery grave. I had been hunting, of course, many times: the bugle calls brought this to my mind, though they were not the same. But I knew they must be telling the soldiers something. None of the men within my sight moved; they stood and waited — for what, I did not know.

Could I risk moving from the hedge? The soldiers did not seem interested now in the boy in the red coat whom they had chased. It seemed they knew that I was not Henry Parish, the deserter and thief. Our plan had failed.

Only then did I think of removing the red jacket and my soldier's hat. With my foot, I scraped a shallow hole in the wet earth beneath the hedge, and pressed the garments as flat as I could into the shallow dip, covering them with sticks and dead leaves. No longer was I Henry Parish. Although I confess to feeling some relief, I believe there was more sadness and anger.

Now, I could only hope that, somehow, they would not catch Henry. Could I dare hope for so much?

Bess was out of sight, having disappeared behind

a ridge. I wanted her with me now. I did not wish to lose sight of the soldiers, nor did I wish to leave Sapphire, but I must find Bess, to discover what was happening and for what reason. I moved along the line of the hedge, toward the very brow of the hill. Surely the soldiers would not see me here, even should they look. And if they saw me, who was I? Just a lad, a shepherd perhaps? In the distance, I could be anyone, but not Henry Parish, not without my red coat.

I hurried now toward the brow. And there was Bess, riding toward me, cantering now. She was out of breath, her eyes blazing, her face red with exertion.

"Will! Thank goodness I have found you! Our plan failed!" Her voice trembled. She pulled Merlin to a halt beside me and jumped down. She could see Sapphire some way away beside the hedge, and we went in that direction.

"What happened?" I asked. "Why did the soldiers stop pursuing me? I saw you ride . . ."

She was staring down the hill as she answered. I looked but nothing had changed — still the men waited in their groups. "The road was blocked." She shook her head in anger and frustration. "There had been a flood after the melting snow and then a landslide, making the valley impassable. I had to take a different route. When we could not cross the river,

Henry refused to go on. He said he would not put me in danger. I said I did it not for him but for his mother and sister . . . but he would not listen. He burned with fervor. You can scarce imagine his appearance. He said that he would never reach his mother and sister and that even if he did, how could a few bags of flour help? His mother and sister might even find themselves in danger. And so . . ." She paused, looking at me now.

"Yes?" I said, when she did not continue.

"And so, I made Henry Parish a promise."

I was filled with dread. What had she promised?

"I told him that if something happened to him, we would help his mother and sister. And that we would avenge him." I imagined that that part would not have been difficult for Bess to promise. Besides, I felt almost as much hatred for the redcoats now as she did.

But, as for helping the boy's family, why should I wish to? Why should I put myself in danger for them? And yet these thoughts disappeared almost as quickly as they had come — I was not the same as I had been only a few days ago. Much had happened since then. If helping Henry Parish's poor family was what I must do, where my honor led me, then that was the course I must take.

I could still hope that he would escape. I would still hope that. And pray, which I now did.

CHAPTER FORTY-SIX

Bess gasped. She pointed. At first I could not see what she had seen. The sun had burst through the clouds, and we were almost facing into it. I squinted. Did I see movement? Did I see someone? Someone running? Did I see horses following? Did I hear a bugle, ringing out time and time again? Did I see the waiting soldiers stir, take positions, load and prime their muskets?

Did I see the sun glinting on steel?

I know I saw some horses, splashes of red above them, moving at speed, back from the way they had come. But I did not see at first whom they pursued.

I know I heard Bess cry out again. I know I saw her put her hand to her mouth. But her eyes must have been sharper than mine, for still I did not see what she saw.

"Where?" The word breathed from my mouth, as though by whispering I could change anything. If by shouting I could have changed the course of events, I would have shouted. If, by running down the hill and waving my arms, I could have turned those horses, changed their riders' minds, I would have done so gladly.

I know Bess grabbed my arm, pointed my hand to the other side of the valley. I know she did not let go and that her fingers dug into my wrist like steel. And then, I know that I, too, gasped, and held my breath, frozen in horror.

"The fool!" whispered Bess. "I knew he would do something like this!"

It was, of course, Henry Parish. He had run from some woods, not from the hillside where I had seen Bess appear, nor the place to which she had directed the soldiers, but perhaps half a mile away to the southwest. But he was not running away. He was running down into the valley, into the open, into the arms of the waiting soldiers.

"Why does he not run away?" I asked, in disbelief. "Can he not see the redcoats? Can he not see them everywhere?" And, indeed, in every direction were those horrifying splashes of red. Tiny bloodstains. As though some wounded colossus had shaken his head across the land.

There were not many of them, perhaps fifty or sixty, but one would have been sufficient, if he ran straight toward him.

"Yes, he can see them," said Bess bitterly. "He is running to his death."

"We must do something!"

"No," she said quietly. "We cannot. This is Henry's choosing."

"How can we let him? How can we give up?"

"Because nothing we can do here will help Henry. We can only help him by continuing what he was trying to do. I should have known this was his intention. There was something possessing him when I left him, a fervor I had never seen. We were on the hill over there, and we saw you being pursued. Henry could not bear it. He said he could not live if you died for him. And so I left him there, telling him to run away as fast and as far as he could. Then I rode back, approaching from a different way, and told the red-coats I had seen a frightened boy. And they believed me. Henry could have escaped — but he would not. He had given up."

It was more than Bess could bear to watch. But I must watch. Still I hoped, against all hope, that something would happen. I prayed for some miracle that would save poor Henry Parish. I prayed to God — as strongly as ever I have — that, if there were any justice in the world, He should save Henry Parish. God can do such things, can He not? If He wishes to.

I watched.

I have been hare coursing, many times. Often the hare escapes. I have watched, just as I did then, from the brow of a hill, as the scene unfolds beneath me. But with hare coursing, the hare has as much chance as the hounds. One cannot say which will win.

Henry Parish had no chance. He gave himself no chance. They gave him none.

He ran, more and more slowly, down the hillside opposite us, his thin arms flailing, his head thrown back. As he came closer, I fancied I could see his wide eyes and his mouth open in what was almost a laugh. At the bottom of the hill, he came to a stream, which he crossed in one leap. On the other side, he looked around, deciding which way to go.

The soldiers moved closer. They went at walking pace, carelessly. Their prey had no weapons. They had nothing to fear. The horses now stopped galloping, soon slowing to a walk. I could distinguish the man with the mustache, the one who had so insulted Bess. If I could have taken him with my bare hands, I would have. But it would have been for nothing. I boiled with hatred for him and for men like him.

Bess was watching now. I could hear her breathing. On occasion, sounds came from her lips, little gasps of horror. It was unbearable. And yet, how much worse for Henry? Bess clutched my arm. I put my hand over hers. Her knuckles felt tight, sharp, cold.

The soldiers came slowly closer to Henry. He moved up the hillside a little and then turned to his right, no longer walking toward us. And then he stopped. He simply stood there as the soldiers moved closer. I counted them — not because it made any difference, but because I wished this recorded on my mind. I wished never to forget. I wished to recollect them in detail. I wished each to bear guilt. I did not know what went through their minds — I did not wish or need to know. I hope they felt guilt, but I suspect they did not. I suspect they had not learned to think. After all, I had not learned to think until such a little time before. So how should they?

Closer and closer they came. Now they were some fifty yards away from their target. Henry was soon within range. Slowly, so slowly, they moved around, so that now they fanned him in a semicircle.

Henry knelt on the ground.

"No!" cried Bess. I held her arm tightly. But she turned away. Finally, she could not watch. And so it was that I was the only one who witnessed Henry Parish's death. I was the only one who saw him clasp his hands to God. The only one who saw the officer raise his pistol and check the priming. I saw the man flick the hammer with his thumb, I saw him pause, I fancy I saw him smile, I saw him shoot. Bess winced as she heard it. Henry did not fall, though I saw his body jerk and a spray of red spread across his shoulder. I saw the officer lower his other hand, and as he did we heard the horrible crash of fifty muskets firing, and Henry's small body splintered and disappeared.

So it was that they killed Henry Parish. The redcoats shot him dead, down like a dog on the hillside.

And I would not forget. I would never forget.

CHAPTER FORTY-SEVEN

It is hard to talk about my feelings. It was hard even to understand fully myself what those feelings were. I know they were raw, and confused, as though something inside me had been shattered, as though the bullets that killed Henry had hit me, too. Yet Henry lay there dead, in pieces, destroyed, asleep forever. And I was still here, whole and yet not whole.

I cannot know what Bess felt, for neither of us spoke much as we made our slow way home. But I think she felt as I did: an unbearable mixture of horror, anger, sorrow, and guilt. Henry had died in order to save us and his family. He had been braver than I could ever be.

If I wished one thing, it was that I had said something kind to Henry Parish. When we had parted,

I had said nothing. If Henry's soul listened now, I wished him to know of my respect. That he was a better man than I. But that I would be true to our word: we would help his mother and sister. And we would avenge him.

I imagine that the same thoughts passed through Bess's mind.

Our journey was slow. Bess rode, slumped exhausted in the saddle, the reins slack against Merlin's neck. I, meanwhile, walked slowly, leading Sapphire as she limped.

The wind had blown the clouds away and the sun shone, weakly but with a welcome warmth. The snow was melting more rapidly now. Once, we stopped for water at a stream, letting both horses drink and splashing our own faces in silence. A small patch of crocuses quivered in a sheltered hollow. I saw Bess notice them, hesitate, but then say nothing.

On an impulse, meaning nothing except an act of kindness after what we had endured, I stooped to pick one, and handed it toward her. At first, she hesitated for so long that I thought she would not take it. Then she reached her hand toward me and took it, smiling her thanks. Somehow, I thought she knew all that I meant by it: an act of friendship and understanding. I did not know then that it meant something more to her.

We walked on, and at last we came once more to Bess's cottage. This time, although tired, we were cautious before entering. We checked for signs of intrusion, but there was nothing. The broken and scattered items were a painful reminder of the redcoats, and Bess's shoulders tightened when she saw them again. She began pushing things aside roughly, trying to hide them. Though she said nothing, I observed the way her lips narrowed, and she clenched her jaw.

I thought that such anger would not help her. Her home had been sullied, and I did not like to see her distress.

"I need hot water, Bess. For a poultice for Sapphire's leg."

She nodded and set about relighting the fire and carrying water to it. In the stable, I fed and watered the horses, spreading clean straw for them. Their warm breathing and their trust were a comfort to me. I rubbed them both down and found my own pleasure in such simple acts. When Bess brought the hot water, she sat and watched me as I mixed it with bran and placed the mash onto a fresh cloth, binding the warmth around and around Sapphire's swollen fetlock, tucking the edge in firmly. Sapphire would mend, but not quickly. I did not like to think how long it would be until she might be fit again.

"You have a good way with horses," said Bess.

She wore her proper attire now, I saw. I said nothing, but worked quietly, pleased with her remark. I found rugs hanging up and threw them over both animals, fastening the buckle beneath them. They would be warm enough and now needed time to recover after their efforts.

We left the stable, closing the door firmly, and walked across the yard to the cottage. Inside, the fire blazed. Together we began to pick things up, to put them in their rightful places, to sweep up broken pottery.

"We should eat," said Bess. I had no stomach for food, but she was right. With the door closed and the oil lamps burning even though it was daylight outside, we sat and ate and drank, talking little. We did not speak of Henry Parish. I know I could not, and I wager Bess felt the same. We kept our thoughts inside. There would be a time to talk of him later.

After a while, as the fire crackled and the cottage became thick with applewood smoke and the scent of ale and the steam from damp clothes, Bess curled her feet beneath her in the fireside chair, tucking her skirts around her. Staring into the fire, recent illness still etched beneath her eyes, she spoke. "Tell me your story. Who you are. How do you come to be here?"

My story seemed so far away, part of a different

world. At first I did not know how to begin. I could find no words.

"You were running away when I met you. Why?"

Only Bess would be so direct in her questions. But that was something I was beginning to respect. Why not be direct? Life is not long enough for winding journeys if there is a shorter way. Though there were some things I would keep back.

"I was running from home. Then I was running from the militia, because I had stolen a purse."

"And where is your home? What is your family name?"

"I wish to forget them both."

Her face seemed annoyed at this. "Well, no doubt they would mean little to me, ignorant girl that I am."

"I am sorry. They are of no interest. And it is perhaps better you do not know."

"You think the redcoats might beat your secrets from me?" Her eyes met mine, challenging.

"They are cruel. They might do worse than beat you. But besides that, I wish to forget my family name, and this is my home."

"If I choose for you to stay!"

"If I choose to stay," I retorted.

For a moment, petulance twisted her lips, but then her face changed. "I am sorry," she said. "I am tired and you are right: I do not need to know your name.

It would make no difference to know who you are. But tell me, please, why were you running from home? A rich boy, in a comfortable home, I dare say — why should he run away?"

"I seem to remember your father did not stay at home long either."

"That's true. And I told you my father's reasons. Are you going to tell me yours?" Her words seemed harsh, yet her face was soft as she said them.

"I ran away because my father and my brother insulted me. They called me a coward. Many times."

"So you ran away! To prove you were not a coward!" Her eyes were laughing.

I blushed. "I ran away because I would not be insulted further. What would you have had me do? Nothing?" I was silent for a while, thinking, before I spoke again. "No, you are right. It was a cowardly act. I should have stood firm. If I was there now, I would stand and be a man."

She seemed about to say something, but when she did not, I continued. "My father is a cruel man. My brother is like him. They take pleasure in the weakness of others. My sisters and my mother did not mind being seen as weak, but then they are women and —"

"Why should women not mind being seen as weak? Are all women weak? Have you seen what women in the country bear? Did not your father have strong servants, women who could lift three of you and fling you high into the air and doubtless catch you before you fell and grazed your knee?"

I saw what I had done. "Yes, but I did not mean that. I mean that highborn, gentle ladies have a weak disposition, whereas —"

"Whereas? Whereas those who find themselves of lower status, as I do . . . ?" She did not need to finish her sentence.

But I would not allow myself to be flustered, to be browbeaten by her. "I was telling my story. I was telling you what it is like in the life I was born into. I've left that life now, a life where ladies are delicate, and men are sometimes cruel but brave and chivalrous, and seem happy if they die for a king they have never met, in a land they do not care about. But there are good men, too. Not everyone of my birth is cruel and arrogant. You do not know everything. Besides," I continued, "you cannot rightly make a claim to virtue when you spend your nights in robbery."

Bess opened her mouth to retort, but was silent.

I continued. "I left my family because I could not bear to be treated as I was. I left in anger and fear and shame. Perhaps I should not have done, perhaps I should have stayed, but I am glad I left. Shall I tell you more? You asked to hear my story."

She nodded. So I continued. "I told you that my brother is cruel like my father. His name is Alexander, and he is five years older than I. I know not why he hates me. Perhaps he hates weakness, as does my father. And I know that I am — was — indeed weak compared with him. With my friends I could be strong, but with him and my father . . . somehow they took my strength. Alexander excels at everything. Being so much older, he could always beat me, whatever we did. And he took pleasure in it. So I was frightened of him, ever since I can remember. He once held my head under water until my senses left me. I think if it had not been for a servant finding me, I would have died. And I knew that he would do it again if he willed.

"Perhaps a year ago, he noticed that I could ride as well as he, and from then he hated me more. I think he never forgave me for beating him once when he challenged me to a race on horseback. I may have been weaker than him in other ways, but on a horse I was his match. That evening, someone fed my horse — a beautiful mare, Serenade — with deadly nightshade, and she died. I know that it was he. But I could do nothing.

"Then, two weeks before I left, I heard cries from the stable. No one else was nearby — it was Sunday, and the family was at church. I was in bed with an ague, and I heard the cries from my window. I went down to the stable, and I found my brother with a serving girl. He was supposed to be away at university, but he had come back for some reason that I do not recall. The girl was crying. There was blood on her mouth where he had hit her. Her dress was torn from her shoulder, the bodice ripped. And when I walked in, he had one hand around her throat and the other on her skirts.

"But the look on his face was worst of all. There was madness in him, I think. He let the girl go, and she ran away crying. My brother drew his sword and walked toward me. I thought he would kill me, so I turned and ran. I could not look at him."

"Did you tell anyone?" asked Bess.

"I did not know whom to tell," I replied. "I knew my father would not believe me, nor my mother. I tried to speak to the girl, but she avoided me. She was ashamed of what I had seen. But I knew it was not her fault, and I wanted her to know that. I even tried to speak to my brother. I told him that if he went near the girl again I would tell our father. He laughed. He told me I was too young to know about such things, that I would never be a man, that I was no better than our sisters, that he was not afraid of me, and that he would do exactly what he wished because he was the heir. And the worst thing was that he was right in every way."

I took a mouthful of ale before continuing. Bess was silent. There was nothing in my story to make me proud, to make her admire me. My brother was right. I was weak and a coward. I had done nothing to help that girl or to stand for what was right.

"A few days after this, my father called me into the library. My brother stood there, sneering at me as I entered."

I did not furnish Bess with the details but I can picture him now, standing with his back to the fire, one arm along the mantelpiece, his chest puffed out, one small foot resting on the fender. My brother had strangely small feet. He was, indeed, smaller than an average man — I was taller, despite being younger. I recollect my father not looking up as I entered. There was something in his voice that day as he bade me good morning. And in the way he played with a silver knife on the table. I had never liked his hands. White they were, and somewhat flattened at the tips, and soft. He was sitting in his usual chair. His pigtail was newly coiffed — I could detect the apple scent of pomade — and his sideburns were fluffy. His white stockings fitted, as usual, with never a wrinkle, the black buttons in a straight line down the side of his thick calves. My buttons would never remain straight, and how often he berated me for that!

I continued now. "I do not recall how the conversation began, and the details are unimportant. But what my father had to say made my heart beat hard and my mouth go dry. It concerned the serving girl. Rebecca was her name. My father said that it had come to his attention — and at this point it was impossible not to notice the smirk on my brother's face — that I had been making myself a nuisance to her. There had been complaints, he said. Other servants had been talking, though the girl herself denied it. 'I do not expect you to confess it,' said my father when I began to protest. 'You are a mere child and know nothing of such matters. But it has been suggested to me that it is time you began your career in my militia. I have arranged for you to take a commission. You shall be an officer. This will make a man of you, if anything ever will.' My heart sank. I had known this would happen one day. I tried to refuse, but the more I did so the more my father and brother sneered, and the more it sounded like cowardice. Perhaps it was: I confess that the idea of fighting, perhaps of dying, was horrible. I can say that now.

"But there was something else I did not like about his militia. I did not like the way he ruled it. I did not like the way he cared nothing for anyone who did not love it as he did. I think now that his militia was more important to him than life itself, and that anyone who got in its way was as nothing. I thought my refusal to join looked simply like cowardice — I now think that he took it as an insult. And anyone who insulted his militia deserved nothing better than death. I cannot prove that, but it is my belief."

I would not tell Bess everything they said to me. I would not tell her how my father said that I was no son of his if I would not stand and fight for my King, and how he told me that my mother often wept from disappointment at my cowardice. That was when he told me it would have been better if I had been born a girl. At least he had one son, he said, to carry on his line and produce strong heirs.

I did not know what to say. Inside I felt anger, but I would not show it. It would not have been respectful, nor would it have improved my lot. And I was afraid. For these reasons, I must keep my fury in. I stood and took their sneers in silence. Without doubt, they took that for cowardice, too.

Afterward, my brother followed me out of the room as I bowed obediently to my father. Servants were outside, so we said nothing, but once we were out of sight, he pulled me into a doorway and grinned up at me. "Do you wish me to help you?" he asked. I knew not what he meant, so I said nothing. "Do you?" he repeated in his nasty voice, squeezed from the back of his throat. When I still said nothing, he continued. "I could speak for you, should I choose to.

Perhaps I might tell my father that it would be better to wait until you are older, stronger. I could do that for you." I did not understand, though I knew there was a trick. A fleck of spittle sat on his bottom lip, and he did not wipe it away. His face was so close to mine that I could see the minute veins in the whites of his pale eyes, see each ginger hair in his mustache, each pale freckle on his nose, a patch of red under one eye; I could smell his pomade, too, almost disguising his nasty, warm breath.

I did not tell Bess those details, only what happened next.

"Afterward, my brother challenged me to fight him with swords," I said. "He said that if I won he would put in a good word for me with my father and make him delay my commission in the militia. But I knew my brother too well. Had he not killed my first horse? Had he not nearly killed me once before? I was skilled with a sword, but not as strong as he; I knew he would try to kill me in the fight, and that, if by some chance he did not, he would not keep his promise. And besides, nothing I did would change my father's contempt for me. The thought of my mother's disappointed face and my sisters' silly laughter was too much. I decided to leave, to run away. It is something I had thought of before, dreamed of sometimes, but this time I knew I would do it. A few days later, I did so. And that is how I came to be here. That is my story."

"I do not know if you were a coward before. But you are not now. You were right to leave."

I looked at her, startled. "I feel like a coward. I could not have done what . . . what Henry did."

Her face clouded over. "Who knows what we might do when faced with such a choice, but I know that neither of us was a coward today."

I considered this. And I believe she was right. I had not been a coward. Perhaps nothing is as bad as the contemplating of it. And now, even with the shocking death of Henry Parish, the sorrow and the injustice, perhaps I could look forward. Perhaps we could bear what had happened. Perhaps that was bravery.

One other thing I knew: if my father could say that he wished I was not his son, then he had his wish. I was no longer his son.

CHAPTER FORTY-EIGHT

The following morning, the sky was clean, swept by a fresh southerly breeze, warmed by a strengthening sun. The snow had all but disappeared, except for shaded patches beneath trees and in hollows where the sun could not reach. Bess and I busied ourselves with tasks around the cottage and with the horses. Sapphire's foot showed no improvement, but I replaced her poultice with a fresh one and let her rest.

We did not speak of Henry Parish, though occasionally I saw Bess stop what she was doing, her eyes drifting away, and I wondered if her thoughts rested with what had happened the day before.

But perhaps not, because I soon found that there was something else on her mind.

I came in from the yard carrying two buckets of water. I had thought to heat some so that Bess could bathe, if she wished to. And if she did not, then I did. But when I came in, her back was turned to me and before I could speak I saw that she held in her hands the crocus I had given her the day before. It had wilted, and she was touching it gently with her finger.

I was confused, thinking at first that she would not wish me to see her. What did she think as she touched the flower so? Did she understand more by it than I had meant? I felt myself blush. She had not heard me come in. Very quietly I crept backward toward the door. But she heard me and turned around.

"It requires water," I said, for anything to say.

"It is my favorite flower," she said. "The crocus. You know not what it means to me."

Now I blushed further. "I did not mean . . . I mean . . ." But she cut short my flustered words with her smile.

"No," she said. "I do not mean that. I mean that you did not know that tomorrow is the anniversary of my parents' death, and then I pick crocuses. I go to a place I know, near here, a place that my father loved, where they grow above a waterfall. I pick them and drop them down the waterfall and watch them disappear. Will you come with me?"

I was learning to know and respect her directness further. She did not tangle her words with webs of deceit and confusion. So, if she said she did not mean any attachment because I had given her a flower, then she did not mean it. And for that I was relieved.

"I would be honored," I said. "If you are certain."

"I am certain. Besides, being a woman, I am weak, and may need your assistance. Unless, of course, since I am of lower birth, I may be less than delicate?"

I smiled at her. We understood each other now.

Life at that moment seemed as good to me as I can ever recall it. We occupied the remains of the day making use of the clear weather, repairing parts of the thatched roof, cutting wood for the fire, caring for the injury to Sapphire's fetlock, and cleaning out the stable. The warmth from the sun seeped into the earth and began to dry up the damp chill of winter. New light bathed the hillsides.

Bess walked to a nearby farm for eggs and milk, and while she was gone I stopped on more than one occasion to breathe in the sweet air and to think quietly of poor Henry Parish. I told myself that he was better in Heaven than down here, where he would be forever on the run. He had faced terror and death and faced it bravely. And now he was at peace.

He did not have to endure anything again. We, on

the other hand, must surely have many dangers ahead, and we could know nothing of what they might be.

Did I envy Henry Parish? No, I did not. It seems we are born to cling to life until it is dragged from us, and I would cling to mine. Did not one of our poets say, "Hope springs eternal in the human breast"? I think he did, though I do not recall who. And so, I believe hope lives in us until it can live no more.

CHAPTER FORTY-NINE

Even in her skirts, Bess was quick and strong. Not once did she slip on the rocks and pebbles that were strewn across the path. We were clambering our way up the hillside the following day and there was a light in her face, a smile at the world, despite the purpose of our journey.

With sunlight spearing the trees in front of us, with gulls wheeling and crying overhead, with new grass underfoot, I followed Bess toward the summit. There was a hot pounding in my head, and I could speak only with effort. But it was good to run without someone running after me. It was good not to have to look behind me, to wonder where soldiers were. To feel free.

I stopped, turned, and looked down the hillside, resting my hands on my knees as I gasped for breath.

"Hurry!" shouted Bess above me.

"No, wait!" I replied. "Look!" and I pointed toward the east, almost at the sun. In the distance, like a line of silver thread, was the sea, glinting. Before it, there stretched the gentle slopes of newly enclosed land, in places somewhat like a patchwork, in others more natural. When I looked more closely, I could spy houses, scattered, a shepherd's hut, the dark shadows of woods and forests. On a twisting road I could see tiny figures of people walking, and a carriage with horses. How small they looked! How unimportant!

"What is it?" asked Bess impatiently.

"Everything," I said. "Everything. All this. We are not important, are we? All this will be here when we are long gone."

"You are wrong," said Bess. "That is why we're important. *Because* we're not on this earth very long. The place is not important. People are important. What we do is important. Nothing else matters."

But she stood and looked with me all the same. And I thought about what she'd said. It sounded new and bold and strange. Was she right? All my life I had been taught that we are unimportant — although some are more unimportant than others — and that God will judge.

But on what will God judge us if we do nothing important?

Eventually, out of breath, hot-faced, we came to the top of the hill, and Bess hurried toward the place she was looking for, gathering up her skirts as she deftly made her way along an almost invisible path. "Here!" she called, and I followed her. I could hear the noise of the waterfall now, could see its silver ribbon falling farther down the hillside, but it was only when we scrambled over one final rock that I saw it fully.

Below me, as if from the cliff face itself, the water dropped from a hidden spring, crashing onto the rocks as it fell before twisting down the hillside. I could feel a fine spray across my face, lifted by the sifting wind. A seagull flew up from a ledge, squawking in anger, and wheeling and circling over the tumbling water.

Bess pulled my arm. She pointed over to our left, and I followed her.

And there, nestled in a hollow, facing south where the sun would strike first, protected from the wind on three sides, was a patch of royal-purple and gold crocuses.

Now Bess became quiet. I kept my distance, sitting on a rock, watching her, feeling the breeze in my hair, the warmth of the sun on my face, allowing the sound of the waterfall to crash over me. She picked a large handful of the flowers, one by one, slowly, without speaking. Then she walked to the top of the waterfall, and I watched her stand there. She paused for a few moments, fingering her father's locket on the chain around her neck, before she threw the flowers into the torrent.

Her hair, black and twisting, blew in the wind, like tumbling water itself. I could see her face from the side. She did not look sad. She looked alive. And I thought how fortunate she was to have someone to whom to bid farewell, someone to join one day.

Bess walked to me, her eyes shining, watering in the sunshine or the wind. "We shall remember Henry, too," she said. And she bent to pick more flowers. I did likewise. And together we walked to the edge of the waterfall and together we dropped crocuses into the torrent for Henry Parish, to show him that we had not forgotten and that we would never forget. For as long as there were crocuses and for as long as we had breath in our bodies, we would not forget him and why he died.

As we made our way back to the cottage, talking of this and that, we saw in the distance a long line of soldiers taking a road along the valley. Their red coats marked them for who they were. We stopped and watched them ride.

"How I hate them," said Bess quietly but with bitter venom in her voice.

I kept my silence. I hated them too, perhaps as much as she did. But it was what *we* did that was important, was it not, not what they did or even what they did to us?

Bess and I were better than them, I knew that. And we would do the right thing, whatever that might cost.

That evening, Bess took a stringed instrument from a heavy chest. A cittern, I knew — and all too well, since I had had to endure the unnatural playing of one of my sisters on many an occasion.

Bess held the cittern easily against her body and began to draw her fingers softly across the strings, turning the pegs at the end until it made the sounds she wanted. I could not tell which notes were the right ones — I had no skill in music making. Without strangeness, though smiling to me in acknowledgment that what she did was for me to hear, she began to sing. The words were not familiar to me, but then I had not heard ballads sung before. And as she sang, I saw that there was another reason I could not know the words — this ballad told of Henry Parish, and these were Bess's own words. As she sang, sometimes repeating or changing fragments so that they might better fit the rhythm, I marveled at this skill: to put a man's life and death into words and to reach a listener's heart. That is an art indeed.

Her voice was light and strong, soft at the edges, a voice of gentle warmth. It was like nothing I had heard, but then I suppose I had only heard my sisters' thin and wavery voices. Perhaps I had never before heard anyone sing from the heart. But soon I found myself thinking not of Bess or her voice, but only of Henry Parish. How surprised he would have been to be immortalized like this. And, perhaps, how proud.

I recall her words:

'Tis of a fearless soldier-boy
A story I will tell
His name was Henry Parish-o
In England did he dwell.

'Twas for the King he stood so bold
'Twas for the King he dressed in red
'Twas for honor he lived so true
'Tis for honor he lies cold dead.

Ten years and four had Henry breathed,
A mother's only boy.
Hear, hear ye now his sorry tale
And judge ye then her joy!

'Twas for the King he stood so bold
'Twas for the King he dressed in red

'Twas for honor he lived so true
'Tis for honor he lies cold dead.

As Henry fought for King and truth,
His mother lay near death,
His sister, too, for lack of flour,
How close her dying breath!

'Twas for the King he stood so bold
'Twas for the King he dressed in red
'Twas for honor he lived so true
'Tis for honor he lies cold dead.

He could not see his sister die
So Henry took his share,
But the flour that our poor must eat
Men need to white their hair.

'Twas for the King he stood so bold
'Twas for the King he dressed in red
'Twas for honor he lived so true
'Tis for honor he lies cold dead.

How raged the soldiers' fury then!
How cruel their steely eyes!
How cold their hearts, how true their aim
How fast poor Henry flies!

'Twas for the King he stood so bold
'Twas for the King he dressed in red
'Twas for honor he lived so true
'Tis for honor he lies cold dead.

And so upon the wintry moors,
The redcoats closed around.
As Henry stood there, brave and true,
They felled him to the ground.

'Twas for the King he stood so bold
'Twas for the King he dressed in red
'Twas for honor he lived so true
'Tis for honor he lies cold dead.

Where spilled his blood there is no sign,
No mark of his last breath,
But in our hearts he lives on still:
Remember ye his death.

It was through hearing the *Ballad of Henry Parish* that
I did, at last, begin to remember him well. I understood now his life and his death.

CHAPTER FIFTY

A little over a week later found us in Scarborough once more. This time the horses were not with us: Sapphire's injury was healing but she was not fit to ride many miles, and Merlin, too, needed to rest. So Bess decided we should walk to the road and hope for a horse and cart to pass and take us to the town. Why we must go to Scarborough I did not know — it seemed too far and my memory of what had happened there last time was all too fresh. But Bess had something on her mind and when Bess had something on her mind there was little I could do about it, as I was coming to learn.

She had said we would find a cart to take us, and this is indeed what happened. And so, shaken, sickened, and cold, we soon found ourselves breathing in the sea air once more. We climbed down gratefully, thanking the carter, and I followed Bess toward the tavern where One-Legged Jack lived. This time, I was permitted to follow Bess inside.

I was assailed by noise and heat and the roar and shouting of men, the smell of ale and gin; the air was thick with fire smoke and roasting meat and tobacco. Several dogs lay beside their masters, one of them gnawing on a hollow bone. But the men seemed scarcely to notice us. I felt my arm being pulled — it was Bess. I had not heard her calling to me. She guided me through the crush of bodies and through a doorway, into another room. She dragged the door closed behind us.

Here, one man only sat, by the fire, smoking a thick cigar, one leg before him, the other leg no more than a stump sticking straight out. Seeing Bess, he lowered his tankard with a crash that splashed dark beer onto the table. Placing his cigar on a plate, he held out his arms toward her, and she went to him and let him kiss her hand. While they greeted each other I had time to examine this man, One-Legged Jack, as I assumed him to be.

I could not decipher his position in society. His face was coarsened by dark stubble, yet the line of his jaw and his cheeks were strong. His jacket, though long and well cut, was tired, its claret color now dull and somewhat dusty, yet a stiff lace collar, as white as I had ever seen, garnished his throat. Two large gold rings sat upon his fingers, and the embroidery on his waistcoat was ornate, but his hair was undressed, hanging almost to his shoulders, not quite straight, neither bewigged nor curled nor even tied in a pigtail. His voice, however, was strong and mellow and spoke of education and good birth.

"And whom do we have here? This must surely be the lad of whom you spoke?" He gazed directly at me, his green eyes bright and inquiring. He looked me up and down, slowly.

"Yes, this is Will," said Bess. "You can trust him. He has proved himself true."

"You did not tell me that fortune had smiled when she made his face. That his eyes were dark and steady, his nose and jaw strong and straight. Is it possible that this had escaped your notice? Are you not your father's daughter? He had an eye for beauty."

I blushed under such comments and know not what showed on Bess's face.

"It matters only that he can be trusted," she said with perhaps a certain sharpness.

One-Legged Jack still looked at me, and I stared straight back, though trying not to look insolent. "I am pleased to make your acquaintance," I said, holding out my hand, which he took. It was a firm grip, which lingered while he looked into my eyes before letting my hand go.

"Who is your father? Bess told me that you are wellborn, which I can see for myself, and she told me that you are a runaway. Where are you from?"

"He will not say," Bess answered for me.

"He shall say now," said One-Legged Jack.

"I am from near Hexham. Beyond Durham," I added unnecessarily, somewhat flustered by his questions.

"Yes, I am aware of the whereabouts of Hexham. But you did not answer my other question. Who is your father?"

I paused, just slightly, before answering. I did not wish to tell them. Had I not left that life behind? And yet, I knew that I must say.

I took a deep breath.

CHAPTER FIFTY-ONE

"My father is George de Lacey."

A gasp came from Bess. One-Legged Jack became very still all of a sudden, his eyes narrowing. He looked at Bess. "You should have asked."

"I did ask. He would not tell me. I did not think . . . I could not have thought . . ."

"You should have thought. Remember what your father taught you: knowledge is all."

"What do you know of my father?" I asked, confused, startled by their manner on hearing his name.

"He is a High Sheriff, is he not?" When I nodded, he continued. "But your father is not all he seems. He is also the Member for Parliament, of course. A popular man, then, you would attest?"

"I don't know. I don't know of such things." I could not imagine my father being popular. Nor could I imagine him caring for such things as popularity — although of course, he would wish for the necessary votes. I had never thought on it. I simply knew my father was the Member for Parliament and that the absences this caused were the happier parts of my life.

"He is indeed a popular man. More popular than a man of his corruption should be." The man was looking at me, judging my reaction. I did not rightly know how to react. I did not understand what I was hearing. He continued. "Do you know what we mean by a pocket borough?" I shook my head. "It is where the constituency is in the pocket of the Member for Parliament. To be precise, he buys the votes, generously giving money to those who vote for him. As for those who choose to vote for another, he might throw them off their land. His land — because it is, of course, all his land."

Why did I feel such shame? Why did I care so when I heard what my father had done? Had I not already decided I was no son of his? You might think I should be pleased to find good reason to despise him, but I can assure you it gave me no pleasure at all. I was of his blood and his shame was my shame.

Bess was looking down at her hands. She knew all this already — but she had not known that this man was my father. What did she think of me now?

One-Legged Jack was still speaking. "But there is more. There are people whom I know. People who will tell me things. And then I tell the people I trust, people who will carry on the work that I can no longer do." He gestured toward his leg before continuing. "Seeking out corruption and fighting it in the only way we know. We have heard tell of many men, wealthy men and men of the middling sort, lawyers, magistrates, and the like"— his mouth twisted in distaste as he said this —"who use their positions to rob from the poor, storing up ill-gotten rewards for themselves. We merely work to redress that balance. And your father, the honorable George de Lacey, High Sheriff, is only one of many men who have come to our attention in recent months. And my people have told me more about him. Do you wish to know what we have discovered?"

"Yes," I replied. "I do."

One-Legged Jack looked at me for a long moment, and I made my shoulders as strong and tall as I could, set my jaw as firmly as was possible, waiting for whatever I might be told.

"You will perhaps not know, in a position of such privilege, of the taxes that ordinary people must pay? You will not know, I venture, that the high prices of soap, of wool, of spirits, of sugar, even of flour, and many other necessities, are caused not by scarcity of those goods but by the taxes set on them by our government. The government wants our money, and they prefer to take it not from the wealthy but from the poor."

"Is this my father's fault?"

"No, but those who collect the taxes are in his pay. We have heard rumors, stronger now than ever, that he keeps part of the taxes they collect, to fund his militia and to buy his votes. And we have heard more." Now he turned to Bess. "I told you of our suspicions when last we met — now I know them to be true. I have sworn evidence from four men. He has been giving pardons to convicted felons — for a high price, of course. And once they are freed, he has them arrested again on another charge in another county. His net is wide, his accomplices as corrupt as he."

Jack and Bess looked at me. Anger and shame struggled inside my heart.

I had not known! Not even a small suspicion of his greed and dishonor had I had. Should I not have known? Should I not have questioned how he could afford to fund his militia? But I did not know or think of such things. They had not been my concern. I had thought only of my own feelings.

Strangely, however, among all this was a new shiver of pleasure, of rightness. This was my father;

this was the man I hated. With even better reason than I had thought. And if I had felt any trace of guilt at my lack of respect for him, I felt no guilt now. Though I did indeed feel shame for my blood, my family, my inheritance. How could I prove myself better than them?

"We must act!" And once I spoke, my anger could not be held back. "We must act to stop him. We must tell someone. Surely such evil cannot go unpunished. Tell me what to do, and I will do it!"

"Be patient," said Jack. "This will require careful planning. And cool heads. I had thought to wait until a time closer to the next election, but the knowledge that you are de Lacey's son changes matters, changes them considerably. I believe I shall lay aside my other plans and see this one to its conclusion first. You may have knowledge that will help us." He stroked his chin, looking past me, into nothingness.

"Ask anything," I said. "I will do anything."

Bess had kept her silence for some time, but now she spoke. "Will must surely know his father's movements, when he goes to the assizes, when he may be carrying money, his traveling companions. With such information, we could hold up his carriage. Think of that — not only do we take back money that is not rightfully this man's, but his son plays a part in it! That would be justice indeed!" Her face shone.

Any lingering trace of her earlier illness had now disappeared, and she seemed full of fire.

"I had been thinking so myself. How good is the boy with pistols? How skilled is he on a horse? How do you know you can rely on him in danger?"

Bess answered at once. "There's no one better on a horse, and he has proved himself strong in danger." She looked at me.

Jack spoke to me now. "And pistols, lad? Can you handle weapons?"

"Yes, sir, I can. I know how to use pistols, although I have never . . . I have never had cause to use one in anger. And I am schooled with a rapier, of course."

"Have you ever killed anyone?"

"No, sir," I replied, somewhat sickened by this sudden question.

"Do you hope to?"

"No, sir, I do not hope to."

"Good," he replied. "I hope you will not need to. It is enough that you know how to. I would not like a hothead as Bess's accomplice."

One-Legged Jack called for ale and meat, and soon there arrived a steaming calf's-head pie and liver sauce, with hot pickled cabbage making a vibrant red splash on the enormous wooden platter. My mouth watered as I smelled its flavor, and I recalled that this was the first hot meat I had eaten since leaving home.

It was, I think, the food I have most enjoyed in my whole life.

As we ate together, we talked more of our plans. It was a strange feeling, very strange, to be talking so seriously of a crime we would commit, and yet talking of it as though it was the right action to take.

Was it right? Certainly, what my father was doing, if Jack were to be believed, was wrong, very wrong. But did that mean we were right to act wrongly against him? Can a wrong deed ever be right? Shall we be judged on what we do or on what is in our hearts? And what if someone were hurt or even killed in our action? Did we have the right to make such a judgment?

A part of my mind did not think we were right. And yet I was caught up in it and willingly, too, I confess. It was easy to tell myself that what we did was just, to repeat it over and over in my head, to listen to Bess and One-Legged Jack, to go with my heart, and to hear what I wanted to hear — but it was less easy to believe it fully. It was less easy to banish the small, dark doubts that crept up on me every time I stopped to think.

And so I tried not to think too hard.

CHAPTER FIFTY-TWO

As we left that place, Bess and I were in two very different conditions. She was burning with enthusiasm and certainty, talking more than I had ever heard her. She did not stop to see whether I shared her fervor.

I, on the other hand, felt a heavy burden upon my shoulders. This time, it was not a burden of fear, but of doubt and confusion. I had known what I thought of my father before — I feared and disliked him. It had been very simple, though perhaps it had not felt so at the time. But now, it was not so simple. For now, mixed in with fear and dislike, I felt also shame. It was no longer a matter of what he thought of me. It was a matter of what he was.

And, therefore, what I was.

One-Legged Jack's final words to me were ringing

in my ears. He had clasped my hand and looked deep into my eyes. "Be true, Will. Be true to yourself. And take care of my friend's daughter. Take care of Bess." Then Bess had said something, that she did not need to be protected. And Jack had smiled sadly at her and touched her cheek as he said, in a voice quieter than usual, "A friend is a good thing to have, Bess. Your father was a friend to me. Why, I even forgave him for being of Scottish birth! He cared for me and never was I ashamed of his help. You have need of a good friend, too. Look after each other."

Now, Bess was walking fast toward the New Brough Barr, the entrance to the town of Scarborough. It was a market day, and many folk walked and rode in the streets. In the spring sunshine, faces shone and men and women stopped to gossip with acquaintances, not hurrying hunched in the cold but raising their faces to the new season.

Bess stopped for me to catch up. By her face, I think she saw that my spirits were low.

"Let us have some entertainment, Will. I have an idea which will make you think on good things. There were two reasons I came here today — only one was to speak with Jack. The other was . . . well, you shall see. Follow me!" And she took my arm, smiling so that I could hardly remain looking sad.

Where were we going? What was Bess's plan?

CHAPTER FIFTY-THREE

I knew the streets by now. And I kept my hands in my coat pockets in case of quick-fingered thieves.

My attire marked me as neither wealthy nor poor: I wore a working coat belonging to Bess's father, my own brown breeches, clean stockings, and buckled shoes; my hair was tied in a simple pigtail, topped with a soft, flattened hat. Bess was wearing her skirts again. She had a plain shawl of dark red around her shoulders and pattens to keep her feet above the mud. And mud there was on those streets, slippery, stinking pools of it. The dung of horses and cattle and dogs, together with rotten potato peelings and thawing carcases of dead cats, mixed with human waste thrown from high windows, filled the gutters, sometimes spilling up onto the pavements.

Sunlight, darting through the gaps between buildings, glittered in our eyes as we hurried along. It was not easy to watch where I placed my feet or to avoid knocking into persons traveling in the opposite direction. Every now and then, shouts from a postilion would alert the crowds to an oncoming carriage, and passersby would leap aside with shouts of anger as stinking mud splashed up from the wheels.

I began to long to be back on the empty moors, which seemed like home to me now. In the town humans, animals, seagulls, carriages all jostled together, vying for space. On the moors, there was air to breathe and space between everything. Here, the ugly mark of humankind was etched everywhere. On the moors, people passed unnoticed, leaving no shadow, like the ghosts and spirits that shared the air. I could not imagine ghosts in the town, in these busy streets.

We were approaching the place where the market was. The stalls were set out much as before, some on the pavements, others in the street. Bess was watching in both directions, looking from one side of the street to another, until suddenly she stopped, pulled me into a doorway and pointed. I saw at once what she was pointing at.

The gap-toothed crone. I had forgotten her! In all the fear and horror of the last few days, I had forgotten the old hag. How unimportant she seemed now! Yet I remembered how I had vowed to repay her for her treachery. She had deserved it, but perhaps this mattered less now. It seemed somehow unimportant. And yet . . . and yet, how I did hate her.

"Stay here!" said Bess. "Keep a close watch on her." And before I had had a chance to ask her what she intended, she had gone. I saw her black hair, neatly dressed beneath her bonnet, disappear around a corner, and then I was alone in the crowds.

I shrank back into the doorway and watched the old woman. I watched her grin as each buyer approached, and I watched her weak eyes darting here and there, watched her gnarled hand put coins in her bag, watched her spit rheumy liquid onto the ground, watched her hook a finger into her ear and gouge out what was there.

Nowhere did I see Bess. How long was I to wait here observing the old crone?

I let my thoughts wander. I no longer worried about being recognized. Already, I felt invisible in this busy, unseeing place. My old home, my old life, my family — all seemed entirely strange to me now.

I cannot say for certain what feelings I harbored for my family at this time. Did I feel sadness when I thought of them? Did I regret that I might not see them again? I cannot say clearly. I did not believe they thought with sadness of my absence, and I did not like to think on this. So, I put such matters from my thoughts.

One thing I do know: whenever I thought of that place, I could not help but think of Blackfoot, my horse, and wish he were with me. And my spaniel puppy. I believed that the servants would look after them well. I hoped that Saul, the stable boy, would be entrusted with Blackfoot. I hoped that my sisters were not spoiling my puppy. He would need to be trained properly. For certain, I could not trust my sisters to do that. I could only hope that the good people on my father's estate would watch over them. And there were good people, I knew.

I hoped my brother would play no part at all in the care of either my dog or my horse. My skin went cold at the thought, as I remembered how he had poisoned my first horse, Serenade. And how he kicked his own hunting dog when it did not understand his commands, or when he simply wished for something to kick. . . .

Had I put my animals in danger by running away?

There was Bess! Her shawl was wrapped around her head now, and she walked purposefully toward the old woman's barrow. The distance was too great for me to hear what was said, but I could see the crone's face. I saw her wildly wandering eyes light up at the prospect of another purchaser. I saw Bess handle some jars and pots. My heart jumped when I saw her toss a pot into the air and catch it before it reached the ground. I saw the old woman's eyes narrow in distrust and, perhaps, anger. She watched Bess, who was now rummaging in her deep pockets. I saw the woman frown, open her mouth to say something, and then look down at what Bess was holding out to her. I saw confusion pass across her face, as she took it.

What was Bess doing? I could not see the object in the crone's hand. But I could see her confusion turn to fear. I could see her step back, try to speak, try to return the object to Bess. But Bess was gone, hurrying away, through the crowds, leaving the black-mouthed crone shaking, looking around from side to side, her eyes wide. Another purchaser came to inspect her wares but rushed away, disturbed no doubt by her ghoulish look, her staring eye and open mouth.

Soon Bess was back at my side, her face bright with excitement. "Did you see?" she asked.

"Yes, but what did you do? Why is she so afraid?"

"I have put a curse on her. I went to a woman I know, a friend of Aggie's, who knows about such things. I bought a cursing stone, and I have given it to her. But I have not finished. There is something that you must do. I told her that the curse will only come to pass when she sees someone whom she has wronged. When she sees you, she will know that the curse is working. All you need to do is approach her and let her see your face. She will remember you. And then we shall watch her suffer!"

"Do you believe this? Do you believe in such curses? The men of the church say we should trust in God, not in witches."

"I do trust in God. I trust in many things. When I gave the money to Aggie's friend, when I made the curse, I prayed to God as well. God and witchcraft can both help us, can they not? And we need do nothing. If God does not wish to see the old woman punished, then doubtless He will ensure that the curse fails. Who knows why these things happen, but I know that they do. Now go and let the woman see you."

I hesitated. Bess urged me on. "You wanted her to suffer, did you not? You deserve this much, after what she did to you. You could have died, and she would have cared nothing. All that will happen to her is some illness or pain or misfortune. Go on!"

I walked toward the crone, my palms sweating. There were no soldiers or any persons of that sort to be seen. There was nothing to concern me.

Should I do this? I could not be sure.

And yet, I hated her! As I came nearer, I recalled her evil look when she had called the soldiers. And then I recalled the scream of the falling horse and the look in its eyes before I shot it dead. That horse would not have died, had it not been for her treachery.

So, full of anger, I walked toward that gap-toothed hag, stood in front of her and watched as she looked up. And, with a thrill of true pleasure, I saw the horror spread across her face as she recognized me. Her hands flew to her mouth, and she let out a moan, collapsing onto her stool.

"Do you recall me?" I asked. She nodded, mutely. "I, too, recall you," I said, and turned away from her, slipping among the crowds.

As I ran back to Bess and as we made our way from that place, we heard a crash and a commotion from the direction of the old woman's barrow. Briefly, we stopped to watch. We could not see clearly, but it seemed as though she had collapsed across her wares, scattering broken jars everywhere. We heard her high-pitched keening and the shouts of people as they tried to help her.

We disappeared from there as quickly as we could. And, I confess, I felt joy as I thought of the justice of it. I do not know whether it was the curse, or her fear, and I do not know what happened to her next. But I care only that she deserved to feel that horror, to believe that she had been cursed.

It was justice. And I took great pleasure in it.

My pleasure did not last long.

CHAPTER FIFTY-FOUR

We heard the shouting of the news crier, sensed the movement of people toward him. What had happened? At first, I felt only slight interest, the interest of the crowd as we allowed ourselves to be swept along. By the time we reached him, people were passing snippets of the story to each other.

There had been rioting. Civil unrest. In Hexham. The militia and the people were rioting against the authorities.

Even then, I could not know the whole truth. Why was everyone so angry? Did they not like riots? I had heard that the masses like to riot.

People had died. Many people. Some said twenty. Others said dozens. Shot by the militia from neighboring Yorkshire, because the militia of Northumberland would not shoot their own people. But the orders had been given by the authorities in Hexham. To shoot the rioting people and militiamen of Hexham.

And why had they rioted? Because they objected to the unfairness of the ballot that took men away from their families and enrolled them in the militia. My father's militia.

Only then did I begin to understand.

But there was worse.

The authorities had hanged a man for his part in the riot. An old man, seventy-four years old, they said. They had hung him without trial. They had not waited long — he was hanged, in public, the morning after the riots. They would not listen to the truth: that the old man had not even been in Hexham that day. He was innocent. They had hanged him and left his body on the gibbet as an example to others.

An innocent old man, hanged at dawn, without a proper trial.

And the man who was responsible for this atrocity?

The High Sheriff.

My father.

Chapter Fifty-five

Then, indeed, did ice truly grip my heart. Bess took hold of my arm and guided me, sensing my distress. She pulled me away from the crowds and hurried me back toward the New Brough Barr, till we were outside the town walls.

"Say nothing," she urged. "We will talk when we are alone. Say nothing now." And she led me away.

I willingly followed. I wanted more than anything to be far from this place, away from these people who would have strung me by my neck from a tree had they known who I was. Whose son I was.

Gulls screamed overhead as we hurried along the road, and the smell of salt and sea freshened the air as we left the sickening animal smell of the town behind. I found myself hurrying toward the dark moors as though they would give me sanctuary. I think I did not breathe properly until we were away from the sounds and smells of Scarborough town and within sight of the familiar hills. I wanted to cleanse my mouth of spittle, to rid myself of its poison.

Yet the poison was not in my mouth. The poison was throughout my body. My father's blood beat in my heart. How would I ever forget that? How could I rid myself of him entirely? Or would I forever carry the burden of what he was and what I was?

We soon found a carter who was willing to let us be carried in his cart for the greater part of the journey. Bess and I sat in near silence as we rocked and swayed our way into the hills, and my thoughts became slowly numb as we rattled along the rough tracks. At last, we came to the place where we must get down and walk alone for the last mile up into the hills.

A light, misty rain began to fall and cold seeped into my skin. I wrapped myself tightly in my jacket and shivered.

It was nearly dark when we came to Bess's cottage once more. Wearily, we walked up the last part of the track. A sharp evening wind rustled the trees and shifted the loose straw in the yard. The horses whinnied in welcome as we looked to their needs. We knew we must tend to them before we thought about ourselves. And, indeed, it was a comfort to do so.

By now, I knew what needed to be done in the cottage, and I set about lighting the fire and closing the shutters against the night, as Bess lit oil lamps and began to fetch vegetables from her stores to make a warming soup. She brought carrots and potatoes from an outbuilding — this, she had told me, was where they had lain bedded in sand to keep them from spoiling over the winter — and some cabbage from a jar of vinegar. I watched her chop them deftly, add a scrag of veal to the pan of water, throw in some dusty herbs from where they were hanging to dry, add a scoop of salt from the box beside the fire, and begin to stir the mixture in the large, battered pot above the flames.

I held out my hand, wishing to help her, and she passed me the wooden spoon. As I stirred, and breathed in the steam from that simple food, I began to feel warm again. I smiled at Bess, out of friendship, not because inside myself I felt like smiling. It was a smile to thank her for her understanding and her silence and for not condemning me for who I was.

I think even Bess did not know what to say now. Bess, whom I knew for her outspokenness, her direct questions, her piercing truth, was silenced, struck dumb by my father's actions. And so I spoke for her.

"That was the man who once was my father," I said. "Can you understand my shame? That my own father could care so little for the life of a person that he would sentence an old man to death, without even a thought? I am ashamed to be his son."

"You should not be ashamed. Only your father should feel shame."

I thought about this. Bess had struck the truth in one simple statement. I could do nothing at all about how my father was, just as I could do nothing about how my brother was. Yet why did I feel the shame deep within me, like a cold fall of snow?

I knew what I must do. I must turn my shame to anger. Only by acting bravely and honorably could I bring justice for that old man, and for the other men and women who had died in the riot. Only anger was the proper response.

And anger was not difficult to summon. Anger was as easy to stir as the steaming soup in front of me. As the wind beat against the shutters of our cottage and the door rattled, as the water came to the boil on the flames before me, as the fire burned on my face and my eyes stung, my shame did indeed turn to anger. I fanned the flames of that anger with my thoughts.

I had seen or heard enough of injustice now — the poverty of the blacksmith's family, the death of that soldier's horse, the brutish murder of poor Henry Parish, as well as the tragic deaths of Bess's mother and father. It seemed that the only way to justice was through human actions: the death of Mad Dog Tim the ostler and the curse on the gap-toothed crone felt like justice to me. Even the choice of victims by Bess and One-Legged Jack felt like a better sort of justice than that meted out by corrupt sheriffs and magistrates and men who cared only for their own sort. What did those men think of people of the lower orders? What did they care? And who would fight for the weak and the poor?

I would fight for them. Because I was among them now. But also because in my heart it felt right.

All I could do was act as I thought right.

CHAPTER FIFTY-SIX

We talked, Bess and I, late into that night, not wishing to sleep. We placed more logs on the fire, stoking it until it burned with unnecessary fervor, until the flames leaped high into the air and sparks flew onto the stone hearth.

Our plans were laid. My only regret was that we would have to wait so many days before acting. I knew that my father, or one of his servants, took his money to the British Linen Bank in Hexham on a Thursday. We knew, too, that Sapphire's injury would not allow her to make the journey for more than a week. It would be nearly three days' ride, and two nights' rest wherever we could find it, so we would begin our journey early on Tuesday of the following week.

It seemed too long to wait. But we would spend the time in planning, in practicing down to the last detail how we would rob my father of his ill-gotten money before he reached the Bank. And Bess had a great deal she wished to tell me about the art of highway robbery. I had now no discomfort at the idea of being taught by a girl — I understood enough to know that Bess must be listened to. My heart beat faster as I thought about what I would do. It was not fear I felt, but excitement. I wished we could act now.

Sleep did not come easily to me that night, or those following. It was not the hard floor — I was well used to that by this time. Nor was it the shame I had felt earlier, on hearing of my father's terrible actions. It was the knowledge that now, at last, I had the chance to act, to change something, to fight against the injustice of our lives.

When at last I did sleep, on that first night after learning of my father's dishonor, it was with the memory of Bess's ballad to Henry Parish still echoing in my ears. She had sung it again that evening. I had asked her to. To pass the time, for something to do before morning came, we had written out some copies on thick paper that Bess kept dry in a drawer lined with a layer of salt. We cut new quills and dipped them in the ink, as Bess told and retold each line and we wrote the words down together. We planned to make only a small number of copies to sell to printers in towns and villages where we might find ourselves in weeks ahead, but each time we wanted to stop, we thought of Henry Parish, and how one more copy would spread his story to more people, each of whom might tell his story to more. And so we wrote, late into the hours of deepest darkness, till the fire quieted and hissed gently, and the noise of our quills scratching on the paper became part of the sounds of the night.

Outside, the night-loving spirits of the moors awoke and, no doubt, ghosts walked. But we were safe indoors and had no need to fear them. And if some of them watched over us, if the ghostly highwayman looked through the trees at us, then that was the way of things. We could only do what the living can do: hope and pray and act.

And so, as I slept at last, the story of Henry Parish's death, in Bess's true words, settled into my head and grew inside me until he became a part of me. I could not know what would happen, but my life now was tangled with his, and with Bess's, with One-Legged Jack and Aggie and Bess's parents — the highwayman and the landlord's red-lipped daughter — and the old man who had lost his life so unjustly on a chill March morning in the year of our Lord, 1761.

I prayed that God, and whatever spirits He might see fit to allow, would watch over us. I could not know if my prayers would be answered.

CHAPTER FIFTY-SEVEN

A wild March wind whipped the hair into our horses' eyes as we set out some days later. As we trotted, and as I felt Sapphire's stride strong beneath me, I tried to accustom myself to the sword slapping against my leg. It was Bess's father's sword, which I had polished the night before until its jeweled hilt sparkled. I had sharpened the blade on a whetstone, too, till its edge felt rough against the flat of my thumb, its steel warm, its double edge deadly and glinting in the firelight. I would use it if I had to, and I would think of Bess's father as I did so.

I was proud to have a brave man's sword at my side. I hoped I could be as brave as he.

Our bags were packed with as much as we could carry without overburdening ourselves. We had food and water, flint and steel for making fire, spare clothes, a pair of pistols each, full powder horns, and two bags of shot. We had all our money with us, though this was not much — Bess had earned no money since I had entered her life, and she had spent much of what she had on buying Sapphire for me. But this robbery of my father's money was not for us — it was for Henry's mother and sister.

Once we were on the road west, we met few travelers. Those we passed took little notice of us — two well-dressed young men riding decent horses, one of us with a sword, neither of us with pistols in view. We could have been fledgling merchants, lawyers, two doctors, even students. Our dress was not flamboyant, nothing you would recall if asked: thick riding cloaks, with plain, twisted stocks at our throats, hid whatever jackets we might be wearing; our breeches were dark brown and our spurred riding boots long and burnished to a soft shine. Tricorne hats hid the color of our hair. In Bess's case, of course, her hat also hid her feminine tresses.

Our journey would be long and tedious. I wished only to reach our destination. We could not hurry, however, as we must keep our horses fresh. We would need their strength when the time came. And so we rested every hour or so.

After some three hours spent traveling west, we came to a small village. Here, we knew, we had to take the road north over the moors. Now we must pray for our safety — a sudden fog, a fall, a band of footpads, any of these could be our doom. There would be no one to help us.

We turned our horses and took the lane that we saw before us. Behind us, to the south, the sky gleamed like burnished steel where the weak sun was hidden. In front of us the clouds lowered themselves onto the hillsides, settling like a thick fog. Rain began to fall more heavily now, as the moors folded us into their shadows.

The ground was wet here, wrinkled with streams springing from the earth and pouring down the steep hillsides on either side of us. The path took us along the line of a valley, and the slopes steepened until they loomed over us.

Down to our left, we saw the ghostly ruins of a huge abbey, with three rows of arched and empty windows. "Rievaulx Abbey," said Bess. I had heard of it. I would not have liked to visit it by night, imagining the ghosts of monks wandering restlessly through its cloisters. We stopped to look, but the horses did not like this place, and champed and stamped until we moved on.

We did not wish to spend a night on the moors, and so we pressed on as fast as we safely could. We passed almost no one. The occasional shepherd or goatherd stared at us in suspicion as we trotted by; an old woman carrying a basket stepped aside as we approached, nervous perhaps in case we meant her harm; once, another rider came toward us and we readied ourselves in case he had ill intent, but he tipped his hat to us and we to him, and we were alone once again.

I had no fear of the moors now, and they were welcome to their secrets. Only living people held fear for me, and there were few enough of those in these bleak hills. But as darkness fell on that first night, and as we found ourselves suddenly on leveling ground, the hills and lowering cliffs behind us, my heart began to beat faster.

We spent the night in a simple tavern on the banks of the River Leven. The innkeeper's wife brought us a steaming pot-boiled hare, accompanied by sea kale boiled white and carrots stewed in a thin, pale sauce. I tasted little of it, though I remembered to thank her and commend her for her cooking.

She must have taken kindly to the two of us — decent and well-spoken young men as we seemed to be, for she then offered an excellent gooseberry trifle with a custard so smooth and thick that my parents' French cook would have been proud to serve it. We declined her claret, thinking to keep a clear head for the next day, and preferred to drink a pale, malty ale instead.

We slept, of course, in the same room, but I went outside to see to the horses to allow Bess privacy while she prepared for bed. An ostler slept above the stable, and I thought of Mad Dog Tim as I spoke to him. But this one — Joseph was his name — seemed keen and honest, as far as I could tell. He did not have a shifty look, and he called me "sir." For my part, I smiled at him as I spoke, for I wished him to like me and to care well for our horses. A smile costs nothing and seems to me a proper way to behave to a person of any deserving sort.

Only since leaving home had I begun to think how one should behave. At home, I had had no call to think.

CHAPTER FIFTY-EIGHT

I will not pause to tell of the next day, except to say that we covered some forty miles and by nightfall found ourselves, cold, tired, and with aching legs and weary horses, on the edge of Durham, skirting the river that almost surrounds it. Thinking to find ourselves a comfortable bed, we came to a bridge, crossed the river, and proceeded into the city under the glowering shadows of the castle.

Early evening as it was, this was the time when gentlefolk would be in their houses, dining, away from the noisy masses. Workers hurried home or lingered on corners, shouting greetings or insults to each other. I counted at least three beggars slumped in doorways and one hobbling along on sticks, his legs bound with grimy bandages. Suddenly a door opened beside us as we passed and out stumbled three drunken women, their dresses awry, their hair spilling from their mobcaps. One vomited onto the pavement, held by the other two.

The smell of the river, of dankness, of dead fish and rotten matter pervaded everything. We urged our horses onward, taking little care to avoid trampling the drunken women.

Ahead, we could see the huge square towers of the cathedral, looming over everything, and soon the cloisters were in front of us, solid, reassuring, and yet cold and stern. They were like a strict schoolmaster — you cannot approach him for comfort, and yet you know that somehow he has your interests at heart.

Near the cathedral, we found what we were looking for: a tavern with a stable. I did not trust the look in this ostler's eyes, though perhaps I say that only with after-knowledge. Leaving the horses with him and giving instructions to care well for them, we approached the entrance of the tavern.

Noise surged through the doorway. The noise of angry men fueled by liquor.

It is easy to say such things afterward, but it seemed to me immediately that I did not like the look of the men we saw inside, though by then it was too late. Silence fell suddenly, as the men stopped their talk and stared at us with open mistrust. Perhaps we were too well dressed; perhaps simply we were strangers, and strangers may spell danger if evil is being planned. A great deal of drink was being consumed by all, and the air was thick with cheap gin and tobacco and men's sweat.

We kept our bags slung over our shoulders, and we stood close together.

A man was standing, red faced by the fire. All looked to him when he spoke. "We want no strangers 'ere," he said, his voice loud with liquor and anger, his eyes bright with some unknown fervor. "Ye be not welcome."

"I am sorry," I said, speaking as gruffly as I could, trying to appear older than my years, though even I could tell that the modulations of my voice marked me out as someone of higher birth than I wished to show. "We only want —"

But Bess interrupted me. I marveled that she could disguise her voice so well. "Aye, two beds for t' night, an' we'll not disturb ye more." She could have been a laborer on my father's estate.

There was a shifting in the room, a murmuring without visible source. Men looked at each other, scowling, looking for someone to make a decision. "What brings you 'ere?"

"We pass by. Family business. We go northward, to Scotland," said Bess strongly, levelly. Someone spat on the floor.

For a moment, however, it seemed as though Bess's words had satisfied them. But nothing that she might have said or done could have prevented what happened next.

A man, bleary faced, greasy haired, rose staggering to his feet, peering closely at me. He raised his finger, pointing straight. "'Tis 'im. So 'tis."

My heart began to thump, until I was sure that they could hear it.

"Who?" asked some of the other men. All of them stared at me, their anger burning into me, even if they knew not who I was.

Bess and I began to edge toward the door.

Then the leader, the man by the fire, demanded, "What sayst thou, Thomas? Who be this?"

Three of the men stood up now. Their arms hung loosely by their sides, hands open, ready. They were larger men than I had thought, burlier, like oxen, the sinews of their necks rigid and thick. I tried to watch them all, to see which might move first and fastest. Their faces were red and round, burnished like leather in the sun and wind and rain and years spent on the land. The strength of northern hills ran in their blood. Bess and I would stand no chance against them, whether or not they were drunk. I thought of the sword hanging at my side, but I did not move my hand toward it, though I dearly wanted to.

And now, with horror, as I looked more closely at the face of the man named Thomas, I thought I knew him, too. Who was he? I knew him and yet I could not recall precisely. A man who had worked once on my father's estate, perhaps? Yes, that was it. That was it! He was a gamekeeper who had been drafted to the militia perhaps a year before. I remembered that there had been some hard feeling, some sullenness among the servants that day, some voices raised behind closed doors. But the man had gone — he had had no choice. He had been named in the hated ballot, and the fact that he had a wife with three young children had made no difference.

His voice was rough with distaste. A wet pad of tobacco flew from his mouth onto the floor by my feet. "'Tis the Sheriff's son. 'Tis de Lacey's boy."

Then the wind of their anger rushed through the room, and they seemed to swell and grow tall. Chair legs scraped on the uneven floor as they rose to their feet.

"Run!" cried Bess. We leaped toward the door, and I drew my sword as we did so, turning back once more, slashing it from side to side. One man fumbled with a pistol that had lain on the table, but dropped it with a clatter. Two of them stooped to pick it up. The men were slow to move, fuddled as they were by drink and warmth. But they were only moments behind us as we ran for our lives across the dark inn yard toward the stable.

I thanked God for lazy ostlers. This one was eating his supper and had not unsaddled our horses. We grabbed them from in front of his eyes, leaving him widemouthed and stupid, and we flung our bags over the horses' withers. I was about to leap into the saddle when I saw that Bess's was indeed unfastened, and that she was fumbling with the girth. Silently urging her to hurry, I stood with my back to her, slashing my sword in front of us as widely as I could. A man tried to grab my reins, but one thrust of the sword put him in fear of his life and he leaped back.

I could not rest for one moment — as soon as one of them had been repelled, another two or three would leap forward. But none had a sword, and the fierceness in my eyes was enough to show them that I would have killed them if they came too close. And, angry though they were, they were not fighting for their lives and they lacked vigor.

As I heard Bess shout behind me that she was ready, and as we both leaped into the saddles, I could see a man, the one who had seemed in charge, with a pistol in his hand. With practiced fingers, he was loading and tamping down the powder.

Without waiting to put my feet in the stirrups, I pulled Sapphire's head in the direction of the yard entrance. Men stood there, some now with pieces of wood, one with a short knife, blocking our path.

Out of the corner of my eye, I could see the man cocking his pistol and raising it in our direction. I lowered myself as close as I could to my horse's neck, shouting to Bess to do the same, twisting Sapphire around as fast as I could, trying to keep moving, trying to stay in the melee of men.

One of them grabbed my left foot from behind, and I kicked out viciously, hearing a crack as my spur hit him in the jaw. Another man had hold of Bess's leg. She wheeled her horse around, and I saw Merlin in his fear kick out at her assailant.

A pistol shot rang out, and there was a yell, followed by furious shouting.

"Now!" I shouted, and dug my spurs into Sapphire's sides.

We galloped for the gateway, straight toward the waiting men, holding our breath as we waited for the second shot. It did not come, for what reason I would never know and had no time to wonder.

The men leaped aside as we came close, though not before more than one had rained blows on us. One cudgel caught me on the knee with a crack that sent a spearing pain through my whole body. Another landed hard on Sapphire's back, causing her to buck and whinny. My leg dashed painfully against the gatepost as we passed through, but we were safe.

But as we clattered away from that dark inn yard, I heard a voice ring out, a voice full of fury and hatred. "The devil take the Sheriff's son! May he burn in Hell's fire!"

The words fell around my ears, echoing their whispers like ghosts in the night, and a cold finger of fear crept down my back. My skin crawled under the power of his curse. Perhaps the man had God on his side? Perhaps I would suffer punishment for my father's wrongdoing? Did not the Bible say so? "And the sins of the fathers will be visited on their children."

We escaped through the streets, turning this way and that, taking whichever street seemed broader, emptier, until we were sure no one followed us, and then we slowed to a trot and then a walk. We looked at each other and said nothing. We knew that fortune had smiled on us and that it could have been very different.

I did not tell Bess of my fears, not at that time. I tried to shake the dark words from me, to forget them. But I knew it would take more than a strong will to forget their menace. How could I protect myself against the power of the devil? There are things that are stronger than a man.

Bravery is easier by daylight.

CHAPTER FIFTY-NINE

We could not risk being seen by those men again, so we left the City of Durham as quickly as we were able. I think neither of us wanted to be among persons whom we did not know and could not trust. We had too much to hide and too much to lose. And so we rode as fast as we could to the nearest tavern outside the city walls. It was not far, a mile or two, but at least here we felt the empty spaces around us. The innkeeper was not pleased to be woken so late, but he took our money willingly, and the room was dry and sufficient in furnishing.

I knew that I was now not far from my father's territories, some twenty miles northwest, and the thought of him subdued me further. And yet, excitement ran through me, too, each time I thought of what we would do the next day.

We lay fully clothed on our beds and listened to the wind rattling the windows. Murky moonlight shafted through the open shutters; we wished for as much light as possible, in case of intruders. Our pistols lay beside us, loaded, primed, and fully cocked.

"Think not of that man's words," said Bess, her voice breaking the dusty silence of the room. "He does not know your heart."

"His curse seemed strong. Did you not feel its power?"

"You have done nothing wrong. You should feel no shame."

"Perhaps I shall pay, nevertheless."

"Perhaps so," said Bess, startling me. "Perhaps in truth this *is* how you will pay. By taking from your father what is not his, and by returning it to poorer people. By doing what is right. If there is a price to be paid, you will pay it tomorrow. And God will watch over you."

Would He? Or would the devil win? Would the man's curse hold strong? Which spirits of the night had taken his words and were even now weaving them into a binding spell, to follow me the next day, to haunt my footsteps, to make my arm heavy as I wielded sword or pistol, to dim my eyesight, or to confuse my mind with terror and darkness so that I knew not how to act?

I thought of the old hag and the curse that we had placed on her. I saw how strongly that magic had worked. I tried to tell myself that such things are superstition, that God does not heed such magickings. But that is easy to believe in daylight; in the hours of darkness, demons enter the mind and tangle it in webs of ghoulish deceit.

Chapter Sixty

The countryside now became grimly familiar to me. It was not dark like the moors we had left behind, but granite gray, bleak, and cold. The sharp, craggy slopes were peppered with boulders, as though some race of giants had lived here once. A lowering sky threatened rain: rain that we would welcome later but that now would simply serve to chill us to the bone.

As we came closer to my father's lands, some miles from Hexham, around noon, and then reached the crossroads where his road met ours, all my senses were alert to danger.

I knew the place we sought, a little farther along the road toward my old home. I had told Bess that I knew a spot to wait and to watch the road, with a shepherd's hut to shelter and hide us. We did not know what time my father's post chaise would pass by, though we knew it must be before evening. We did not know if it would be my father himself, as it sometimes was, or if his estate keeper would be entrusted on this day, as he often was. I knew only that someone would pass this way, carrying a great deal of money, making for Hexham. My father would often stay overnight in the town after paying the money to the Bank.

To think that I had never before thought of the ugly burden he carried when he made those regular trips! I had seen him return smiling the next day and noticed him bestow on my mother or sisters some small gift or trinket. I had not wondered at our life of comfort, at the fine wines and rare foods that my parents served to guests, at the new gowns my sisters so often had made for them, at my own possessions and the ease with which we lived. I had thought simply that my father was a successful gentleman and that our wealth was no more than we deserved or earned by our position. Now I knew whence it came, and the thought sickened me.

The rain began to fall fast. A heavy mist closed in as we took shelter in the hut, taking the horses inside with us. Bess was shivering as we shook the rain from our faces and hair. Her eyes were dark with tiredness. I think perhaps she had slept less than I the night before. Perhaps she was as afraid as I was.

We took turns to watch the road from a slope just above the hut, under shelter of some trees. I took the first turn, telling Bess to keep as warm as she could. I left her checking the powder in our pistols.

How long would we have to wait? Would they perhaps not come at all? Perhaps my father's routine had changed? Would it be he who came or someone else? Would he be armed? Would he be alert, expecting trouble?

I shivered.

It was on my third turn at the watch, when my eyes were becoming blurred with straining through the mist, when I had begun to think that no one would come, when I thought my fingers would snap with cold and my ears had lost their feeling, that I heard the unmistakable sound of a horse and wheels. I peered through the rain, squeezing my eyes to slits, waiting to see who would come around the corner.

Was it? Surely, it was? It was! My father's carriage, my father's two black horses, one with a white flash on its nose.

With my hearting thudding in my chest, I ran the few yards to the hut and urged Bess to come. "They are here! For certain!"

"Is it your father?"

"I can't tell. But they are his horses."

As quietly and quickly as we could, we climbed into our saddles and made our way to the place where we had decided to wait. We would have very little time before the carriage rounded the corner, carrying my father's money, one week's evil takings.

The mist swirled, and the rain continued to fall in sheets. I was glad of it.

My heart raced, but there was no fear in me now. I was ready for whatever might happen.

We looked at each other, Bess and I. Silently, with my thoughts, I wished her well, and I believe her eyes spoke the same thoughts to me.

Together, we pulled up our kerchiefs to cover our mouths and noses.

With a cry, a pistol in one hand and reins in the other, we spurred our horses forward and into the path of the oncoming carriage.

As the driver saw us, I glimpsed his mouth open wide with shock. He hauled on the reins and brought the carriage to a skidding halt, the horses rearing in fright. I pointed my pistol firmly at his head before he had time to reach for his own.

"Do nothing hasty, gentlemen, and you will not be harmed," shouted Bess, her voice strong, indistinguishable from a man's.

I held my pistol steady, protecting the flint and powder from the rain with my cloak. Only a fool would ignore the maw of a double-barreled pistol, and the coachman was no fool.

"I should be obliged to see your hands. Place them outside the door, if you would be so kind," Bess called to the occupant, her horse dancing beneath her. Rain fell in rivulets from the corners of her hat. Not a movement came from within the carriage. "I will not wait long," she said calmly but with menace in her voice, "before I shoot your servant. You need him, I fear, to carry you safely home tonight."

A hand, gloved, appeared at the window. And then the other. They were my father's hands. I knew his gloves. They had been a gift from one of his officers, maroon leather with great cuffs and a brass button at each wrist.

"Open the door, gentle sir. Touch not your sword, for your own safety. Hold your money before you while you step down. Take good care where you place your feet — there is a deal of mud underfoot." Bess kept her horse somewhat behind the door, close to the side of the carriage, so that her victim would not see her until she was sure he carried no pistols. She had explained this to me many times, as we planned every moment of this in the days before.

I kept careful watch on the postilion. His face was

white and wet, his eyes wide. A pistol lay on the floor beneath his seat. He would not be able to reach it before I shot him, I knew. But I did not want to shoot him. He was blameless in all this.

The door opened and out climbed my father, slowly, carrying a wooden box. He was wrapped around with a thick winter cloak, clasped at the neck with a familiar jeweled buckle, and beneath his three-cornered hat I could see the waves of his white wig held behind with a scarlet ribbon. His legs were thickly built, strong, encased in white silk stockings above the shiny, buckled shoes. I remembered them all. Hatred flooded through me as I saw his face. I had almost forgotten his face. I had forgotten his eyes. His pale eyes, small, like a fish's. I had forgotten their power.

And yet, was it hatred? Did I not wish, above all, that I could remove the covering from my face and reveal myself to him, tell him that I had shown myself not a coward after all? Yet again, how could I prove this? He would think nothing of my trying to save Henry Parish. There was nothing I had done that he could praise. He would consider none of it bravery.

He watched Bess angrily. How he must wish that he had had his pistols ready! He looked then at the postilion, and his face darkened in scorn. He must wish the man had been more alert, though there was little the poor wretch could have done. I regretted that he would be punished later, but I pushed that thought away.

"Open the box. So that I may see. I would not like to have to injure you with this pistol, but I will do so if I believe you hide a weapon in that box," warned Bess. He obeyed, opening the lid toward her. Would he have acted with such caution if he had known she was a girl? No, he would surely have laughed. Bess nodded, satisfied that there were no weapons inside. She held open her saddle bag. "And now, good gentle sir, place your money in here, if I may trouble you one more time," she said, keeping the pistol pointing at his head. Though she spoke softly and calmly, this was the dangerous part, I knew. This was the moment when he might lunge, and Bess's horse might be startled. This was the moment when a highwayman must keep his nerve.

And keep her nerve Bess did. Very slowly, my father handed over the bags of money, placing them in her open bag. Very slowly. Why so very slowly? There was something odd in his face, a strange look, a lack of fear, almost the slightest smile at the corner of his mouth. Should he not be afraid? This highwayman could shoot him. Surely he should be moving with greater haste, so as to escape as soon as he might? Surely he should be shaking with fear, anxious to please his robber? Surely at least he should be blustering and arguing? I did not think to see my father acquiescing so easily to a highwayman's demands.

I looked at his face through the gray air, while still trying to guard the driver. There was a fleeting flicker of . . . knowledge. My father knew something, something to his advantage. But what? Did he have a pistol in his belt? Was someone else inside the carriage? I strained all my senses, narrowed my eyes, tightened my muscles.

That was when I heard it, just as I saw my father glance almost imperceptibly over Bess's shoulder. Through the pattering rain, I heard it. Unmistakably. A horse's galloping hooves.

My father had known! This was why he had moved slowly! He was waiting for a rider to catch up. A rider whom he had expected.

I was about to open my mouth to speak, but I could see that Bess had heard it, too. I saw it in the flicker of her eyes above the kerchief.

Without warning, the postilion dived for his pistol. Instantly, I fired mine, without pausing to think. I did not hit him, I know — and for that I was glad even then — but his horses reared in fright, and he was thrown hard to the ground, landing with a terrible scream and rolling over. He stayed on the ground, moaning in agony and clutching his shoulder. The rain spattered onto him as he lay there, and splashed into the mud around him.

The sound of the galloping hooves came ever nearer, and now I could make out the vague shape through the mist. The rider was shouting at the horse, his voice coarse with anger.

"Ride!" shouted Bess to me. Still she kept her pistol aimed at my father, but she was wheeling her horse around in the mud. She had the money. We had won! We could escape now and there was little chance that a lone horseman would give chase. Not when we were armed with pistols, and there were two of us.

My father stood foolishly, powerless to stop us, the rain now soaking his leather gloves, running in rivulets from his hat and his cloak. His hair was in thin strands, like mice's tails, plastered onto the sides of his face, his sideburns straggly, too. "God damn you! God damn you to Hell!" he cried furiously, his cheeks tight with anger, his eyes blazing. But now he shouted to the approaching rider. "Damn you! Hurry, man!"

With a sudden desperate and foolhardy movement, seeming to care little for the pistol pointing at him, he lunged toward Bess, grabbing hold of her leg. She struggled to free herself, but my father is a large and strong man, and fury added to his strength.

Would she shoot him? But as she pulled her arm back to angle her pistol at him, he made a wild grab toward her hand, knocking the pistol aside. It flew from her gloved fingers and spun through the air. He dived toward where it lay in the mud and picked it up, pointing it at her with a terrible smile on his face.

In a moment of horror, in which I was frozen, powerless except to scream, "No!" I saw her eyes open wide. Then my father, still smiling, cocked the pistol expertly with his thumb and fired.

She did not have time to move.

CHAPTER SIXTY-ONE

Nothing happened, no flash, no sound other than a dull click. Had I had time to think, perhaps I should have known that the mud and rain must surely enter the powder box, but a pistol is a fearsome weapon to face, even in those conditions. I was thankful once more for the rain now, which fell ever more heavily.

Yet I too held a pistol, and mine would almost certainly be useless, too. I could not waste time in finding out, so I thrust it into my belt. I still had my sword. But I would not need it: my father was powerless, his postilion injured, no weapons to hand. We should escape now, and they would not catch us.

But now the rider was almost upon us, sliding to a halt, calling to my father, trying to grasp the scene before him through the rain.

"Come!" cried Bess to me. "We have what we came for," and with that she swung her horse around and spurred him into action. She did not stop to wonder why I did not follow.

There was a reason I stayed. The rider was riding my own horse, Blackfoot. I could never mistake him, his gentle and brave eyes, his white flash. I did not like the way he was being ridden. His sides were bloody from sharp spurs, and the rider had been lashing his flesh with a stick as they galloped toward us. My horse's nostrils were wide with fear and exhaustion.

The rider was my brother.

Chapter Sixty-two

I did not call Bess back, but she must have sensed that something was amiss. I thought of nothing other than my horse and my hatred for my brother. And if what I felt for my father was perhaps not pure hatred, what I felt for my brother was exactly that. Deep and dangerous and raw as a recent wound.

He must not use my horse in this way. He must not use my horse at all.

I drew my sword, my eye catching the glint of steel, seeing the rainwater gather and spread and scatter on the slanting blade. If ever the ghost of Bess's father watched over us, I needed him now. But if he did not, then I would fight hard and I would fight long.

My father scrambled to his feet, his clothes covered in mud. He shouted curses at my brother, railing at him for lagging so far behind, and my brother answered him with that thin and spiteful voice that I knew so well. It seemed he should have followed our father more closely, but Blackfoot had thrown him after shying violently. As he said this, he lashed once more at my horse's side with his stick, and Blackfoot threw his head back, eyes staring wide in distress. My brother struggled to regain control. The reins were held too tight, and Blackfoot's neck was arched and taut.

I could not bear this.

I would fight my brother. But not on horseback. It was too dangerous for the horses and more difficult than fighting on foot. I leaped to the ground. I had no other thoughts, no eyes for anything else, though I was dimly aware that Bess had returned. I would trust her to watch over the other men. But I would fight my brother.

Although I had been afraid to fight him when he had challenged me only a few weeks before, this was different. Then, I had never fought except in practice; now, I was fighting with my heart. Now I was not afraid.

Moving forward, my sword before me, my intention clear, I gathered the words I would speak. I cared nothing for the money now, nothing for my father; I thought only of saving my horse from my brother's cruelty.

But before I could say anything, my father spoke, shaking with anger. "Be off with you, you scoundrel, footpad, you blackguard, you!" The whites of his eyes were wide and wild, as he spat his words. "You have what you came for — now be gone! And be sure I will not sleep until you have been caught and hanged."

"Get down from the horse, and fight like a man!" I shouted to my brother. I did not care now if they might know me from my voice, but I do not think they did.

My brother merely grinned and urged Blackfoot forward. The horse threw his head back and reared up, feet thrashing the air. My brother dug his spurs into the bleeding flanks, and Blackfoot jibbed and bucked, pain in his eyes and in his flaring nostrils. But Blackfoot, my Blackfoot, did not move forward. Skittering sideways, his feet raised high in agitation, he would not obey.

"Fight like a man!" I shouted again. And as I did, recognition dawned in my brother. It spread in a smile across his face. He lashed Blackfoot one more time and when the horse still refused to charge forward, he, too, leaped from his saddle.

My brother drew his sword. "So, you must hide behind a handkerchief? Ever the coward, William! You may have thought you and your accomplice could overcome an old man, but now you have more than met your match!"

As I pulled down my kerchief, I was only dimly aware of the gasp from my father, and of the noises behind me of Bess controlling the horses. I was very clearly aware of my brother's gleeful face and the rain on his ginger moustache and his small, ferretlike eyes gleaming.

With a cry, he leaped forward, thrusting his sword toward my face. I ducked sideways, parrying, and the echoing crash of our swords rang through my body. My brother was strong and furious, and with every blow, every parry, every step backward, I felt his power. His arm moved so fast, with such strength, that all I could do was defend myself, leaning back, twisting my sword this way and that, now across my face, now down at my feet. His blade flashed fast until all I could see was the crisscross pattern of steel stripes in the air before my eyes.

I could hear his breathing, his grunts with every blow, see his maddened glare, his grimace as he threw every effort into beating me into submission. And then I understood: my brother would kill me, with no more thought than he would kill an animal.

CHAPTER SIXTY-THREE

With rain across my eyes, and my vision spinning, I stumbled, falling to one knee, holding my sword above my head. And still my brother beat his weapon down on mine with fury, the blows falling faster and faster onto my blade. Pain jarred up my arm, thudding into my shoulder.

"Cry mercy, little brother!" he shouted.

But I would not. I should rather die than ask for mercy from him. Now, from somewhere deep inside me, came a voice, my own voice: "Think of Henry Parish! Think of injustice!" And, through a mist, I saw flashes of red before my eyes — the bleeding wounds on my horse's flanks. Or was it the memory of the redcoats before they killed Henry?

With a roar, gathering every remaining ounce of my strength, I rose to my feet and brought my sword crashing down on my brother's as he paused for breath. He stepped backward, taken by surprise, parrying my blow. I pushed forward, now bringing my sword crashing down, now thrusting it forward, now slashing down from the right, now pushing forward, now swinging from the left, now thrusting forward again. In rhythm we moved, my brother and I, weaving a deadly dance. According to my rhythm, not his. Did my father watch me now? I think he did.

My body was wearying but I would not give up, and I would not show any weakness. I could see my brother's eyes, could feel him begin to doubt himself, begin almost to fear.

But with his fear would come extra fury — I sensed that, too. I must act quickly.

Without warning, I broke the rhythm of our blows and, with a sudden twist and flick of my wrist, I sent his sword spinning out of his hand. It landed on its point in the mud several feet away and stuck there, shuddering. Bess leaped toward it, grabbed it, and in several swift movements sliced through the traces that held the horses to the carriage.

But my eyes were still on my brother. I advanced on him, my sword pointing steadily in front of me. He stepped backward. I thrust the sword forward. In his haste, he stepped back too quickly and his feet slipped from under him.

My brother was sitting on the ground, drenched in mud and rain, staring up at me in fear. With the point of my sword against his throat, I could do anything.

I pushed the sword slowly, gently forward, and he sank back until he lay first on his elbows and finally flat on the ground.

"Don't!" he cried. His voice was choked, thin, weak. "Don't, I beg of you!"

I had not intended to do what he feared. But I wanted to see his fear and, indeed, I could see it in his watery eyes and hear it in the way his voice shook. It was enough.

I moved my sword away, and said nothing. While Bess stood over the men with my brother's sword, I tied my father and brother tightly to the wheels of the carriage, using their own neckties and the belts from their breeches. Bess looked inside the carriage and removed a pair of pistols, which she threw far away — within moments they would be too wet to use. The postilion I did not tie — from his shocked white face and his teeth closed in pain, he would be no help to them. None of this had been his fault, and we put him gently in the carriage for shelter and some comfort.

My father, shivering now, spoke at last. I could not tell what emotion was in his voice, whether it was anger or fear or surprise. "Why have you done this? To your own father?"

"I have done it for justice."

"How so? Justice?" He was sneering now, the father contemptuous of his son, assuming everything.

"I have done it for the old man whom you ordered to be put to death. The innocent old man. I have done it for the good men you take from their families without thought for them. I have done it for a young boy who died because men like you think that the lives of the poor are worth nothing. I have done it because I believe it is right and your way is wrong."

And with that, I turned around and went to Blackfoot, my beautiful Blackfoot, where he stood patiently. I stroked his nose, and I know that he remembered me. Perhaps that is why he would not obey my brother and help him against me — I do not know. Strange things happen in the bond between horse and man. But I know that he knew me. There was a thick feeling in my throat as I stroked him and smelled his familiar warmth.

"Come on, Will," urged Bess, holding Sapphire and sitting on her own horse. "We should go now."

She had watched me fight, she had trusted me to win without her help, and I was glad of that, more than she could know.

I mounted Blackfoot, careful not to touch his wounds, and gently squeezed him to encourage him onward. He did not need to be asked twice, and we trotted away from that place, leaving my father silent and my brother railing at us until I heard my father's voice ring out in anger against him. I did not hear precisely what he said, but I think he called my brother a coward.

I think he did not use that name for me. No longer would he think me a coward.

I smiled. And as the rain stopped at last and as the evening sky brightened to the west, I threw back my head and I laughed.

As we rode away, I looked around at the grim countryside. Did the ghost of Bess's father watch over us here, too? Perhaps. Yet, I do not think we had need of him that day.

CHAPTER SIXTY-FOUR

We rode fast, taking the road back the way we had come. We had no need to lead Sapphire — she followed us willingly, as riderless horses do. Every now and then, I looked at Bess and we smiled. For the first time, we felt power: a sense that we could fight and win.

A fresh wind dried our faces and our cloaks as we rode. Once, the sun broke through over a distant hill and a bright patch spread across the slopes, moving fast in front of the clouds.

We came to where the road forked and took the southerly direction, wanting to put many miles between us and my father's place before sunset.

Perhaps two hours later, we came to a small farm and approached cautiously. A conversation with the man and his wife soon secured us a place to rest and feed the horses. These people had little enough to call their own, and even the chickens that ran around their feet were scrawny, but they welcomed us.

The woman prepared a paste for Blackfoot's wounds, and I winced for him as she spread the ointment into the torn flesh. Some of the wounds looked older than others, and I cursed my brother for his cruelty.

The good people would take no money, however hard we tried to press it upon them. But I had an idea. I led Sapphire toward them.

"Take this horse — we have no need for her now." At first, they would not agree, though I could see from their faces that such a horse would mean much to them. But we persuaded them, and I felt considerably better once this deal was done. They would look after Sapphire kindly, just as she had served us well, and we had no use for her now. She would, perhaps, have a longer and safer life than she might have with us.

That evening, we sat by the fire, feasting on pigeons spitted over the flames and old potatoes baked long in the embers, oozing freshly churned butter. Our clothes dried and our faces became pink in the heat, as the smell of roasting meat and tired bodies and hot cider mingled in the air. When I looked at Bess and thought of what we had done, and when I watched her eyes sparkle as she chewed meat from a pigeon's leg in the manner of the man that they still thought her to be, I felt something like real happiness.

Surely, nothing could harm us now? Surely God and fortune would favor us at last?

CHAPTER SIXTY-FIVE

Nearly two days later, we came back into the valley where Bess's cottage sat. We were tired, and the horses now walked slowly, but we were glad to be coming home. And, indeed, it felt like home to me. I looked forward to summer in the cottage, to growing vegetables, to making repairs, to learning to live in the countryside without servants to do everything for me.

We would have another journey to make before that, of course. For we had not yet taken my father's money to Henry Parish's mother and sister, as we had vowed to do. But we needed to rest a day or two first, and to rest the horses. They had ridden hard and far, and we must not overuse them.

And so, eagerly, with light spirits, sometimes laughing together, we rounded the brow of a hill and looked down on Bess's valley. We pulled our horses to a standstill and they stood there, blowing steam in the afternoon air. Our eyes moved along to the trees above her dwelling. And then down toward the cottage.

I gasped. A low moan escaped from Bess's lips.

Where her cottage had been, were now plumes of smoke.

"No!" she cried. "No!"

She kicked Merlin to a canter and a gallop and hurtled down the slopes, scattering clods of mud, ignoring paths, racing straight for her home.

I followed, a little more slowly, darkness in my heart, not wishing to see what I knew we would find.

I scanned the hillside for signs of danger. Any redcoats. For I understood, and I suppose Bess did too, that this was their work. A stone-built cottage does not burn down by accident or chance of nature.

But I saw no redcoats. I saw only the forlorn dampness of the moors, the darkness of the trees, the somber, careless scattering of rocks.

As I came to the cottage, Bess was there before me, standing in the yard, her shoulders stooped. Smoke spiraled slowly from empty windows. The roof had gone, fallen into the main part of the building. There could be nothing left undamaged in there.

She walked toward the blackened doorway.

"Bess!" I called. "Wait!" And I dismounted quickly and went to her.

I took her hand and we walked toward the door together, holding our breath against the acrid smell. Bess tried to go in, to climb across the ruins, but I held her back. Burned timbers and smashed rafters were piled in confusion everywhere.

I could just make out parts of the table, with sections charred as though chewed by a hungry beast. Bess stooped to pick something up — it was the end of a quill pen, one that we had used to copy her ballad to Henry Parish. I knew then, that if the redcoats had doubted whether or not we had tried to shelter their prey, they would have known for certain once they found those written words. We had not even thought to hide the papers.

Bess turned to me, her face covered in tears.

"We can write them again, Bess," I said.

She shook her head, whether in disagreement or despair I could not tell. "Did they mind so much? Did they care so much about the theft of a few bags of flour?"

There was no answer.

Suddenly, a chill swept down my back. I sensed a quick darkening of the sun and a whisper of wind in the trees. I glanced toward the woods. Did I see a shadow there? A figure moving and then vanishing?

I do not know. I shall never know. If Bess's father watched us, how could he help us now?

Then she spoke, her voice low and small. "I shall write more, many more. I shall tell everyone." There was soot across her cheek, smudged from her hand.

"Bess, we must go. The redcoats may come back. Do you know somewhere we can go? Somewhere safe, someone you trust?"

"If they come back, I will kill them!" The venom in her voice was quiet but deadly. I knew she would do as she said, even though she might die doing so.

I took her arm and gently pulled her away. "Bess, we have to find somewhere to go. You must think. We can decide what to do tomorrow."

"I cannot leave! This is my home!" Her face was shocked, white, wet with tears. But her eyes were blazing, with fury as well as desperation. Without thinking, she touched the locket around her neck, her fingers fluttering.

I pulled her gently again, and she allowed me to lead her away. "We cannot give up, Bess! We have both lost our homes now. We have nothing but our horses and each other, but we need nothing more. You cannot give up! It is what we do that matters — you have said that to me and you were right!" I made her look at me, to listen to me.

She nodded, numbly. "I know where we can go,"

she said, though with no strength in her voice. "I know a place where we can take refuge for the night. They were friends of my father. We can trust them." As we walked slowly away, her voice grew stronger. "I will never forgive this. I will never forgive them."

She did not look back, not once. But I did. I stopped and turned and as I looked one last time, I recalled all that had happened there, in that sad heap of stones: how I had been led by the ghostly horseman; how I had met and fought with Henry Parish; how I had despised what seemed like his weakness; how I had wished for him to go and to take his troubles with him. I remembered sitting by the fire as Bess had recounted her story, the tale of her parents' death and her own struggle. I thought with anger of the intrusion of the redcoats, how they had misused Bess and her home and how, finally, they had destroyed it through spite and brute force. And then I recalled Henry Parish's bravery and how we had watched him die, shot dead, down like a dog on the hillside. I recalled friendship and anger, love, loyalty and shame, brutality and honor.

And I knew in my heart, knew as I looked at that smoldering ruin, and then as I turned and saw Bess's straight, strong back riding before me, I knew that somehow, right would win, goodness would prevail, and God would look in kindly fashion on us.

We would never rest while men like those redcoats and men like my father and men like my brother believed that their lives were worth more than the lives of others. We would not rest until the redcoats had paid for their cruel deeds.

We would have to leave this place forever, I knew. We would finish Henry Parish's journey for him, taking the money we had won with honor to his family, and we would relate to his mother how her son had died bravely. Then we would go far away, to some place where no one would know us or follow us. But wherever we went, however hard the struggle, we would be on the side of right and goodness.

Why? Because one truth I had learned: it is not only what we do that is important.

It is also why we do it.

Afterword

This story came about during a conversation with my editor. "Why don't you do historical adventure again, something really dramatic?" she said. "What, you mean perhaps something about a highwayman?" I said. That afternoon, I wrote the first chapter.

As soon as I started thinking about highwaymen, I was drawn toward my favorite poem, perhaps my favorite piece of writing anywhere: "The Highwayman," by Alfred Noyes. For me it is perfect — emotional and dramatic. I *still* can't read it without feeling a catch in my voice and a tugging at my heart. It's just SO beautifully tragic!

I don't know if you will love it as much as I do. Maybe you won't at first — maybe it will grow on you. The best thing is to listen to an actor or someone with a beautiful voice reciting it. Here it is:

The Highwayman

PART ONE

The wind was a torrent of darkness among the gusty trees.
The moon was a ghostly galleon tossed upon cloudy seas.
The road was a ribbon of moonlight over the purple moor,
And the highwayman came riding —

Riding—riding—
The highwayman came riding, up to the old inn-door.

He'd a French cocked-hat on his forehead, a bunch of lace
    at his chin,
A coat of the claret velvet, and breeches of brown doe-skin.
They fitted with never a wrinkle. His boots were up to the
    thigh.
And he rode with a jewelled twinkle,
    His pistol butts a-twinkle,
His rapier hilt a-twinkle, under the jewelled sky.

Over the cobbles he clattered and clashed in the dark inn-yard.
And he tapped with his whip on the shutters, but all was
    locked and barred.
He whistled a tune to the window, and who should be waiting
    there
But the landlord's black-eyed daughter,
    Bess, the landlord's daughter,
Plaiting a dark red love-knot into her long black hair.

And dark in the dark old inn-yard a stable-wicket creaked
Where Tim the ostler listened. His face was white and peaked.
His eyes were hollows of madness, his hair like mouldy hay,
But he loved the landlord's daughter,
    The landlord's red-lipped daughter.
Dumb as a dog he listened, and he heard the robber say—

"One kiss, my bonny sweetheart, I'm after a prize to-night,
But I shall be back with the yellow gold before the morning
    light;
Yet, if they press me sharply, and harry me through the day,
Then look for me by moonlight,
    Watch for me by moonlight,
I'll come to thee by moonlight, though hell should bar the way."

He rose upright in the stirrups. He scarce could reach her
    hand,
But she loosened her hair in the casement. His face burnt
    like a brand
As the black cascade of perfume came tumbling over his
    breast;
And he kissed its waves in the moonlight,
    (O, sweet, black waves in the moonlight!)
Then he tugged at his rein in the moonlight, and galloped
    away to the west.

PART TWO

He did not come in the dawning. He did not come at noon;
And out of the tawny sunset, before the rise of the moon,
When the road was a gypsy's ribbon, looping the purple
    moor,
A red-coat troop came marching—
    Marching—marching—
King George's men came marching, up to the old inn-door.

They said no word to the landlord. They drank his ale instead.

But they gagged his daughter, and bound her, to the foot of
her narrow bed.

Two of them knelt at her casement, with muskets at their side!

There was death at every window;

   And hell at one dark window;

For Bess could see, through her casement, the road that *he*
would ride.

They had tied her up to attention, with many a sniggering jest.

They had bound a musket beside her, with the muzzle
beneath her breast!

"Now, keep good watch!" and they kissed her. She heard
the dead man say —

Look for me by moonlight;

   Watch for me by moonlight;

I'll come to thee by moonlight, though hell should bar the way!

She twisted her hands behind her; but all the knots held good!

She writhed her hands till her fingers were wet with sweat
or blood!

They stretched and strained in the darkness, and the hours
crawled by like years,

Till, now, on the stroke of midnight,

   Cold, on the stroke of midnight,

The tip of one finger touched it! The trigger at least was hers!

The tip of one finger touched it. She strove no more for the rest.

Up, she stood up to attention, with the muzzle beneath her
    breast.

She would not risk their hearing; she would not strive again;

For the road lay bare in the moonlight;

  Blank and bare in the moonlight;

And the blood of her veins, in the moonlight, throbbed to
    her love's refrain.

Tlot-tlot; tlot-tlot! Had they heard it? The horsehoofs ringing
    clear;

Tlot-tlot, tlot-tlot, in the distance? Were they deaf that they
    did not hear?

Down the ribbon of moonlight, over the brow of the hill,

The highwayman came riding —

  Riding — riding —

The red-coats looked to their priming! She stood up,
    straight and still.

Tlot-tlot, in the frosty silence! *Tlot-tlot,* in the echoing night!

Nearer he came and nearer. Her face was like a light.

Her eyes grew wide for a moment; she drew one last deep
    breath,

Then her finger moved in the moonlight,

  Her musket shattered the moonlight,

Shattered her breast in the moonlight and warned him —
    with her death.

He turned. He spurred to the west; he did not know who stood

Bowed, with her head o'er the musket, drenched with her
     own red blood!

Not till the dawn he heard it, his face grew grey to hear

How Bess, the landlord's daughter,

   The landlord's black-eyed daughter,

Had watched for her love in the moonlight, and died in the
     darkness there.

Back, he spurred like a madman, shouting a curse to the sky,

With the white road smoking behind him and his rapier
     brandished high.

Blood-red were his spurs in the golden noon; wine-red was
     his velvet coat;

When they shot him down on the highway,

   Down like a dog on the highway,

And he lay in his blood on the highway, with a bunch of
     lace at his throat.

               ✿   ✿   ✿

And still of a winter's night, they say, when the wind is in the trees,

When the moon is a ghostly galleon tossed upon cloudy seas,

When the road is a ribbon of moonlight over the purple moor,

A highwayman comes riding —

   Riding — riding —

A highwayman comes riding, up to the old inn-door.

Over the cobbles he clatters and clangs in the dark inn-yard.
He taps with his whip on the shutters, but all is locked and barred.
He whistles a tune to the window, and who should be waiting there
But the landlord's black-eyed daughter,
* Bess, the landlord's daughter,*
Plaiting a dark red love-knot into her long black hair.

ALFRED NOYES, 1880–1958

Lots of teachers use this poem to teach creative writing. I did that myself when I was a teacher. We talk about the sounds of the words, the rhythm, the repeated phrases. But what I remember as a reader are sheer passion, drama, excitement, and tear-wrenching sadness but rightness of the ending.

So, when I knew I was going to write a dramatic story about a girl who was a highwayman, I immediately knew she had to be connected with that brave couple. So I decided that Bess, the landlord's black-eyed daughter, and her lover had had a baby, and that the story of their deaths would affect that child as she grew up. I knew that the young Bess would be brave and beautiful like them, but human and real, too, with problems and depth and character.

Of course, it's the things teachers talk about — sounds of the words, the rhythm, the repeated phrases — that help tug at our hearts. As with all good writing, it's not just the story that matters: it's how you tell it.

When I write, I always try to manipulate the reader with the sounds and rhythms of language, with precise word choice to influence your emotions. The tragic death of Henry Parish is supposed to make you feel just as I still feel when I read "The Highwayman." Henry's death echoes the poem, with phrases like "down like a dog on the hillside."

But there's a difference between the deaths in the poem and the brutal killing of Henry Parish: Henry is based on a real soldier. There are different versions of the story but his cruel execution in 1795, during a time of hunger and poverty, caused great anger among the public, who then called on the army to change its policy of whitening soldiers' hair with flour.

And so, just as Will and Bess vow to remember Henry Parish and his death, so do I. I hope you will remember it, too. There are people whose lives are short and tragic but have meaning and they should be remembered. The lives and deaths of people in stories and poems, whether true or not, make us think about the world and — perhaps, if we are brave enough — change it.